TALON of the UNNAMED GODDESS

By

C.R. Daems & J.R. Tomlin

ISBN-13: 978-1463662394
ISBN-10: 1463662394

Check out all our novels at:
crdaems.com
jrtomlin.com
Visit J. R. Tomlin's Blog:
http://jeannetomlin.blogspot.com
Or follow her on Twitter:
@JRTomlinAuthor

The Four Kingdoms
Granya, Valda, Salda, Jaddah

TABLE OF CONTENTS

CHAPTER ONE

The Aerie: The Ordeal

I knelt on the hardwood floor with the other five remaining members of my seventh year aerie. We waited for Master Jiang to speak. He was a thin man, average height with long gray hair and goatee, and the piercing gaze of a deadly bird of prey. I froze when his eyes settled on me for a moment.

"You six are what remain of the one hundred and four candidates we admitted seven years ago. You have demonstrated your suitability to be considered for membership into the Raptor Clan through your hard work, adherence to our rules, and by surviving your first four Ordeals," Jiang said, pausing as if considering his next words. "One more Ordeal awaits you. The three who triumph will be allowed to continue training. The other three must leave."

I detected no hint of an apology or concern as to where the others would go. Each Ordeal purged half of the remaining students, the clan's method of extracting the best. Ninety students had failed to survive them, and eight were asked to leave because of poor performance in their studies, laziness, or failure to obey the rules. I loved my life as a student, but I hated the Ordeals.

"Your Ordeal will begin tomorrow at first light." He waved his hand to dismiss us.

I bowed and rose. My aerie exited the room in a solemn line.

As the door closed behind us, Kolek grabbed my arm. "Aisha, where will you go after you lose tomorrow?" He smirked. "You survived by luck and treachery over the years. Many made the mistake of feeling sorry for you, and you took advantage of them. I hope you're my opponent tomorrow. You'll get no sympathy from me."

My stomach twisted. I had arrived at the Raptor Clan's remote fortress, the Aerie, with vengeance as my only thought. Raiders had destroyed my life when they raided my village, killed and kidnapped my people. I was off in the forest exploring when I should have been working in the village. I returned to smoking ruins and dead bodies, the only survivor not dragged into slavery. After burying the dead, I made the week long trek through the mountains to the home of the legendary Raptor Clan, hoping to be accepted as a student, to become a skilled fighter, and to find and kill the raiders who had killed my parents and kidnapped my younger brother. If I failed tomorrow's Ordeal, I had nowhere to go, no family and no village.

"I'm not lucky enough to draw an easy opponent like you, Kolek." I refused to back down, although he was one of the better fighters. He said something under his breath as I walked away.

I had been frail when I came to the Aerie. I could not have competed against any of the others in a fair fight, so I learned to outwit them. I've become stronger than most women because of my rigorous training and developed excellent reflexes and balance. My speed makes me a good knife fighter. Constant training keeps my figure lithe and trim. My face is typical of the mountain people of the Camori: long and narrow with high cheekbones, dark-brown almond-shaped eyes, straight nose, full lips, and pointy chin. I love my long midnight black hair worn in a horsetail with a small blade woven into it.

* * * *

I stepped out of my room onto the portico the next morning. Students in their simple brown cotton tunics and pants crowded the edges, a zealous audience. A group of clan members, clad in black were among them. I stopped for a moment to survey the courtyard where my Ordeal would soon start, a two-acre square yard, covered with white gravel. A portico led from the yard to hundreds of rooms that abutted the massive gray walls of the fortress, their roofs forming a wide parapet. Above the walls, I could see the snow covered peaks of the Camori Mountains.

The sun shone brightly in the cloudless sky. Above the foothills the mid-summer air carried a chill. I stepped onto the gravel of the courtyard where the rough surface improved our sure-footedness. I would need that today.

Normally the area would have been swarming with activity: students exercising, stretching, and practicing fighting

2

techniques with swords, knives, bows, or with nothing at all--using only the natural weapons of the body. Today, only my seventh-year aerie was there as I walked over to join them.

We waited without looking or speaking to each other. After a few minutes, Master Jiang strode toward us, followed by three masters. He would control the Ordeal from inside the circle. The others would judge it from the outside.

"Seventh-year students," Jiang said. "The Ordeal today is with knives. The winner is the one who draws, in our judgment, significant first blood or who forces their opponent out of the circle. You will cease fighting immediately upon my command. If a contestant dies, it will be the decision of the judges whether the death was intentional or accidental. If it is determined to have been intentional, Master Dragos will decide the student's punishment. Is this clear?"

"Yes, Master Jiang," we said in unison. Ordeals are serious contests. Real blades increased the risk. My hands shook. Only the best would move from student to Talon, from nestling to bird of prey.

"We have paired the three strongest students with the weakest. This is in keeping with the Clan's intent to select the best to become a Talon." Jiang pointed to two students to enter the circle, marked off in the gravel. The student considered the best would be paired with the fourth best, the second best with the fifth, and the third best with me. I felt no surprise when Tellac, tall and lithe, entered the circle although I would have thought Olsim, his opponent, would have been rated lower than forth.

The two opponents circled each other. Olsim seemed cautious, his motions jerky. He scored first, a scratch to Tellac's arm but received two cuts to his arm in the exchange. The contest ended a few seconds later when Tellac darted in to leave a shallow slash from Olsim's neck to his belly.

Several minutes later, as I expected, I wasn't summoned into the circle for the second contest, but my stomach knotted when Kolek wasn't called either. He was a skilled knife fighter, fast, aggressive, and sadistic. My blood pounded in my chest as he looked at me and his lip curled into a contemptuous smile.

I didn't fear being hurt. I feared being forced to leave the

Aerie and having my dreams smashed. *Think Aisha. Keep your wits about you.* I struggled to slow my breathing. I was prepared for this Ordeal even if my preparation had been with cunning. I couldn't help but smile and felt his glare.

Time after time, Master Jiang had told us, "Emotions kill." Kolek always got excited when he fought. He enjoyed causing pain and often lost his temper. I could use both against him, but I would need time, skill, and my wits.

I must gain control of my raging emotions. But how? I could do that by not caring, but I did care. The Aerie was my life. I forced myself to think calmly about what fueled my fears, losing the Ordeal, having to leave, or not being a Talon. I needed to blur my feelings, to stop thinking about what might be. I focused on slowing the rapid beat of my heart.

"Too scared to move, Aisha?" Kolek said, jolting me back to reality. The second contest was over. Melor had won, as expected. His opponent's blood dripped in a line on the gravel as he was carried out injured but alive. "Take a good look. That's you in a few minutes."

"I'm more worried you'll cut yourself, Kolek," I said with a chuckle. I had reached a strange place. My vision had changed, expanded. I drew my knives at Master Jiang's "ready" command and could sense Kolek's confusion at my composure.

"Begin," Jiang said and moved away from us. I looked towards Kolek but not at him. I could see more than I had ever seen before. I saw Kolek's slight coiling as he prepared to lunge and sidestepped him as he thrust at me. I made a puny thrust with my left hand. I could have cut his extended arm when I sidestepped him but held back. It would only have been a shallow cut.

"Dung face," I muttered loud enough for him to hear, hoping to enrage him. It did.

Only seconds later, he lunged at me with both knives, going for my throat. I sensed this was more an attempt to scare me than to score a winning cut. He didn't move in close enough for a killing blow. He needed me to be scared. He craved it. I parried and jabbed his arm hard enough to draw blood. He answered with a slash that left a few drops of blood running down my hand.

4

I held back any left-handed blows I knew wouldn't end the match. The longer we fought the stranger I felt, as if I watched from above. I saw Kolek's subtle shifts in weight and muscle tension as he prepared to slash. I heard his breathing. He muttered a curse. Behind me, I heard Jiang's movement as he shuffled out of our way.

Kolek dove in, scoring another nick to my right arm. His right hand dropped. I knew his anger had overcome caution as he plunged his knife in a fierce thrust toward my stomach. I twisted sideways, using my left knife to block his blade. With an upward move, I slashed across his wrist. A gush of blood splattered over my hand and onto the gravel.

I stepped back as Master Jiang shouted, "Stop."

Snarling with fury Kolek threw his knife down and grabbed his wrist. "Damn you, Aisha!" His face twisted in anger. He turned towards Jiang. "She cheated."

"You're right, Kolek. I had a sharp knife." I had won. With one stroke of my knife, I had become clan.

Master Jiang walked over to Kolek and examined his wrist. "The gash is deep but not fatal. Aisha, you, Tellac, and Melor are declared the winners of the fifth Ordeal."

The three masters left the courtyard. Jiang motioned for me to join him. "Aisha, do you know why I placed you in the last rotation?"

"Because I was the weakest."

"No, we considered you third best, Kolek, last. You have a distinct disadvantage if I consider strength or reach. You are smaller than the average woman and much smaller than the average man. But you are two steps ahead of most students. You survive because you are always thinking, 'What if?' I believe you could have defeated Tellac had I paired you with him." He cocked his head and a smile twitched his lips. "Was your left blade ever weak or did you always fake that?"

I grinned. "I faked."

"Tellac, too, would have relied on that supposed weakness. And you are fast. At times I almost felt sorry for you letting student after student beat you using your pretended weakness. You almost convinced me until I saw you practicing your left handed techniques on your own a few months ago. I knew then that you were already planning for the next Ordeal. Tellac would have been a real loss to us."

I blinked in surprise.

"No more faked weaknesses, Aisha. For the next three years, we need to know everyone's real strengths and weaknesses. If one of you has a weakness, we must eliminate it. A Talon can have no weaknesses."

* * * *

The next three years flew by in a glow of happiness. I no longer worried about having to leave. I belonged, and I was learning the secrets of the Talon.

The state of mind I had achieved during the fifth Ordeal was called "battle mode." Talons quiet their mind. In so doing they achieve a heightened awareness of their surroundings. And the strange finger motions I had seen from the Masters and clan members were the Talons' battle language. The hand and finger signing allowed the Talons to communicate in silence. I learned about herbs for healing injuries and for killing, along with secret fighting techniques and tactics unique to the Talon. By the end of my tenth year, I could shoot a short bow and could put an arrow or throwing dagger into a target from twenty paces. And I made good friends.

Before the fifth Ordeal, I had kept a distance between me and the other students, my future opponents. The Ordeals made real friendships too painful. Who wanted to be responsible for a friend being asked to leave? Who wanted to have to say goodbye to good friends, or possibly kill one? With the Ordeals over, Tellac, Melor, and I became close.

We trained, studied, and ate together every day. It was a joy to watch Tellac use weapons. Each seemed to become a part of him, but with knives, he was already a master. He practiced every day with Melor and me so that we became deadly with all of our weapons. Melor took to book learning and helped coach Tellac and me in our studies of battle tactics, and the customs of the four kingdoms. I found battle mode easy. We often sat together on the gravel of the courtyard as I taught them how to reach a quiet place inside to heighten their senses.

And for the first time we took our meals together and spent time exchanging stories about before we came to the clan.

6

Then the pranks began. One morning it was honey in Tellac's boots, another, salt in the syrup I put on my porridge. We talked among ourselves. It must be one of the younglings. But I awoke late one night to see Melor sneaking out of Tellac's room after pouring water into his bed. Our studious Melor was the prankster.

Tellac sat on him in his room while I ran out with his books. Once Tellac let him up, he followed. He swore he'd reform, although I didn't quite trust the twinkle in his eyes. Yet that was the last of the tricks he played on the two of us.

As we approached the end of our tenth year, Master Jiang introduced us to hi'Blessed Tasilaba, the ancient one. Her gray hair hung in a braid down to her waist and, although straight and slender, she leaned slightly on the tall staff she held in her hand.

"Hi'Blessed Tasilaba will be your instructor for your remaining time as students. It is she who will pronounce you a Talon." I was shocked. We had all seen her around the Aerie for years but had never thought to inquire about her function. Talons didn't have maids or cooks, but we still assumed she performed some unimportant task.

"Come students, I find the Aerie confining." She led us out of the gate and up the mountain slope on a narrow rocky path. A chill breeze blew from the heights, but she didn't seem to mind, nor did the steep trail slow her. At a wide spot, she stopped and sat on a flat rock, gesturing for us to take our places around her. The view was beautiful from this vantage point, looking down into a valley where a tall waterfall fell in a veil into a distant river. Above towered the majestic snow-covered mountain peaks.

"What do you know about the living sigils," she asked. Melor and I just stared at each other shaking our heads.

"My father has one," Tellac said. "It's a Truth Sigil. I know he got it at a temple. He said it keeps him from being cheated. He's a trader."

"Hi'Blessed Tasilaba, those are the red scar-like marks the Talons have on their arms?" Mellor asked.

"Yes, those are the sigils of which I speak. And one is a Truth Sigil as Tellac said. In all, there are six. We believe six gods and goddesses created them sometime in the dim unknown

7

past. Six shrines, each devoted to a single sigil, were rediscovered by accident two hundred years ago. Only in the past hundred years have we learned how to use them."

For the next four weeks, we learned about each sigil, where it was found, the god or goddess associated with it, and the powers that the sigil provided for its holders. The War Sigil, which enhanced the holder's ability and skill with weapons and fighting, fascinated us all. It had been found in Valda and was the sigil of the god, Dai. After class, we spent much of our time sneaking looks at Talons' arms. We concluded that many had the War Sigils and sometimes one other although that varied considerably.

One day, weeks later, when we filed outside the gate to climb the trail and meet hi'Blessed Tasilaba for class up on her favorite spot. She waited for us outside the gate.

"Melor and Aisha, come back tomorrow. Tellac, follow me."

We trudged back to a study room and spent anxious hours waiting for Tellac to return. When he did, his excitement showed as he jumped around pointing to the reddish scars of the War and Energy Sigils on his arm.

"Look, look! hi'Blessed Tasilaba said I was officially a Talon." Tellac couldn't make another coherent statement all day from excitement. But we were able to talk the quartermaster out of a small pitcher of ale to celebrate. I managed, I think, not to seem too jealous.

The next morning hi'Blessed Tasilaba told me to go home. I sulked all the way back to the Aerie. "It isn't fair." I mumbled it over and over. But the following day it was my turn.

Hi'Blessed Tasilaba met me on the trail and in silence led me further up the mountain to a cave. I had to stop several times to catch my breath while she, an old woman, seemed unaffected. The Energy Sigil I imagined. Inside, the rough unfinished cavern stretched into intense darkness. We walked about fifty paces into it before she stopped in front of a wall with a golden sigil emblazoned into the rock. I stared at the curved symbol, trying to decipher it. I had never seen this sigil, definitely not one of the six.

"Sit, Aisha," Tasilaba said. She fetched six clay bowls on a tray off a large flat rock that served as a shelf. Knowing the ritual, I extended my left arm. She reached in the first bowl, painted with the War Sigil, placed a reddish lump of something cool on my arm and bowed her head over it. I had longed for the War Sigil and hoped for another, maybe Illusion. I felt nothing, although I knew it should have burned, leaving a reddish scar. Tasilaba tried five more times with the same result. Nothing!

"Aisha, take off your shirt."

Petrified, I sat frozen as she brought a seventh bowl forward. She reached into the bowl and pressed something cool to my back. Something moved in a pattern under the spot. It grew into discomfort and then into pain. The pain was intense as it worked its way under my skin. I wanted to run, to scream, to stop her. I sat still and gritted my teeth to keep quiet.

When the burning eased, I brought myself to say, "What did you put on me, hi'Blessed?"

"The living sigil of the unnamed goddess. Many years ago when I was young, I found her here quite by accident and have dedicated my life to her. Until today she had not yet allowed me to pass the sigil on to anyone."

I cried knowing none of the six sigils would be mine. When I looked at hi'Blessed Tasilaba, she was crying too. I wanted to die. Could I be a Talon without any sigils? This was unheard of. With the back of my hand, I wiped away the tears but they continued streaking down my face.

"Aisha Talon, you are hi'Blessed," she whispered as if in reverence and turned towards the bowl with nothing painted on it. She knelt with head bowed.

"Hi'Blessed? You mean they all took? But I thought--"

"No. None of the six sigils took."

"But you said hi'--"

"You are immune to all sigils. They cannot be used against you. The unnamed one has blessed you with the seventh sigil, Negation!"

"Hi'Blessed, why do you call her the 'unnamed' one? I wanted to know the goddess I should honor for my gift."

"Because, if we name her, the world would be negated. That is her power. Would everything be unmade? I am not sure, but her power is great." And so she swore me to secrecy.

She pulled back the sleeve of her dark gray silk tunic to expose an intensely red Energy Sigil. As I watched, it moved slightly under her skin.

"You know what it does. My energy and vitality were always high, even as a girl. Now it never flags, even in my age."

My mouth dropped open as I realized that I could sense the Sigil on her arm. It was like a melody, one I had always known.

"Now think on your own Sigil. Nudge it with your mind," she said.

This was new and seemed hard until I realized it was little different from the battle mode I was so used to. My sigil responded with almost a sigh and hers grew still. I watched it for a moment, waiting for it to continue its slight movement, but nothing happened.

"Did I hurt it?"

"No, it only sleeps. Release yours and you will see."

In a few moments, her sigil again began the small motions that showed it was at work. I knelt and she gave me her blessing before I began the trek back down the mountain with much to think about and consider. How would I keep this secret from my good friends?

Tellac and Melor made an honest attempt to tell me I didn't need sigils and that I was good without them. That was when I began to understand my gift. Since Melor had received the Truth Sigil in the cave, he should have been able to tell I was lying about my experience. I only thought of my sigil and could feel it moving. I sneaked peeks at his and realized that his Sigil of Truth had stilled. Even with his War Sigil, Tellac was still hard pressed to beat me much to his amazement. Each time he used his War Sigil I could see it moving as if coming alive, but it stilled as though sleeping when my back came alive. It was beautiful to watch the sigils as they twisted and grew. In time, they would become more vivid and colorful. I wished I could see mine.

* * * *

The days of our student alliance ended soon after we had been declared Talons.

"Aisha, we have a contract!" Tellac shouted as he and Melor charged into my room and slid to a halt in front of me. I had been studying a manuscript of herbs. "Melor and I are being assigned to the kingdom of Valda as guards to the hi'Lord Radulf."

I was happy for them but disappointed I hadn't been included. I worried that Master Dragos might have trouble finding a contract for a young woman.

"That's wonderful. I only wish I was going with you. I'll miss you two." My stomach twisted and I felt tears in my eyes that I held back. They must only see my joy, not my fears.

Two days later, Tellac and Melor started out for their assignment. I walked with them for a while, trying to put off saying goodbye.

"Don't worry Aisha," Tellac said. "Master Dragos will find something for you soon. After all, there must be many assignments where a female Talon is uniquely qualified, and you are the only one available right now." I gave Tellac and Melor each a long tight hug, not wanting to let them go. They turned and continued their trek down the mountain trail. I waited until they were out of sight before returning to the Aerie.

"From Tellac's lips to the goddess' ears," I mumbled as I climbed back up toward the fortress.

* * * *

A week later I knelt in front of Master Dragos, bowed, and waited for him to speak. He wore black silk. His sash had three beautifully embroidered four-talon feet of a raptor, which proclaimed him the master of the Raptor Clan. Talon masters had two, four-talon feet on their sash. A Talon like me had only one.

"You continue to confuse me, Sister Aisha." Dragos said, his voice soft. "You had been designated the weakest at each of your first four Ordeals, yet you are still here. Master Jiang says that you are always the best prepared, whereas the others rely on their skill alone. That is high praise from the head instructor at the Aerie. Now hi'Blessed Tasilaba calls you hi'Blessed. Did you receive all six sigils?"

"No, Master Dragos."

"Let me see your arms," he demanded.

11

I rolled up both sleeves to show my naked skin.

"None? Why did she call you hi'Blessed?" His frustration leaked through his otherwise calm exterior.

"You will have to ask her, Master Dragos." I felt trapped.

"She refused to tell me. Relax, Aisha. Hi'Blessed Tasilaba is a force unto herself. The clan could replace me in a day, but they couldn't replace her in a lifetime. If she says you are hi'Blessed, I will accept it without question." He paused, pursed his lips and paced with his head down. "I can only hope they are both right."

He stopped for several seconds and fastened his piercing gaze on me before he continued. "Is it fair that I will place a great responsibility on one young and untried?" He shrugged. "I have no choice. Bakaar has already accepted a contract, and this calls for a female. But this assignment will require more than just skill. The Raptor Clan has been shamed. While Talons guarded the family of the hi'Lord of Granya, his wife, son, and oldest daughter were murdered. Only his youngest daughter survived. I am sending you to protect her. It is up to you to regain the honor of the Clan." Dragos never lifted his voice, but his eyes blazed with fury.

"Valen!" His aide entered the room with a bundle that he unwrapped and laid out neatly on the floor in front of me: a composite bow and quiver, a double-edged sword, two daggers, six throwing knives, and two survival knives. Each piece was an exquisite work of art. The bow was made from antler, sinew and a rare dark blood-red wood found only in the Manipur Mountains. The sword and knives were Astrakan crafted with black-wrapped handles and legendary patterned-textured blades, capable of cutting through rock. The traditional weapons given to a new Talon are worth more than the average commoner could earn in ten years.

My expression remained serene, but inside, my blood pounded in my temples. I was bursting with pride, a deep love of my clan. I bowed so low, my head touched the floor. "Thank you, Master Dragos. I will protect her with my life."

"Fail not in your duty, Sister Aisha."

I bowed again, rose, and followed Valen from the room and down the portico to his room.

"These are the terms of the clan's contract with hi'Lord Varius, the ruler of Granya. You are to memorize them along with Master Dragos's written instructions, attached to the contract. When you are ready, a guide will be at the gate to accompany you down the mountain. A caravan will escort you to Savona, the capital of Granya."

As he left the room, his fingers signed, **Glory is yours to earn.** Valen's parting gesture was the closest anyone in the clan came to wishing another luck. They believed a person determined their own success or failure. If one were prepared, they shouldn't need luck. I agreed, but I would never snub a helping nudge from Huan, the goddess of luck.

I spent the next hour studying the contract and Master Dragos's instructions before putting them back on Valen's table. The contract intrigued me. I would be a bodyguard to the heir of a kingdom but pretend to be her chaperone. In a way it was perfect for me. The goddess had heard Tellac's words. I had survived my early years at the Aerie by my wits, pretending to be clumsy, weak on one side or the other as I fought, somewhat stupid and slow with instructions.

I returned to my quarters and packed my meager possessions into two canvas kits. One I would leave at the Aerie, and one I would take with me to Savona. While posing as a chaperone I would keep my identity secret, hoping an assassin would dismiss me as harmless. I could take nothing that might identify me as belonging to the Raptor Clan except my weapons. Those I'd conceal on my body in hidden sheaths or give them for safekeeping to my Talon brothers who guarded the Granya ruler and his daughter.

I stopped on the portico outside my room to watch the students in the courtyard, as usual a bee hive of activity with ten years of students engaged in the many arts of becoming Talons. I stood there and purposed an outward serenity of a well-disciplined Talon while my heart pounded, my face flushed, tears formed in my eyes, and I bit my lip. This was my home and I would soon leave it.

Master Jiang approached. "Good hunting, Sister Aisha." A traitorous tear escaped my left eye and began its trek down my cheek.

13

"Emotions can get you killed, Sister Aisha." He reached up and brushed the tear away. "And that would be a shame after all the effort I've devoted to training you."

Glory is yours to earn, Sister Raptor. Jiang signed. The term "Raptor" was a high compliment from any clan member and an honor from a Master. He turned away, and I strode to the storeroom.

"Master Bakaar, I need to store a kit while I'm on contract," I said, handing her my bag. Bakaar always amazed me. Small and skinny, she looked like she would be easy to overpower. But I had seen her in the practice yard. She was as quick as a viper and just as deadly, a good reminder not to assume anything about potential opponents from their looks. Assumptions could kill you.

"Sister Aisha, I have a kit for you from Master Dragos." Bakaar handed me a well-worn kit. When I looked, it contained peasant clothes for traveling, the special sheaths for weapon concealment, a generous sack of silver and gold scrules for expenses, and two letters for hi'Lord Varius. I emptied my kit into the well-worn one, changed clothes, and went to find my guide off the mountain. I found him waiting at the gate.

When my guide saw me, he bowed and exited the small door in the gate.

"Duty, adventure, a new life awaits me outside those gates," I mused as my steps quickened in anticipation.

CHAPTER TWO

Road to Savona: Duty calls

"Quinius, these past six days have been amazing," I said as we walked alongside the eight pack horses piled with burdens of trade goods. The caravan included the Merchant Quinius, two Talon guards, six members of Quinius's extended family, and me. My heart thumped with excitement. Today we would finally reach Savona, the capital of Granya. "Remember the first village we stopped at? I thought it was huge."

Quinius laughed. He was tall, wiry, and not unattractive, though he was at least ten years older than me. "All one thousand peasants. If they didn't produce such exquisite leather work, I wouldn't have bothered stopping."

"You made a good profit on those goods in the next town."

"That is what traders do. We buy in one place and sell in another."

"The second village, when we crossed into Granya, was what I imagined Savona would be like." I laughed at my inexperience. I'm sure Quinius thought me a naïve mountain woman on her first trip off the mountain, which, in a way, I was. Fortunately, it fit with the mountain woman chaperone image I had been told to assume. In fact, I had been raised in a tiny mountain village, and my home for the past ten years had been the Aerie, an isolated mountain fortress. "It did have a castle."

"That wasn't a castle, merely the home of a minor Fifth Lord," Quinius replied still laughing. "You really are a gem in the rough, Aisha. I wish you would join my house. I'm wealthy and would take good care of you."

"What would your wife say?" I grew curious in spite of myself.

"She wouldn't mind. She's well cared for, and I would bother her less. Besides, she never accompanies me on trips as you would."

Quinius had been trying for six days to lure me into his

bedroll. He tried charm, gifts, money, employment, and now second wife. I admit I was flattered by the attention. Someone trying to entice me was new, and I enjoyed the feeling. At the Aerie, I was a student: neither male nor female. I had been an object to be studied, pushed, and prodded to watch perform. He was attracted to me and showed it. This was fun, even though Quinius didn't interest me in that way.

"I am committed under contract to hi'Lord Varius. I don't think he would like me or you if I broke my word," I said for the twentieth time.

"I'm sure we could work something out."

We stepped past the last straggling trees of the forest and saw a huge white edifice in the distance. "What is that?" I said with a gasp.

"That is the city wall. It's close to twenty paces high and over a league long, spanning all the way between the banks of the East and West Mystic Rivers." Quinius swept his hand from one side to the other.

Walking several hours, we passed small farms and a scattering of stone houses with wisps of smoke drifting from chimneys above thatched roofs. These abruptly ended as we neared the wall. The ground in front of the rampart was cleared for several hundred paces, a killing ground for any enemy attacking the city.

"Now that is a castle." Quinius pointed ahead.

I saw the city and the castle above the wall. They were built into the side of a steep hill at the apex of the triangle formed by the fork in the Mystic River. Quinius was right. Even from a distance, the castle was a spectacular structure sitting atop the hill, sparkling white in the morning sun.

We entered the city through a massive arched tunnel with several iron gates, now open, and many killing slots for archers and burning oil. The guards knew Quinius and passed him and his caravan through with a wave. As we wound our way up the main road, the houses and shops increased in size, better repaired and more elegant and elegance, better maintained. The houses down the side streets looked smaller and a bit ramshackle.

About half way up the hill, Quinius turned onto a side

street and into a small fenced-in courtyard. "Aisha, if you get tired of hi'Varius's daughter, you are welcome to come live here."

"Thank you, Quinius. I will consider it," I lied, easier than telling the truth. The exciting part was that he believed me. He had to. He wore a Truth Sigil. I had noticed the amulet around his neck days ago and recognized the sigil as one of the weaker that could be purchased instead of having the mark on his body. It wouldn't have mattered, because I could sense its presence and even its kind. I could activate my sigil merely by thinking about it. Though I was lying, Quinius believed me because his sigil didn't detect my lie. Hi'Blessed Tasilaba was right. The Negation Sigil was better than having one or two sigils of my own.

Resigned that I was leaving, Quinius assigned his nephew to see me to the castle. I gawked at the houses as they got bigger, many with large fenced courtyards, as we continued up the hill.

The castle had its own rampart, twenty-paces-high, multiple turrets, and another killing tunnel entrance. The guards passed me through the gates but had me wait for their sergeant. The castle was breathtaking. White granite, the keep stretched fifty paces long and rose six stories. Three attached towers ascended an additional two to four stories. Several smaller three story buildings extended off the main one with its own eight-story towers, massive and beautiful.

When the sergeant arrived, I was passed from sergeant of the guard to officer, to captain, to minor noble, and finally to Minister Lucas. The Minister kept an icy silence and sniffed as though he stood too near the privy.

I couldn't help staring at the opulence of the hallways and offices as I was led through the castle. Hundreds of tapestries, sculptures, and wall carvings adorned walls, ceilings, and floors. The Aerie was stark by comparison. Lucas at last led me into the hi'Lord's private study which was paneled in golden oak. Varius sat in a massive ornate gold chair behind an equally ornate desk. A young girl sat in a large chair to his right. She was elegantly adorned in a dark blue velvet over dress, pinned at each shoulder with a gold broach. The lace edging of her underdress showed around her feet. Three Talon guards stood with hands on their weapons, ranged about the room.

"Hi'Lord Varius, this young woman--" Lucas said with a scornful twist of his lip, as he handed Varius the letter. "She is in possession of the letter you sent to the mountain tribe leader, Ferka, requesting a chaperone for your daughter. Your pardon, hi'Lord, but I still don't understand why you didn't choose someone from the Granya nobility. A mountain woman will lower your daughter's prestige."

"Thank you, Lucas. That will be all." Varius gave the document a cursory examination and laid it aside. Lucas turned suddenly, lowering his shoulder and stepping into me. My first reaction was to twist sideways to redirect the force of his shoulder, but I forced myself to freeze. He rammed into my chest. I intentionally stumbled backward, tripped, and landed on my rear as my kit went flying. I thought my performance was spectacular.

"Ow!" I shouted and did my best to look hurt and shocked. "You are very clumsy, Minister Lucas."

"Let me help you up." He extended his hand.

"No, thank you, sir. I will just sit here for a moment while I catch my breath." I refused the proffered hand.

I continued to be amazed by my Negation Sigil. This is the first time I had been near so many people with sigils. I could not only detect their sigils but even their holder's power to a degree. Varius had living Truth and Energy Sigils, both moderately strong. Lucas had Truth and Charm Sigils, both rather weak. Master Taras and the other two guards each had strong War Sigils. I guessed, partly by the weakness of the sigils, that Lucas had purchased amulets from the Blessed ones, who made comfortable livings selling sigils at their temples. One of the Talon guards, the senior one, judging by the two four-talon feet embroidered on his sash, walked over and looked at me. After a moment, he reached down and lifted me easily to my feet, handing me my kit.

"I'm sorry hi'Lord, I didn't know she was that close to me," Lucas muttered in apology to Varius, not me. I knew that the collision was intentional. *But why?*

"You can go, Lucas. I'm sure Mistress Aisha will be all

18

right." Varius openly scrutinized me. He looked me up and down as he smoothed the heavy silk of his dark blue tunic over his substantial stomach. He waited for his minister to leave before continuing. "You are clumsy for a Talon."

"Talon?" Rhiannon said. "Father, she can't be a Talon. She can't even protect herself. How is she going to protect me?" Rhiannon jumped to her feet and pointed an accusing finger at me.

"I feel just awful," I said, beginning to enjoy my charade. After all, I was supposed to be a chaperone, not a bodyguard. I looked shyly at Rhiannon, but inside I couldn't help laughing at the young girl's outrage. My new charge was not afraid to express her opinion. Rhiannon's complexion was fair although now it was flushed. She had blond hair, blue eyes, small full lips, and a round face. At sixteen she was several centimeters shorter than I was, a bit chubby. I wondered whether it was a family trait or from too much food and too little physical activity. Her father was a big man with a square, overweight build, sandy hair, blue eyes, and the same rounded face.

Don't overdo it, Sister, the Talon who had picked me up off the floor signed, after he had returned to his place next to the hi'Lord.

It's my first time off the mountain. I signed back, which got a slight twitch of the lip from the other two Talon guards. Everyone knew the Talons signed, but it was against clan law to disclose the meaning of the hand movements.

"Taras, is this a joke?" Varius demanded. "I'm not paying for a Talon maid as a bodyguard for my daughter."

"Your minister intentionally stepped into her. I believe he was testing her."

"Why would Lucas be testing her? Even if he was, I agree with my daughter. She doesn't look strong enough to protect herself, much less my heir." His voice rose until it was near a shout.

"I can only guess. He was probably trying to determine if she was really a chaperone or a bodyguard."

"It's my heir's life we are talking about, Taras. Can you guarantee me she is a fully trained Talon?" Varius glared at me.

"We don't have maids, hi'Lord. She is well armed under

19

those peasant clothes."

At that, I stepped forward and handed Taras the letter with Master Dragos's seal. Taras was an older man, judging by the gray in his hair and lines on his face, but he moved with the ease and grace of a predatory cat.

"Our Senior Brother sends greetings, Master Taras," I said. Taras took the letter, examined the seal, and opened it. He scanned it then read the terse contents aloud.

"To hi'Lord Varius. This is Aisha Talon. It is signed Master Dragos."

"Taras, does that satisfy you that she is a trained Talon?" Varius' eyes still focused on me.

"If Master Dragos calls her Talon, your daughter is safe in her hands. We will not fail you in this." Taras nodded in my direction. While Varius and Taras talked, Rhiannon walked over to where I stood.

"Show me your knives," she said, her hand outstretched.

"What would a chaperone be doing with a knife, pri'Rhiannon?" I used the prefix, "pri," accorded to the heir to a kingdom. Her mouth formed into a pout which I ignored. I turned my attention back to Varius.

"Mistress Aisha, your job is to protect my daughter, with your life if necessary. You will accompany pri'Rhiannon on our journey to negotiate an alliance with hi'Lord Radulf of Valda." Varius continued to assess me. Finally, he shook his head. "I can't believe you're Talon." I ignored the remark. The hi'Lord's opinion of me meant little.

"Hi'Lord Varius, I accept that responsibility. However, no one must be told that I am a Talon. If anyone finds out, I must be told immediately. If I am to ensure your daughter's safety, we must keep my identity secret." I looked Rhiannon in the eye until she nodded nervously. My comment got the first relaxed expression from Varius.

"Excellent. Maybe it's an advantage you don't look or act like a Talon. We'll need to get you settled immediately. Taras, accompany Mistress Aisha and my daughter to her seamstress. As Rhiannon's chaperone, she will need appropriate clothing."

We made a stop at the Talon's quarters where I left my knives and harnesses. Taras agreed to watch my kit while I was

20

being fitted for new clothes.

Rhiannon and I spent over an hour at the seamstress, where I was measured and examined like some strange bug.

"You're very thin and muscular, Mistress Aisha," the seamstress Karla commented after her examination.

"Mountain life is very hard, Mistress Karla."

"What are these scars on your back?" Karla turned me around again.

"It's to keep the evil spirits away." I said this as if everyone should know such an obvious fact.

"We will have to make sure your clothes don't show that," Karla pinched her lips together and wrinkled her nose in disapproval.

Afterward, Rhiannon selected designs, colors, and cloths for ten different outfits, stealing looks in my direction. I played the naïve mountain woman agreeing with Rhiannon and complimenting her on her good taste. I had to admit that I liked her choice of colors, and it was obvious she knew the clothing I would need for each occasion.

"Mistress Karla, pri'Rhiannon's choices are beautiful, but I need you to make the skirts shorter, a hand above my ankle. I will need to move quickly as her chaperone."

The seamstress gave me a blank look of shock. "Only peasants wear short dresses!"

I smiled. "I'm a mountain woman. I am used to being thought a peasant. And please see that they all have pockets so that I can carry anything I might need for her."

The seamstress gave me long dark looks, but agreed to what I asked. I knew that I could split the pockets so that I could reach my knives hidden under my skirts, and I needed them short enough not to trip me if I needed to defend my charge. I refused only two of Rhiannon's selections because they would have impeded my movements too much in a fight.

When we finished, Rhiannon escorted me to her suite of rooms. They were elegant, a bit frilly, with lacy draperies and soft silky rugs on all of the floors. I would be living there along with two teen-aged girls who were part of Rhiannon's retinue. Silva, the daughter of a Fifth Lord, and Raya, the daughter of a Forth Lord, were her ladies-in-waiting. A third lady, Irenka, who

21

was married to a son of a Third Lord and was in her late twenties, was Rhiannon's senior lady-in-waiting and her advisor. The younger girls were friendly, but Irenka was reserved and defensive as Rhiannon introduced me.

"Siress Irenka, Siress Raya, and Siress Silva, this is Mistress Aisha. Father has hired her to be my chaperone for the trip to Dassel." Rhiannon pointed to each woman while saying her name. The title "Siress" meant they were noblewomen or, like Irenka, married to a noble. I knew from my studies that Dassel was the capital of Valda and the residence of the hi'Lord Radulf and his family.

"You look too young to be a chaperone, Mistress Aisha," Irenka swept me up and down with her eyes narrowed. Only discipline kept me from laughing. Irenka had a Charm Sigil concealed somewhere on her person, judging from its low power. Living sigils, those under the skin, were strong, since their strength came from the internal energy of the holder. They grew stronger over time and with use. The Charm Sigil made people more inclined to like you and want to be with you, which obviously wasn't Irenka's strong point. I wondered if Rhiannon knew.

"A good chaperone is not measured by her looks, rather her responsibility, Siress Irenka. Your hi'Lord felt it best to have a chaperone who had no ties to Granya or Valda. And because I'm a mountain woman, it will be easy to explain my lack of court manners if it becomes necessary to hurt someone's feelings." It was obvious to me that Irenka would like the position of chaperone and was not above trying to discredit me to get it. "Besides, that will leave you and the other young ladies time to enjoy yourselves without having to worry about pri'Rhiannon's honor."

The sleeping arrangements were simple. Irenka had a room elsewhere in the castle with her husband. Raya and Silva had the room next to Rhiannon for easy access to her, and I was given the unused room next to Rhiannon's sitting room a few steps down the corridor. I would have preferred to have the room next to Rhiannon, but Talon guards were on duty night and day at each door, which provided direct or indirect access to Rhiannon.

As I was getting ready for bed that night, there was a knock at the door.

"Enter." Each hand sought a knife, one for throwing and one for fighting. However, I relaxed as Master Taras entered with another guard. Taras closed the door.

"This is Brother Leszek, the senior Talon on pri'Rhiannon's guard detail." Leszek was blessed with the strongest Energy Sigil I had ever felt.

"Good evening, Sister Aisha." Leszek took a seat. " I'm pleased you are here. Are you aware that Lady Varius, her oldest daughter and only son were murdered several months ago? That is the reason for the nine Talon guards currently assigned to pri'Rhiannon."

"Yes, Master Dragos explained our precarious position with hi'Varius."

"As a consequence, one or more of us accompanies her everywhere we can, but it is not always possible to have her directly in our sight, for example, when she is sleeping, dressing, or washing. I feel more confident with you here that we can now adequately protect her." Leszek sighed with relief.

"You are just the Talon I needed to see, Brother Leszek. Please require your guards to introduce themselves to me at each shift change, no matter the time. I want no confusion if trouble arises." I had a concern that I didn't know them, couldn't tell friends from enemies. "And can you get me a map of the castle?"

Leszek and Taras spent the next hour bringing me up to date and drawing a map.

I went to sleep pleased. I was finally out in the world supporting the Raptor Clan and enjoying every minute of it.

     * * *

I exited my room through the side door into the sitting room and crossed to the adjacent door to Rhiannon's bedroom. As I walked I patted the knives from the Aerie that I placed in the special pocket sheaths in my bloomers.

"Good morn, pri'Rhiannon." I put on a broad smile for the morning greeting. Rhiannon was still in bed under several puffy blankets.

"You are supposed to knock before you enter." Rhiannon soured her face and protested the intrusion. "Chaperones are terrible people, pri'Rhiannon. They follow you everywhere, stick their nose into everything you do without asking permission and allow their charges no privacy. Terrible people. And mountain women are the worst." I sat in one of the two red-velvet arm chairs facing Rhiannon's huge, pink-canopied bed.

"I demand respect. I am the hi'Lord's heir!"

"Mountain women only respect age. When you are older than me, I will give you the respect you deserve."

"But I will never be older than you!"

"We should get along well, now that you understand the problem." Perhaps I should have reasoned with her, explaining how a bodyguard worked. However, I suspect that would have taken all day and involved numerous arguments. This was easier. "I'm in charge. I decide, not you."

"You're terrible." Rhiannon mumbled something and pulled the covers over her head. I remained seated as her retinue arrived and prepared Rhiannon for the day. I was fascinated by the life she led. Irenka discussed her schedule, what she should wear, and who would be at each event, while Silva and Raya helped her wash, dress, and prepare her hair. I heard in great boring detail the castle gossip about how someone had been seen flirting with a Fifth Lord and another expected her betrothal to be announced soon. None of the names meant a thing to me.

Rhiannon's first meal was served in the sitting room where two Talons stood guard. Two maids and a junior cook delivered more food than I thought we could eat in several days, including some dishes I didn't recognize. The young cook Ferox offered Rhiannon a small tray with a variety of condiments.

"Honey, Ferox," she said and waited as he ladled a spoon full of honey over her hot barley and oats porridge. The way he looked at her out of the corner of his eye made an alarm go off in my head. I was certain it was trouble when Irenka asked for honey and Ferox ladled it from a different place on the tray. I reached over, put my finger into Rhiannon's dish and tasted a faint bitterness under the intense sweetness of the honey, cyanide. I thought it would not be enough to kill her but wouldn't take the chance.

"That's disgusting! If you wanted to taste it, you should have had Ferox put some on a plate." Rhiannon's face flushed with indignation

"What can you expect from a mountain woman," Irenka said, her face pinched in disapproval. Irenka had added a Truth Sigil today, as weak as her Charm Sigil. I felt a little sorry for her having to resort to sigils. On the other hand, it wasn't very honest for a lady-in-waiting. I mentally activated my Negation Sigil to inactivate hers.

"I may not have liked it. But I'm sure she doesn't want to eat it now." I scooped the plate up from in front of her and handed it to a servant. I needed to act fast. Turning away from the women, I signed to the guard.

Detain Ferox and his tray after he leaves. Be careful with the tray and its contents.

Do you need another guard in here?

No.

CHAPTER THREE

`Savona: Treachery at work*

"I find your behavior unacceptable. Your manners are atrocious. You act like a barbarian, show me no respect. I am the heir to the Granya Kingdom and you are nothing." Rhiannon glared at me with her hands on her hips. "And you embarrassed me in front of my ladies."

"I would have your father replace her," Irenka said. Her face screwed up in an expression of disdain. "Someone who respects you and your position. She is obviously not the right person."

"I'll go pack," I said. I stood and turned toward the remaining guard. **Don't leave her alone.**

Out the door, Irenka sneered at me like she had won. Leszek waited for me in the hallway.

Where did they take Ferox, Brother? I signed. Although I saw no one, hallways have ears. You never knew who might be just around the corner or behind one of the many closed doors. I couldn't afford to be careless, especially now that I knew an attempt had been made on Rhiannon's life.

They have taken him to the Talon's quarters. Leszek signed in response. I remembered the map Leszek had given me. The Talons had rooms on the lower level in a building adjacent to the main castle.

We wended our way through the maze of hallways past guards in their armor and finely dressed courtiers going about their business. I still felt a bit intimidated by the elegance of the place with its statues in nooks interspersed with colorful tapestries of feasts and battles. In five minutes we reached the Talon's area.

Greetings Sister, the guard signed as we approached.

Greetings, Brother.

We entered a spacious room, crowded with eight bunks, kits, and a large table which currently held Ferox's condiment tray.

"What did Ferox do for you to have him kidnapped? Did he antagonize you, Mistress Aisha?" The guard laughed at his own quip.

"He should pray to the goddess Yun he doesn't. I'm a terrible person as pri'Rhiannon will tell you." Nearby, another Talon watched Ferox, standing between him and the tray that was in the middle of the table. "Leszek, I would like to talk with the master herbalist."

I felt certain cyanide had been mixed with the honey in the second of the two bowls; however, I needed someone to corroborate my findings. Hi'Varius might not believe me. I had to wonder if Master Taras might be right; I had overdone my acting. No, if I'm not consistent, I will eventually make a mistake and someone will deduce the truth. I must act the chaperone all the time.

"That would be Master Hormiz," Leszek said.

"Can you bring him here?"

"I'll find him." Leszek turned and left the room.

"Please take Ferox to another room," I said to the outside guard.

"Ferox, come with me." The guard gripped the young man's arm and guided him toward a side room.

"I didn't do anything. Why are you keeping me prisoner? What did I do?" Ferox protested. The other Talon also started to leave as Ferox was led out.

"Please stay. I need you to guard the tray. Hi'Varius is likely to think I gave her poison myself if I were left alone with the herbs." He smiled at my gibe.

"Hi'Varius has always been very protective of this daughter, more so since the assassination of his wife and other children. Siress Irenka encourages pri'Rhiannon to take advantage of her new status and her father's concern. I don't envy you having to deal with them."

As one of Rhiannon's guard detail, he had been exposed to her for well over a month. He confirmed what I had observed. I nodded but did not respond. Instead, I examined the tray of

27

spices still sitting on the table. I recognized every item, not from having been served them on my food, but from my studies of poisonous and non-poisonous herbs. I smiled. At the time I had thought I was learning how to poison someone, not how to recognize being poisoned.

Leszek entered a short time later with a small, bent-looking man with shaggy gray hair, a wrinkled face, and stained hands. I detected a living Healing Sigil but nothing else. From the strength of the sigil, I knew he was talented in his profession. He had the robe of a Master Apothecary, gray with silver trim. By the look of the scowl on his face he wasn't in a good mood.

"I am Master Hormiz. I demand to know why I was forced here!"

"To tell me what condiments are on that tray." I pointed to the tray, deciding that talking nice to him wasn't going to appease him.

Hormiz walked over to the tray, looked, and turned back to me. "Any junior cook could have identified those. Parsley, pepper, dill, garlic, chives, honey chili, raisins, honey--"

"Please humor me and taste each condiment before you name them," I said. Hormiz's lips pursed in disgust. He looked defiant until Leszek nodded towards the tray, relented and shuffled to the table where he began sampling the contents of each bowl.

"Parsley...pepper...dill ...garlic...chives...honey...chili...raisins...honey--" Hormiz stopped in mid-sentence. His hand trembled as he dipped his finger back into the second bowl of honey, then smeared it on the back of his hand and bent to sniff and inspect it. "This honey has a powder mixed in with it." He tasted it again. "It's bitter...Cyanide! Did someone give this to hi'Varius? Is he ill?"

Well done, Sister. Leszek signed from behind Hormiz.

"Master Hormiz, let me introduce you to pri'Rhiannon's chaperone, Mistress Aisha. She is a mountain woman and well acquainted with poisonous herbs. This tray was used to serve pri'Rhiannon this morning," Leszek said.

"May the blessed god Jian save her. What do the healers say?" Hormiz asked. His hands jerked in nervous spasms as if no longer under his control.

"The dose was small," I said, "and pri'Rhiannon appeared well at her morning meal. I believe this is a new attempt on her life. I detected it before she ate enough to cause serious damage. The healers haven't yet been informed, in order to give the Talon time to determine who is behind this attempt on her life before they know we have spoiled their plans."

"I understand." Hormiz clasped his hands together to still their twitching and calmed himself.

"I'm grateful to you for confirming my suspicions, but for now, I must swear you to secrecy in both word and action."

"Yes, of course. You will notify Master Healer Luminita soon?" Hormiz asked, his eyes moist with concern. "I realized that many in the palace must be upset and grieved with the deaths of hi'Varius's family so recently."

"Yes, she will be notified today." Leszek led Hormiz towards the door with his hand under the man's elbow.

Bring me Ferox. I signed when Hormiz had turned away.

When Leszek returned with Ferox, the young man's shirt showed rings of sweat under the arms; his face was pale, and his eyes darted everywhere like a caged animal. "Why are you doing this to me?" he half shouted as Leszek closed the door behind them.

"Do you know what you have been serving pri'Rhiannon, Ferox?" I asked. Only she had been served from the second bowl of honey; therefore, Ferox had intentionally given her that mixture.

"No…yes, medicine! I don't know what kind." Ferox's eyes darted back and forth between the tray and me.

"Cyanide." I hoped to discover something from his reaction. In a way, it would be nice to have a Truth Sigil even though it would only show what he thought was the truth. However, as convenient as the Truth Sigil was, it did not indicate the truth of the statement, only whether the individual believed it to be the truth. Because of that, I knew that depending on one could be risky.

29

"No! The healer told me it was medicine to cure a -- a woman's problem she had. Ferox squirmed like an animal caught in a trap. He said I shouldn't let anyone else know because it would embarrass her. That's why there are two containers of honey. One with the medicine and one without. Pri'Rhiannon and Siress Irenka always have honey on their porridge."

"Which healer?" I thought he was telling the truth judging by his defensiveness and fear; otherwise, he was a superb liar.

"Master Healer Luminita's assistant, Healer Herk. I only followed his orders. He said Healer Luminita had prescribed it for her."

"Did you mix the medicine with the honey?" I wondered how he failed to recognize the cyanide.

"No, mistress. Healer Herk gave me the honey already mixed and marked the bowl to make sure I used the right one. See, the bowl has a small nick on the rim." Ferox walked over to the tray and pointed to the edge of the bowl. "I've got to get back to work. I'm going to be in a lot of trouble if I don't."

"You have been very helpful, Ferox, and I tend to believe you didn't mean to poison pri'Rhiannon. You will, however, have to wait for a while longer. Don't worry; I will make sure you don't get in any trouble for being away from your work." I still needed to verify his story before I could let him go, and I had to figure out how to stop him from talking about the cyanide.

The guard took the hint and escorted Ferox back to the other room.

"Leszek, get me Healer Herk. The game is getting interesting." I was making progress.

"Very interesting," Leszek said. "I also hear pri'Rhiannon is with her father, wanting you reprimanded or maybe whipped." His lip twitched as he tried not to smile. "I've never seen a Talon whipped."

"Chaperones are terrible people, Brother Leszek. Go now. You're delaying my whipping." I smiled. Neither Leszek nor anyone else would live to see a Talon whipped.

I sat on one of the bunks, considering what I had learned about the intrigue surrounding the hi'Lord and his daughter. I hadn't realized how much I would enjoy playing the chaperone and the clandestine routing out of the enemy. It was my duty. I would protect Rhiannon with my life, but I found it more exciting than I had ever imagined. It was developing into my first entertaining game of wits, a game I intended to win. My thoughts were interrupted as the door opened and Leszek dragged a middle aged man into the room.

"I demand to know why you have dragged me here, and who is she?" Herk pointed at me. "Hi'Varius will be notified of this offensive behavior towards his healer."

"She is Mistress Aisha, pri'Rhiannon's chaperone. She will determine whether you live or die." Leszek's mouth thinned to a sharp line and his nostrils flared.

Herk froze. The color drained from his face as his eyes darted to the tray of herbs on the table. His lips trembled. He had a living Illusion Sigil and a purchased Healing Sigil. I thought that was strange as he was a healer, and a potential assassin. Just then he gave me my first demonstration of an Illusion Sigil in action. As I watched, the bowl with the poison disappeared. Although I hadn't activated my sigil, I could see two images, the real one and the illusion. The illusion was misty while everything else was clear.

"You can do this the easy way or the hard way, Healer Herk. The easy way would be for you to explain to me who you are aiding in your attempt to kill pri'Rhiannon and beg my mercy. The hard way would be for you to refuse to tell me what I want to know. In the latter case, I'll turn you over to the Talons who will demonstrate their skill at causing you severe physical damage and excruciating pain." I emphasized each word. "Oh, your illusion is very nice, but we know where the second bowl containing the poison is located on the tray."

Herk remained silent, but his eyes widened. I could almost hear him weighing his limited options: "they" will kill me...or...the Talon will kill me.

"I believe Healer Herk needs a little demonstration," I said when Herk continued to remain silent.

Leszek gripped him by the neck and pressed his thumb into the nerves. The man jerked helplessly and screamed. Leszek released him.

31

"I didn't do anything wrong. I'll see you whipped," Herk shouted. At that, I thought I saw Leszek lips twitch.

"I guess Healer Herk wasn't impressed with your demonstration, Leszek Talon." I sighed. "He appears more scared of his accomplices than the Talon. Or, perhaps the Talon are over-rated, Leszek Talon?"

"Perhaps if I cut out an eye or two," Leszek said as a knife appeared in his hand, and he stroked Herk's cheek with it.

"No! I'll tell you what you want to know." Herk screeched, his voice rising as his eyes tried to track the blade sliding down his cheek.

"The truth please, Healer Herk. The truth will get you mercy. Lies will earn you a short lifetime of darkness and suffering." I pointed at one of the bunks toward which Leszek pushed the sobbing man. "Now, Healer Herk, start at the beginning. If I detect any lies, I will stop the questioning and turn you over to Leszek Talon. I believe he would look forward to proving the Talon's talent with knives."

"I was approached three weeks ago by a man claiming to be a messenger from an unknown Lord. He said change was in progress. A prominent Second Lord would replace hi'Varius. If I would help expedite the change, I would become the head healer for the new hi'Lord. I was told the change would happen with or without me." Herk's voice trembled, barely above a whisper. Sweat beaded on his forehead, running down his face, and he turned a ghostly white.

"Who was this messenger?" I prodded when he failed to continue. He swayed and paled even more.

"I don't know. Honestly! I insisted on talking with the unknown Second Lord. A meeting was arranged, but Third Lady Castor and several nobles I didn't know showed up instead. Tri'Castor insisted that the Second Lord remain anonymous. She offered me fifty gold scrules as a sign of good faith. They gave me the cyanide and an advance of twenty-five scrules. I didn't think I had a choice. Tri'Castor would have had me killed if I had rejected her offer." Herk's voice lowered to a grating whine. I suspected that Castor would have eventually killed him in any case.

32

"When did you give the mixture to Ferox?" I needed to know how many doses of cyanide Rhiannon had been given.

"Three days ago."

"Based on the concentration, how many doses would it take to kill her?"

"It depends upon the exact amount she ate at each meal. Somewhere between fifteen and twenty days," Herk said, his voice becoming a little firmer as he talked about his own field of study.

"You will be held by the Talon until we can verify your story. If you have told me the truth, the Talon will give the mercy I promised." I doubted that Varius would show him any. I turned my attention to Leszek. "Can you secure Healer Herk while we verify his story?"

"Yes, we have secure rooms of our own."

"I would like to talk to Master Healer Luminita."

Leszek nodded, grabbed Herk by the upper arm, and dragged him from the room.

I slowed my breathing as I sought my center--a place of peace. I couldn't help but wonder what Rhiannon and her father had decided about my behavior. His reaction would tell me a lot about the hi'Lord and his daughter. Perhaps the timing was good. It would be an ideal opportunity to make sure they faced reality.

Master Luminita wore the traditional robe of a master healer, white with gold trim instead of silver. I was surprised that she seemed no more than in her late twenties, young to have a master rank. Thin and very tall, her face was narrow with high cheek bones, full lips, dark complexion, and dark red hair. She seemed tranquil considering she had been dragged here without an explanation. Her living Healer Sigil blazed with power, as did her living Truth Sigil.

"Master Luminita, what can you tell me about Healer Herk, please?" The word please somehow seemed appropriate for someone so calm.

"I know Leszek Talon. The question is who are you, and why is he doing your bidding?" Luminita questioned aloud and paused as she assessed me before continuing. "Pri'Rhiannon's chaperone, mountain woman, and what else, Mistress Aisha?"

Luminita's voice was soft yet clear. Her eyes met and held mine, as she seemed to look into my mind. "Yes, I see…Herk is a good healer but not a Master Healer. However, he believes he should be the head healer for the kingdom. I'm afraid this is nothing you couldn't find out listening to the castle gossip."

"Then you won't be surprised to find out that he was helping to poison pri'Rhiannon?" I maintained eye contact with her. My time had come to try to look into her mind, but she never blinked.

"Cyanide," she stated with assurance after a short pause. "Pri'Rhiannon had stomach pains, as well as a little diarrhea and vomiting yesterday. Symptoms of cholera or, more likely, spoiled food. Or mild cyanide poisoning. I didn't examine her. Healer Herk did. I was scheduled to go to Terni and Livorno over the next two weeks. May I see her?"

"She is all right. We need you to continue as usual, so we don't alert the people that Healer Herk is conspiring with to kill pri'Rhiannon."

"Yes, I understand. I will want to talk with Master Hormiz."

"You may. He is aware that she has been poisoned. He verified the poison in the tray on the table." I nodded toward the tray still in the middle of the nearby table. "And we will find an excuse later today for you to see her."

"Do you know the amount and the number of times she received it?"

"According to Healer Herk and Ferox, it has been served three times. Healer Herk made the mixture and says it would have taken at least fifteen servings." I couldn't help a small smile that touched my lips. "Considering, I believe he was speaking the truth. And I averted today's serving."

"That is encouraging news, Mistress Aisha. You are good at what you do. Pri'Rhiannon is fortunate to have you as a…chaperone." Luminita bowed and turned to leave. I stood speechless until well after she had left.

"I need to talk with Ferox," I said to Leszek when I recovered.

34

He had crossed his arms over his chest and wore a peculiar look on his face. "Come, he is in the next room."

Ferox stood babbling as I entered the room. "How is pri'Rhiannon? Did I kill her? I didn't mean to. I swear it before the goddess!"

"Ferox, how would you like to help me catch the evil people who would do her harm?" I decided I needed additional help if I was going to win this game. Who better than a servant? Servants were beneath a noble's notice, ever-present but invisible.

"Yes, how can I help?"

"By telling me what you hear. I know the nobles don't pay any attention to servants like us. You hear and see things they don't realize you do, right." My assurance made the question a fact.

"That's true, but--"

"I don't want you to spy. I don't want you to do anything different from what you do every day. Just listen. Listen to the nobles, listen to what the other servants are saying, and report what they say to me. That will help me protect pri'Rhiannon, and I will make sure the hi'Lord knows you helped me save her life. It is important that you don't do anything different than you do now. Just listen."

"I'll do it, Mistress Aisha." A smile lighted his face. "I'll do it. I hear lots of things every day."

"Good. Act normal and don't talk to me unless you can do so without notice. In an emergency you can always let one of the Talons know you need to see me. As for today, tell everyone I caused you trouble because pri'Rhiannon was mad at me, and I blamed you. If necessary, Leszek Talon will confirm your story. Don't forget to say some nasty things about me. Now go." I patted him conspiratorially on the shoulder.

When he left I turned to Leszek. "An interesting day, Brother Leszek."

"Yes, you may have averted a whipping." He laughed. "This attempt on pri'Rhiannon's life was just the kind of assassination attempt I feared we wouldn't be able to stop without someone close to her. Even so you exceeded my expectations, Sister Aisha."

35

I smiled. I loved the Aerie, but it was never so much fun or so satisfying.

"Master Healer Luminita surprised me. She has such a presence about her." I thought back on my interview with her. "It felt like she could read my mind."

"Yes, she is an amazing woman, wise beyond her years, gentle and refreshing as a cool, soft breeze from Lake Tiamat." Leszek's face colored as he cleared his throat.

"It sounds like you know her, Brother."

"Yes, Healer Luminita and I are very old friends." Leszek broadened his smile as he opened the door. "We must see hi'Varius before he sends troops to find you."

As I left the room Master Taras strode toward me down the hallway.

"Mistress Aisha," Taras said as I closed the door. "Hi'Varius has had everyone looking for you for over an hour. His daughter wants you sent away."

CHAPTER FOUR

Savona: Hard truths

Master Taras and I walked back to Varius' private study in silence. I suspect Taras was disappointed in me for upsetting Rhiannon and Varius. He had probably gotten harassed over my lack of respect and mountain-woman conduct. I had contributed to his embarrassment by not keeping him informed. But events had escalated quickly. I rationalized in an effort to absolve myself. But I knew I could have sent him messages by one of the Talons.

"I'm sorry, Master Taras," I mumbled, feeling truly sorry. He didn't respond.

Under a cloak of silence the trek to Varius' study seemed to take forever. When we arrived, the Talon guard at the door smiled and admitted us.

"It's about time you decided to join us, Aisha," Varius shouted. "I took Taras' word that you're a Talon and not a clumsy half-trained recruit. You have proven yourself a barbarian with no manners or respect for your rulers. You will show my daughter, my heir, the respect due her, or I will have you whipped. And you will learn to conduct yourself with proper manners in her presence. Master Timotei will meet with you every day for lessons in court etiquette until he and my daughter are satisfied you can be allowed in public."

"I apologize, hi'Lord Varius, for not allowing pri'Rhiannon to eat the cyanide that was ladled on her porridge." I bowed to both Varius and Rhiannon.

"Cyanide!" Varius jerked out of his chair. His mouth moved up and down, but no further sounds emerged.

"My food had cyanide on it… and you ate it?" Rhiannon opened her eyes wide in disbelief. "Why didn't you tell me?"

"Because I would have had to let your ladies-in-waiting know I am not the rude mountain-woman chaperone they have learned to love, but a bodyguard, and that someone tried to poison you. How long before your enemies would know we had

37

discovered their plot? How long before they tried something new?" *Damn nobles thought more about their image than their lives.*

"How do you know her food contained cyanide?" Varius asked, shaking his head. "We only have your word."

Because I ate the stuff, you idiot. You trust me with your daughter's life and yet question my competence. "Leszek Talon retrieved the tray from the cook as he left the room. Master Hormiz confirmed one of the bowls with honey contained cyanide. And Master Healer Luminita confirmed pri'Rhiannon's recent symptoms were consistent with cyanide poisoning." I stared straight into the hi'Lord's eyes. "Master Healer Luminita indicated she has suffered those symptoms for several days, consistent with what I discovered during my interviews. Pri'Rhiannon had a total of three doses prior to this morning."

"My daughter said you ate the food where the cyanide had been ladled. Is that right, Mistress Aisha?" Varius reseated himself, his face, still scarlet, but he was no longer shouting.

"Yes. I was suspicious, but I had to find out without giving away the pretense that I am a chaperone. My mountain-woman persona is your daughter's best protection. If your enemies know I'm Talon, it will give them an edge and further endanger your daughter's life. The amount she ate was not designed to kill her immediately. She was given a small dose designed to kill her over several weeks."

"Ferox!" Rhiannon screamed as she came out of her chair.

"Taras, arrest Ferox! Throw him in the dungeon--" Varius shouted as he got out of his chair.

"No. Ferox is guilty of nothing except following a healer's orders, thinking he was helping pri'Rhiannon with a delicate problem." I wondered if all nobles acted first and thought later, like hi'Varius.

I explained Healer Herk's part in the conspiracy as well as his implication of Third Lady Castor and the possibility of an unnamed Second Lord.

"If you act against tri'Castor or openly punish Healer Herk, you will drive your enemies into hiding. For now, we have the advantage." I looked to Taras who nodded agreement.

"My daughter and I owe you an apology and our thanks, but you must show her more respect, Mistress Aisha." Varius set his jaw in a stubborn line. Now I knew where Rhiannon got her attitude.

"Hi'Lord Varius, you and pri'Rhiannon must decide whether you want a chaperone or a Talon bodyguard. A chaperone will show her respect and protect her reputation. A bodyguard will worry only about protecting her life." I spoke without smiling. "Master Dragos instructed me specifically. I'm a Talon, not a servant."

"Taras, your sister exceeds herself," Varius said. Taras was the senior Talon and my superior. I could argue with Varius. The most he could do was cancel my contract. The Talons were not his subjects. However, I could not argue with a senior clan brother.

"No, hi'Lord Varius. She speaks the hard truth. Your enemies struck again at your heir. This will not be their last attempt on her life. Aisha Talon has proven her worth. My sister may appear clumsy, barbaric, and overbearing, but she already saved your daughter's life, penetrated your enemies' associates, and managed to maintain her mountain woman image. Her cover has been established. Even you doubted that she is a Talon. By now everyone in the castle believes she is an ill-mannered mountain woman. You would be wise to trust her approach. She hurt your daughter's pride, but she saved her life."

"Taras, you Talons are arrogant…but I must admit the girl is effective. And I must protect my daughter." For the first time I saw a look of grief wash over his face. "For now I will let you do it your way. However, Mistress Aisha will keep you informed, and you will keep me informed." Varius then turned to his daughter. "Listen to Aisha Talon, Rhiannon. I could not bear to lose you."

* * * *

"I'm sorry I complained to father about you," Rhiannon said as we made our way back to her rooms. The bluster was gone, and she appeared subdued.

"Let's go to my room, I would like to talk to you alone."

"I've already apologized." Rhiannon whined and pursed her lips. I remained silent as we continued down the busy hallway, passing guards and several lords and ladies. I detected the presence of several weak sigils and one strong Illusion Sigil. The sigil holder was a man walking with an attractive young woman. She smiled as she clung to his arm; I didn't need to use my sigil. I could see a double image, one misty and one clear. The youthful image he had superimposed on his older-wrinkled face was misty; his real face clearly visible. The perfect assassin's sigil, I mused as we walked down the hallway and entered my room. I pointed to a chair and waited for her to sit.

"Pri'Rhiannon, you don't owe me an apology." She looked at me. "You're in a life and death game, and you need to decide what kind of player you are going to be."

"Poisoning me isn't a game," Rhiannon cried.

"Yes, it is a game. A deadly game. You can choose to be an active player or a passive player who merely watches, but you can't choose whether to play or not. Your enemies will not allow you or your father that option." Looking down at her, I felt her pain. I knew what it was like to lose loved ones. She had recently lost her mother, sister, and brother. Now her life was being threatened. She felt abandoned and helpless. As I had done years ago, she would make a choice in the next few minutes which would affect her entire life. My choice had been to fight and that worked out well for me. But I could not choose for her. I could only do my duty and wish for the best.

"You and my other Talon guards must protect me." Rhiannon drew up her lips in a pout.

"So you choose to be a passive player. That will significantly reduce your chances of survival." I shrugged.

"Why?"

"Because I'm merely one player you have to use against your enemies. If you don't care, you won't use me effectively, or your other Talon guards, or your loyal friends. You will give your enemies an advantage, a deadly one, over you and over your father."

"I don't know what to do. I can't fight. I can't hide. How can I be active?" Tears glistened in her eyes. "I don't want to die."

"I will teach you, pri'Rhiannon, if you are willing to learn. I am very good at what you need to learn. If you are serious, you will meet with me each day for one hour before your normal wake up time." *I'm very good at games. I've spent many years pretending to be slow, stupid, or incompetent as I fought to survive. I can teach Rhiannon to survive as well.*

"I'm not strong," Rhiannon said as she looked down at her soft white hands.

"You don't need to be strong, only smarter than your opponent. We Talons will take care of the strong part."

"I'll try, Mistress Aisha." Tears trickled down her cheeks.

"Good. Freshen your face. We will join your ladies for lunch." It had been an interesting morning. I felt good that I had made progress in protecting Rhiannon. I thwarted a plot to poison her, I redirected her father's priorities from protecting her pride to protecting her life, and I secured Rhiannon's cooperation. I was ready for lunch.

"Pri'Rhiannon, you're back." Irenka pointed a ringed finger at me. "What did your father say about her barbaric conduct? I'm surprised he didn't have her whipped."

"Father chastised her, but I think I'm stuck with her." Rhiannon darted a nervous glance at me as I settled into one of the chairs. Neither Silva nor Raya said anything.

Silva seemed a happy young girl who enjoyed being around Rhiannon. She was a pretty girl, slim but filling out in all the right places, with a contented smile and a happy word for everyone around her. Raya was more serious. She seemed to enjoy being one of Rhiannon's lady-in-waiting. The way she enjoyed giving orders to the servants and courtiers gave me the idea she enjoyed the prestige of the position. She was smaller than Silva but far more developed. Irenka, on the other hand, sought to influence Rhiannon. I had already seen her pressure Rhiannon to ask the hi'Lord for favors. I wondered about Irenka. Silva and Raya were passive while Irenka was an active participant. She wanted me gone, but why?

When Master Timotei entered for Rhiannon's afternoon tutoring, I left the room.

"I'll be at the seamstress if I'm needed," I whispered to the Talon on duty.

It felt good to be able to find my way around the castle. Theory was good and necessary, but nothing satisfies more than experience. Mistress Karla was on the second floor of one of the smaller attached buildings, but I found her easily. "Good afternoon, Mistress Aisha. I'm glad you came. I finished one of your dresses. I'd like you to try it on for size."

"Good afternoon, Mistress Karla. I'm looking forward to wearing it. Your work is beautiful."

I slipped out of my roughly made peasant clothing into a calf-length yellow skirt and blouse. They were of a soft silk that felt delightful against my skin. I never thought about clothes, cloth, or material at the Aerie, so this was new and fascinating. I couldn't help but feel pampered. As I had asked, they were not tightly fitted and were short enough for me to move easily, but they still didn't quite fill my needs.

"Magnificent, Mistress Karla. They are the most beautiful skirt and blouse I've ever owned. However, because I am pri'Rhiannon's chaperone, I'll need you to make a few adjustments for me. I hate to ask you to change even one stitch on anything so beautiful but--" I hesitated. "I would like two more pockets, one here and one here, as unnoticeable as you can make them. I'll need to carry things for pri'Rhiannon and the pockets will allow me to keep them hidden. And please loosen up the blouse and skirt another size. I don't want to draw attention to myself and away from pri'Rhiannon."

"I had thought you young for a chaperone, Mistress Aisha, but I see that you are wiser than your years. I will make the changes you requested." Karla frowned again and sniffed.

* * * *

"What?" Rhiannon opened one eye to find me standing next to her bed.

"Time for your lesson," I threw back her blankets.

"It's not light, yet."

"Remember our agreement, pri'Rhiannon? Active or passive?"

"All right, all right. I'll try." As she got out of bed, I grabbed her arm and started walking.

"What do you do now?" I asked when I suddenly stopped.

"I don't know. Fight?" Rhiannon asked, her eyes still filled with sleep and on the verge of crying.

42

"No, you don't know how to fight. You would just get hurt. You need to use your Talons. Every Talon can put a knife in your enemy's throat from twenty paces away. But you must help." I drew one of my throwing knives. "See the flower in the middle of your door?"

"Yes."

I threw the knife. It spun several times and landed with a thud in the center of the flower. Rhiannon's eyes opened wide with awe. The knife vibrated on its mark.

"How can I help?"

"First, you need to be aware of who is in the area. You are looking for Talons. Look for one watching you. Then give him a target."

"How?" she asked.

"That is what we will practice this morning. Falling is the easiest way if your enemy doesn't have you held around the waist."

For the next hour, I went through ten different scenarios and the things Rhiannon could do to expose an attacker: collapsing to the ground, going limp like a faint, or hugging the person, especially if he was tall. Each situation interrupted an assailant's plan and exposed him for a brief moment.

"I understand now what you meant about being passive or active, Aisha. Passive, I do nothing to help you. Active, I help you save me. I'll be ready for practice tomorrow." Rhiannon beamed, her eyes bright with excitement.

The next several days settled into a boring routine. I ate with Rhiannon and her retinue at her morning meals, sat with her during her sessions with tutors and seamstresses, attended dinners, and saw her to bed. If this kept up for long I feared I'd lose my edge. I stretched and practiced in my room as much as I could for an hour every day before I worked with Rhiannon, but this would not keep me at my fighting peak for long.

Rhiannon and I spent each morning on scenarios I invented. I showed her places to poke, scratch, bite, and kick to get free, even if it brought only seconds in an attack. After a week, I switched to people issues.

"Pri'Rhiannon, who can you trust, excluding the Talons?" I measured my voice to sound calm.

43

"Why exclude the Talons, Aisha?"

"Because if we want to kill you or your father, you can't stop us. Therefore, you must trust us, because you have no choice."

Her eyes rose to the ceiling as she palmed her fingers, one by one. "Silva, Raya, Irenka, Minister Lucas... Why? They are my friends and Minister Lucas is my father's friend."

"Someday, you will be the hi'Lady. Some people will be your friends because they like you. Some will be your friends because they admire the way you rule. Others will pretend to be your friends for what they can get from you, but they will turn on you if someone offers them more. And some people will hate you. Who should you trust?"

"Those who are my real friends."

"No, pri'Rhiannon. Those who hate you," I answered.

"Why?" Rhiannon's mouth opened as her eyes grew like saucers.

"Because no one hates another in pretense. Therefore, you know their true feelings and how they are likely to act. Everyone else must be suspect."

"Silva, Raya, and Irenka are my friends!" She shook her head and stared down at her lap.

"Each will benefit from their friendship with you. There is nothing wrong with that so long as you understand that they do. Don't allow their friendship to manipulate you."

"I hate you!" Rhiannon shouted. "You're making me doubt my friends."

"No, I'm pointing out the truth of being the heir to a kingdom. I'm suggesting you use your mind, not your emotions. Active versus passive. Think of Ferox the cook. He is totally loyal to you, yet what he did would have killed you."

Rhiannon was less enthusiastic for the next two days. On the third day when I arrived, Rhiannon was up and waiting.

"I told my father what you have been telling me, Aisha. He actually said something nice about you. He said that he had hoped I would be older before I had to face the realities of being hi'Lady, but with someone trying to kill both of us, it was time."

After that, Rhiannon was up each morning when I arrived.

44

* * * *

Rhiannon had finished her midday meal. "Mistress Aisha, I would like to go to the markets today. We will need castle guards to accompany us."

"Talons," I said.

"Why?"

"Castle guards will watch you and be attentive to your needs. Talons will be watching everyone else to ensure your safety. I'll notify Leszek. We will be ready by the time you finish dressing."

We left an hour later. Leszek had joined us with four additional guards. I thought Rhiannon was as well protected as possible. I doubted an assassin knew we would be going to the markets today and waiting to kill her. When we reached the Savona Temple area, Rhiannon dismounted and began walking among the Blessed Ones.

"Aisha, when you were being measured for your new dresses, I noticed that you had no sigils on your arms. I thought...all of you had at least one sigil."

"Most have at least one. Some have two." I wasn't sure what she had on her mind.

"I would buy you one. A War Sigil." She pointed to one of the Blessed ones who sat at the top of the steps at the temple honoring the god Dai. Amulets, rings, and other objects lay on his table engraved with the War Sigil. Next to him lay a bowl marked with the War Sigil that he used for those who desired a living War Sigil. The Blessed, however, couldn't guarantee the god would grant a living sigil.

As we passed them, Rhiannon pointed out the three temples on each side of the road. In front of us the splotched-red granite temple of War dedicated honor to the god Dai. The sigil imbued the holder with an ability to learn weapons or fighting skills with an expertise far above normal ability. The white marble temple of Truth dedicated honor to the goddess Yao. This sigil permitted the holder to tell if a person was telling what he believed to be the truth. The onyx temple of Illusion dedicated honor to the god Huan. This sigil enabled the holder to project images created in his mind.

Across the road the golden-brown temple of Charm and Luck dedicated honor to the goddess Yun. This sigil caused the holder to be more likeable and lucky. The blue granite Energy temple dedicated honor to the goddess Liu. This sigil imbued the holder with additional energy and endurance. The green granite Healing temple dedicated honor to the god Jian. This sigil gave the holder the ability to sense the exact injury or disease and to administer the correct treatment.

The silver temple of the hi'Blessed towered in the center of the road with the power of six sigils, its eight story spires capped in gold. The street glowed with the power of the gods.

"Thank you, Rhiannon. How thoughtful of you. However, I'm afraid it wouldn't help me. The Blessed ones have been given the power to create god-gifted sigils on amulets or other objects. Some Blessed ones have the gift of only one sigil, some two or more, and the hi'Blessed all six. But none of the Blessed can give a living sigil. Only the god or goddess of that sigil can do that." The concept of sigils was frequently misunderstood. Many believed that the amulets of the Blessed granted the same power as the living sigils. Others believed that the Blessed could, for enough money, give anyone a living sigil.

"I don't understand, Aisha."

"Imagine the perfect bow made specifically for you. If you were an average archer, an amulet would help you become somewhat better than average. If you had a living sigil it would help you become a master. The sigil magnifies the holder's innate talent. An amulet is of limited help, whereas a living sigil is without limits."

"But you're-- Wouldn't it help you?"

"No. I was tested by a hi'Blessed and the gods refused me all six." I spoke the truth, just not the whole truth.

Rhiannon was quiet for the rest of the day.

* * * *

"What are we doing today, Aisha?"

"A knife." I produced a small wooden knife and leather arm sheath I had Leszek make for Rhiannon.

"You're going to teach me to fight with a knife?" Rhiannon examined it excitedly.

46

"No, that would take a year or more. I'm going to teach you how to survive when the Talon can't come to your aid immediately or can't take action directly. You know that I had Mistress Karla sew pockets in my dresses. Reach in my pocket, pri'Rhiannon." I turned sideways for her.

"Your pocket has a hole in ... a knife ... two knives," she screeched as she bounced up and down.

"You could carry a weapon openly, pri'Rhiannon. It is your right as a noblewoman. But concealing it gives you the advantage of surprise." For the next week I taught Rhiannon where to strap her little knife so it couldn't be seen, how to draw it unseen, and how to use it without being obvious. She was like a frisky kitten all week. I looked forward to and enjoyed my time with her.

* * * *

"You have done well with pri'Rhiannon, Sister," Leszek said. We sat in my room late one evening. "More importantly, from what I've been able to determine, your mountain-woman chaperone act seems to be working well. You are probably the most talked about person in the castle, bad manners, rude, arrogant, and other less flattering comments. Mothers will soon be threatening their children with you."

"Mountain-women chaperones are terrible people, Brother Leszek, but they get results." I laughed. "Rhiannon has matured over the past few weeks. She learns quickly. Now she knows enough to help us if she should need to."

"I briefed all her guards on what you have been teaching her, so that they know what they can expect if trouble arises. Your timing is good. We will leave for Dassel in two days."

"Ferox visited me last night. He gushed a fountain of information from over the past week. If the nobility only knew how much the servants learned from their conversations, they would be flabbergasted." I smiled. "I used to think Rhiannon's ladies-in-waiting were well informed. Now I know Ferox is a professional while they are amateurs."

Leszek nodded as I paused. His last report had me concerned. "Ferox has heard rumors that there will be an attack on the trip to Dassel. He couldn't be specific so we must be ready for anything, from a small army to a lone assassin."

"The Talons will be ready, Sister."

CHAPTER FIVE

Road to Valda: Assassination attempt

I wasn't sure what to expect when I entered the courtyard with Rhiannon and her retinue, but it wasn't the massive caravan that assembled, filled with nobles, soldiers, servants, horses, wagons, and people running everywhere, their arms loaded with provisions. It seemed the entire population of the castle intended to go to Dassel. A hundred mounted soldiers and their officers had joined with the royal Talon guards. Men and women in blue livery scurried about the twenty wagons loading them with luggage and supplies. Except for a couple of tapestries, I would be surprised if anything was left in the castle.

I knew how to ride a horse but did not look forward to spending countless hours in the saddle, but bouncing for hours in a wagon would have been worse, even on padded benches.

After several hours of last minute flurry, we left the castle grounds and rode through the town. Well-wishers and spectators lined the streets and crowded our procession. Varius and his daughter smiled and waved to the masses. I searched the crowd for signs of danger, nervous at the potential for assassins to hide among them. Leaving the gates at the city wall, my shoulders ached from the tension.

Taras and I rode with Varius and Rhiannon at the front of the caravan, surrounded by Talons. Looking back, I saw a sizable group of mounted soldiers, a train of wagons and servants stretching back out of sight.

The land had been cleared of forest in the first league, flat and well cultivated. Many small houses dotted the landscape. I soon saw less cultivated areas, and the tree cover grew denser. By midday we reached woodland so dense it muted the evening light. The forest fascinated me, but I found it difficult to scan for trouble through the trees.

"Master Taras, does this forest stretch very far?" I asked.

"Yes, the Hazwood Forest stretches from Savona to Dassel to Soumiri in the Salda Kingdom, although it is called the

Ebowood Forest when we pass into the Valda Kingdom. The forest exists because of the water provided by the West and East Mystic Rivers." Taras lectured amicably, big brother to little sister. I was forgiven for not keeping him apprised of my actions, and gained a little of his respect with my handling of the cyanide incident.

We moved at a pace which barely exceeded a moderate walk. Rhiannon couldn't keep still, moving around and talking to her father, each member of her retinue, and even some of the officers. I stayed alert even though I didn't think there would be any trouble this close to the castle. I still carried my daggers tucked in hidden sheaths. Leszek kept my sword and bow for me. I acted like the nervous chaperone I was supposed to be.

"Isn't this wonderful, Aisha?" Rhiannon said, "An exciting adventure. We are going to stop in Terni and Livorno and will be traveling through the Hazwood and Ebowood Forests. I'm going to see Dassel, the capital of Valda, and meet the hi'Lord Radulf and see his castle." Rhiannon chirped with glee.

"Yes, this will be an exciting experience for you. Not to dampen your enthusiasm, what do you do if there is trouble or you even think there is trouble, pri'Rhiannon?" I knew Rhiannon was too excited to know how to react if something happen, unless I reminded her.

"Look for you, then follow your directions, my horrible chaperone." She laughed heartily and nudged her horse in the direction of Silva.

I couldn't remember ever being as free and light-hearted as Rhiannon. Life in my village had been hard, and everyone did their share to survive. Life at the Aerie had required me to be alert every hour of every day. I enjoyed my assignment with Rhiannon and being out in the world, but my duty still required me to be alert at all times.

Varius ordered the caravan stopped around midday to water the horses and to have a cold lunch the cooks had prepared in the wagons. The night's stop occurred well before sunset so that the servants could set up tents and begin the evening meal. The process was fascinating. The servants and soldiers literally created a small city within an hour. They pitched tents for the

50

nobility, cooks erected fire pits to begin cooking, and the servants hobbled the horses and provided food and drink. I watched in fascination, but still scanned for signs of abnormalities in people's activities.

I spotted the old-wrinkle faced man from the castle, except now he dropped the illusion. He dressed like a minor noble in charge of mounted soldiers. I continued to scan the camp for any sign that would give me a second or two warning, an edge that might mean the difference between life and death. Varius and Taras approached.

"Pri'Rhiannon! I believe your father is coming to visit you." She was deep in an animated conversation with Raya.

"Father, isn't this wonderful and exciting?" Rhiannon said as she ran towards her father.

"Yes, it is good to be out in the country side and to talk with our subjects. A good experience for you." I could see the affection he had for his daughter. He turned to me with a frown of worry that furrowed his brow. "Taras says you received information that we may be attacked?"

"Nothing specific, hi'Lord, only a warning," I replied.

"What good does that do us?" Disappointment rang in the question.

"Better warned and ready, hi'Lord, than not warned and careless." *Nobles would never survive the Aerie*, I thought as I kept my face blank.

"Yes, I guess so. Do you want additional guards?"

"No, hi'Lord. We don't know if the attack will be against you, your daughter, or both. Nor do we know if it will be a few assassins already with us, some who will attempt to infiltrate the caravan, or a large external force. The Talons are sufficient against assassins, but you may want to assign your soldiers to specific people or places to rally around them in the event of an armed attack to minimize confusion." I looked to Taras for support.

"I agree with Mistress Aisha, hi'Lord. Surprise is usually your enemies' greatest advantage. Assigned positions could greatly reduce indecision and improve our response to an attack."

"I will call a meeting of my officers after we dine. We can work out a response plan in the event of an attack. I pray you are wrong Mistress Aisha, but I will not dismiss you again." Varius turned to go.

"Do you really think someone will attack this caravan, Aisha?" Rhiannon asked. Her face grew grim and flashed with fear. "There are over a hundred soldiers and twenty Talons."

"Yes, I do. The assassins have shown that they are determined, and this probably is their best opportunity. I think they'll try a diversion followed by a direct attack on you or your father. What do you think, Leszek?"

"A diversion. If anything happens, pri'Rhiannon, we will rally on Mistress Aisha and you, no matter what else is happening. Do you understand?"

"Yes, Leszek Talon." Rhiannon nodded.

"Leszek, I will leave a kit outside our tent tonight. Have someone put my sword, bow, and quiver into it. I need all my weapons near at hand. Pri'Rhiannon will also prepare a kit. Whoever is on guard duty will keep both kits." My mind raced as I tried to plan for any possible need.

"What do I put in my kit, Aisha?" Rhiannon asked.

"Comfortable shoes and clothes, so you can run and hide, a blanket for sleeping on the ground, something to hold water and make fire, and trail food."

"We won't need to run or hide or sleep out!" Rhiannon wrinkled her nose and looked skeptical. "And I don't have anything to make a fire or trail food."

"We will find them for you. We must be prepared for anything that might happen. Leszek, please add those along with my weapons."

Leszek nodded.

I turned to Rhiannon. "Humor your chaperone. She worries about your health."

"Yes, Mistress Aisha. I still think you are being too cautious." Rhiannon walked towards her tent.

I agree with her, Sister, Leszek signed.

Brother, I signed, then added aloud, "I survived in the mountains because I was more devious and better prepared than others. Being over-prepared cost nothing, but being under-

52

prepared can cost you your life." I had to be cautious about signing with so many people milling about. Although I mentioned surviving the mountains, Leszek would know I meant the Aerie.

"What about Silva, Raya, and Irenka?"

"They will be fine. Nobody wants to kill them." I had to pity young Rhiannon. The thought of people hunting her must be terrifying.

Rhiannon's tent was large by normal standards, but five women and all their belongings made for cramped quarters. I chose to sleep close to the entrance; an assassin would have to pass me to get to Rhiannon. I lay quietly for a while, absorbing the night sounds before going to sleep. Any foreign sound would wake me, ready for battle.

* * * *

I awoke early and would have loved to work out, but had nowhere I could do so without being seen. The cooks had the fires burning as more and more soldiers appeared, and finally, the nobles. I found it hard to believe the lavish meal set for the hi'Lord, Rhiannon, and other nobles had been prepared while traveling

Rhiannon and her retinue sat to her father's right. I managed to squeeze in between her and a noble I didn't recognize. He sneered at me but said nothing, because he was listening to Varius and couldn't interrupt.

The server pouring the berry drinks caught my eye. His hand trembled. He fumbled as he reached for Rhiannon's goblet. When I saw no one looking, I picked up Rhiannon's drink and tasted it. Setting it down near me, I pushed my drink closer to her. She was involved in conversation with several others and didn't notice, but I detected cyanide in her berry drink. This conspiracy ran deeper than just a few people

"Leszek, please get Rhiannon another glass of berry juice and bring it to the tent." Leszek stood guard behind Rhiannon. Talons didn't normally fetch and carry, and I hoped Leszek realized the seriousness of the request. He would if he saw me switch drinks.

"Yes, Mistress Aisha," he said and disappeared. After eating, I pulled Rhiannon and Leszek aside.

53

"Pri'Rhiannon, put your finger in this glass and taste it."
She surprised me when she did it without question.

"Now, this glass."

"It tastes...different...a little like bitter."

"That taste is cyanide." I poured the contents on the
ground. "From now on, take my drink, as if by mistake, and I
will take yours."

"But what if it has cyanide? Oh, I see." She stared at me
thoughtfully.

The practiced ease with which the servants disassembled
the camp and loaded everything onto the wagons surprised me.
We were off only a few hours after sunrise. We followed the
river south, but I never saw it because of the dense forest. I heard
the rushing water or felt a misty dampness as we passed near to a
waterfall or narrow rapids. The well-traveled dirt road, hilly and
a little rough in places, ran parallel to the river, a half league
inland. I found the forest interesting, comparing it to the Camori
Mountains with its taller pines and barren snow covered peaks.

Rhiannon refused to believe we might have to abandon
the caravan and thought I was being over-cautious. I didn't
blame her for thinking that no one would attack a caravan as
large as this one. I didn't care. I believed Ferox's information
accurate if lacking in detail. I would rather appear foolish
planning for a large attack that didn't come than to be
unprepared. If I survived such an attack, but Rhiannon didn't, I
would rightly have to answer to the clan about why I failed in
my duty, and I would have to live with having let the young
woman die.

On the fourth day the land leveled out as we approached
the town of Terni. I had my first good look at the river since
leaving Savona. Unlike the river at Savona, the river at Terni
was wide and negotiable. As a result, Terni was a busy trade
city. Supplies moved every day between Savona by land and by
river between the southern towns of Livorno in Granya, Dassel
in Valda, and Soumiri in Salda.

As we approached Terni, I decided the town would be
hard to defend. The walls didn't enclose the docks, warehouses,
or most of the merchants' stores, but only surrounded a small

castle and the houses of nobles and rich merchants. The bailey didn't look big enough to bring everyone inside in an emergency.

Second Lord Tadzio, Third Lady Castor and a welcoming committee of other dignitaries met us at the city wall.

"Hi'Lord Varius, pri'Rhiannon," Tadzio said, "I am honored. I have prepared quarters for you and your party. After you refresh yourselves tonight, a celebration will be held in your honor."

Tadzio led Varius and the other nobles through the town and into the castle. The grooms led the horses to the stables, while servants collected the luggage and whisked it off to the assigned rooms in a demonstration of efficiency. Tadzio had advance notice of our arrival and knew exactly who was in Varius' party. Rhiannon was assigned her own room and her ladies-in-waiting an adjoining room. I was assigned a room in the servant's quarters with two of our maids. Much to Irenka's displeasure, I stayed with Rhiannon while she bathed and dressed, and I used her room to bathe and change myself.

* * * *

I still found the nobles' idea of a feast excessive. The food must have cost hundreds of gold scrules. Every noble and wealthy merchant in Terni seemed to have been invited. I had to give Rhiannon credit that she held her composure when Lady Castor came over to talk with her father.

"Do you think she was responsible for the death of my mother, sister, and brother?" Rhiannon whispered to me with tears in her eyes after Lady Castor wandered away.

"I think she was one of them, and she will pay, pri'Rhiannon, I promise."

Rhiannon bit her lip and stared at the woman's back. "Thank you, Aisha." She gave me a small, thin smile. I pretended to be interested in the food and entertainment, which were excellent. Tadzio hired jugglers, acrobats, trained wolves, and several fighting matches, with and without weapons. I focused my real attention on the people, in particular, on Castor and everyone she talked to. She and "wrinkle face" spent time talking in a secluded corner. I doubted they would try anything in their own domain, but if they did, the surprise would be on them.

"You can't sleep on the floor, Mistress Aisha." Rhiannon protested, but I did not intend to use the room I had been given, even though Rhiannon's Talon guards stood watch outside her door.

"I will be fine, pri'Rhiannon. I would be a poor chaperone if I didn't watch you at night."

There came a knock at the door.

"Pri'Rhiannon, a healer at the door wishes to see you," the Talon on guard said. I felt the presence of a strong Illusion Sigil before I opened the door a crack. The image of old wrinkle face was clear; a misty image of a younger face in the robes of a minor healer. I knew this illusion.

"Yes?" I asked.

"I have instructions to make sure pri'Rhiannon gets this juice. It has medicine Master Healer Luminita directed she take each night." The image smiled, the real person didn't.

"I'll take it. Pri'Rhiannon isn't dressed for guests."

"I'm a healer!"

"And I'm a chaperone," I snapped. "I hope the Talon on guard isn't forced to resolve this issue."

"…No. Here!" Wrinkle face shoved the drink at me. "Be sure she drinks it, or you will be responsible for the consequences."

I closed the door and set the glass on the dressing table.

"More cyanide?" Rhiannon asked.

"Try tasting it, with your finger."

She cautiously dipped the tip of her finger into the juice and licked the drop off the tip. "It is! We should have the Talons kill him."

"Later. For now, we want your enemies to think they are winning. But I will not take the chance of leaving you alone." I curled up on the floor, readying myself for sleep. I lay listening to the quiet for the normal sounds of the castle. I knew Castor was one of Rhiannon's enemies, but I didn't think she would attempt something as foolish as a direct attack on Rhiannon and her father while in Terni. But I wasn't going to bet Rhiannon's life on it.

* * * *

Varius decided to stay two nights to give everyone a rest. I accompanied Rhiannon as she and her retinue toured the docks, warehouses, and shopped at a variety of merchants. The morning of the third day, the caravan reassembled for the trip to Livorno.

"How far to Livorno and Dassel, Leszek?" I asked, as servants and soldiers made last minute adjustments for our departure.

"Livorno is thirty leagues south along the West Mystic River. It should take four or five days, depending on the number of stops we make. The wagons slow us, as well. From there, we will continue to follow the river into the kingdom of Valda. The journey from Livorno to Dassel will take another nine or ten days, if the weather doesn't change." So far, the weather had been typical for summer, chilly in the early morning and comfortable by mid-day. The thick forest contributed to the coolness of the days. "If we were on the river, it would be much warmer. West of the river in the Jaddah desert, it would be very hot."

I found the travel to Livorno similar to that from Savona to Terni except the terrain was flatter and the weather, warmer. I saw more of the river and even an occasional river barge. Although the trip was somewhat boring, I kept Leszek and his Talons on high alert with a closer than normal eye on Rhiannon. Duty demanded it. The Raptor Clan had been shamed by the killing of the hi'Lord's wife and two children. I was determined to bring no additional shame to us.

"I told you, Mistress Aisha, no one is going to attack a caravan this large with so many soldiers," Rhiannon said, at least twenty times.

"Better to be annoyed with me and alive, rather than dead. It would ruin your chaperone's day." I blanked my face, though smiled inside. Rhiannon shook her head in obvious exasperation. We stopped only a half-day's ride from Livorno on the fourth night. I couldn't blame Leszek and Rhiannon for thinking of Ferox's rumor as idle castle gossip, not that their doubt deterred me from insisting Leszek remain on high alert.

Everyone was tired from the long days in the saddle, so we retired early, anticipating tomorrow's activities in Livorno.

Something awakened me. I snapped my eyes wide open, listened intently, but heard nothing. As I watched, the tent flap slowly opened, and the night flowed in. I sensed a strong Illusion Sigil. My mind snapped my sigil on and the shadow faded to a small, thin man standing in the entrance. He looked around the room in the dim light provided by the moon and spent a few seconds on each figure. I stayed still, faking sleep.

While he evaluated each bedroll, I struggled with my dilemma. Killing him would be easy, but killing him without giving away my chaperone image wouldn't be. He somehow correctly identified Rhiannon's bedroll and slowly raised his foot to step over me. A professional assassin, I mused, kills only the target and leaves unseen. As his foot touched the ground, I slashed the artery on the inside of his groin. Blood sprayed everywhere, and he fell on me as I struck with my second knife, driving it into his heart.

I lay drenched in the dead man's blood. I screamed and screamed again.

"Talons, Talons," I screamed. I wrinkled my nose at the stench as his bowels voided. Now everyone in the tent screamed. Leszek charged into the tent a couple of seconds later. I actually felt sorry for him standing there with me soaked in blood, a body across me and four screaming young nobles.

"Are you alright, Aisha?" he asked as he dragged the body off me and examined me with a practiced eye. "What happened?"

I waited a moment as the screaming settled down into sobs. "The Talon guarding the tent must have fought with this assassin, and he stumbled into our tent and fell on me."

"Come, Mistress Aisha. Let's get you cleaned up." We went outside to find the body of the Talon guard beside Rhiannon's tent. Three assassins had killed two guards outside of Varius tent as well. The next morning Master Taras pulled me aside.

"Hi'Varius can't stop praising you. He knows the real story about Rhiannon's assassin and realizes your alert probably help save his life." Taras stared down at me. "You are also the talk of the Talons, Sister Aisha."

"Why?" I looked at him with wide eyes, pretending to have no idea what he was referring to.

"Leszek found a living Illusion Sigil on your assassin. That is how he managed to kill the outside guard, without a fight! But he couldn't get by you. How did you detect him?" Taras continued staring at me while awaiting his answer.

"Chaperones are terrible people, Senior Brother, and mountain women the worst." I broadened my smile.

* * * *

Livorno was also a port town with docks, warehouses, and merchants, about twice the size of Terni. The most spectacular part was the view across the river, a shimmering golden sea of sand. The river separated Granya from Jaddah, home to the desert tribes. Much of Livorno's business constituted handling supplies going and coming from Zenjir, Jeddah's capital, so a number of Jaddah tribesmen were usually in town. I would have loved to work out with the Jaddahan warriors. I had been told that many of the Talon's basic knife techniques originated from the Jaddahan, where they favored knife fighting.

Second Lord Lucjan was a gracious host. Varius stayed four nights, resting and restocking supplies for the next leg of the journey to Dassel.

"Mistress Aisha," Irenka said, "there is no reason for you to follow us shopping. It must be hard seeing all the things you can't afford to buy." She primped in front of a mirror preparing to shop for the third straight day. Another time I might have been interested in discovering what was in the markets, but now I wasn't interested in shopping. I was concerned about Rhiannon's safety. An assassination took only seconds. What better opportunity than a crowded market?

"Not at all, Siress Irenka. I love looking at all the things I can't afford." In fact, looking was what Varius paid me to do. I could have warned Irenka yesterday that a cutpurse was about to steal her purse after I had diverted the thief from Rhiannon, but Irenka wasn't my concern. Fair's fair. She wouldn't have warned me either. I chuckled to myself at the thought.

"I'll buy you something, Aisha," Rhiannon said.

"Are you trying to bribe me, pri'Rhiannon?"

"She's a crude peasant, pri'Rhiannon," Irenka said, as she wrinkled her nose in disgust.

"True, Siress Irenka. You can't expect to cut silk from a mountain goat." I smiled at Irenka's attempt to anger me. After ten years at the Aerie, I doubted words could be used to bait me into anger, shame, joy, fear, or hate. "Emotions kill," Master Jiang had beaten into everyone. Only those who could conquer their emotions survived to become Talon. Early on it had become my mantra.

We departed from Livorno the next morning.

The land and the routine remained the same, a morning meal, break camp, a midday break for another meal, stop before sunset to set up camp, and a final meal before retiring to our tents.

"Aisha, I wonder if the danger Ferox warned about is past," Leszek said on the third night out of Livorno.

"That is possible, Leszek. But do we want to wager pri'Rhiannon's life on it?"

No wonder you survived Aerie, my cautious Sister.
"No, Mistress Aisha, we will not fail in our duty to pri'Rhiannon."

CHAPTER SIX

Road to Valda: Royal caravan attacked

The clanging of steel on steel jerked me awake. My knives were in my hands as I leapt to my feet to meet the threat. I used my foot to prod Rhiannon awake as I watched the tent flap. A second later, it was opened with a naked sword, and Leszek peered through the opening.

"Aisha, we are under attack! Hurry. It is a full scale attack by hundreds of mounted soldiers. The invaders will overrun us soon. You and pri'Rhiannon must run." Leszek peered over his shoulder at the fighting twenty paces away. I could see through the opening that the attackers outnumbered Rhiannon's full detail of Talon guards. I saw dead bodies on the ground, mostly the gray and blue uniforms of the attackers, but some Talons were killed in the battle. Every Talon faced two or more assailants. Leszek was right. The Talons couldn't hold long.

I honor you Brother Raptor. It shames me to leave you.

Fail not in your duty, Sister Raptor.

Everyone in the tent was awake and babbling. I grabbed the two kits that we had prepared over a week ago and jerked Rhiannon out of bed, dragging her towards the back of the tent. I used one of my knives to slash a large opening.

"What about us?" Irenka screamed at us as rage reddened her face.

"Stay here and you'll be safe. It's pri'Rhiannon they want to kill." I peeked out through the opening and scanned the area. When I looked back, Irenka had grabbed Rhiannon by the arm, keeping her from following me. I turned and drove my palm into Irenka's chest. She stumbled backward and fell to the ground gasping for breath. Silva and Raya cautiously backed away from Rhiannon and me.

"That wasn't necessary," Rhiannon said as I pushed her through the slit opening. "Once I was out, I paused and looked around. The forest was only ten paces away and the path clear. Before I could move two soldiers charged around the tent. One ran into me before he realized anyone was there. At such close quarters, his sword would have been useless even if he hadn't run right into my knife. Surprise, shock, and pain registered on his face as I twisted the blade upward into his heart. I put one foot behind him and pushed with my shoulder. He toppled backward and my knife slid free. The other soldier raised his sword and headed straight for Rhiannon. The girl ran to him and squeezed her arms around his waist, so close his swing missed. That delayed his strike long enough for me to cut his throat from behind."

"You did exactly what you should have done. Now we must go." I spoke in a whisper, afraid to use her name fearing someone could hear. I was proud of her. Those hours of training saved her life.

I grabbed Rhiannon by the arm and we ran for tree cover. I knew she was in shock as I dragged her through the trees and underbrush. Our survival depended on a good head start. I could outrun the soldiers, but I knew Rhiannon could not.

"Father! We need to go back!" Rhiannon gasped for air and attempted to extricate herself from my grip and stop her stumbling run. I held on. Panic filled in her eyes and fear seized her words. She would do the wrong thing, return to danger to help save her father, her friends--for all the right reasons. Fortunately, she had me, and I had duty. "Your father is alive or he's dead. We can do nothing to help him in either case. We can only hope that your father's Talon guards will be able to protect him. They will not desert him. Your Talon guards died to save you. Right now, your life depends upon us outrunning those soldiers."

I continued to drag her along. After we had penetrated well into the forest and I saw no pursuit in sight, I stopped and opened the kits. Rhiannon's feet were bleeding. Our light colored nightdresses could be seen for a hundred paces or more. "Get dressed, pri'... Anka. Your name is Anka from now until you are safe."

Rhiannon alternatively stared at her kit and back towards the camp. As I looked back, the red haze from fires and the shouts from the fighting broke the eerie serenity of the forest.

"Anka, our lives depend on changing clothes fast and disappearing into the forest." When she didn't respond, I slapped her across the face. She looked up at me, shook her head, and pulled her nightgown off. We stepped into the sturdy pants and tunics I had packed.

I drew my bow, strung it, and put my quiver of twenty arrows over my shoulder. *Too few.* I shoved everything into one kit, including the other kit. They would be able to track us, but I would leave nothing to help them.

"Anka! Your life depends on one focus--me. Listen to me. Do what I tell you to do when I tell you." I took her chin into my hand and looked into her eyes until she nodded. "Good. Follow me."

I headed south through the trees for over an hour, stopping twice to give Rhiannon a short rest. When I stopped the third time, Rhiannon wanted to say something, but I put my fingers to her lips and motioned for her to hide behind a large pine. I crawled off several paces to a clump of bushes. I heard our pursuers thrashing through the underbrush and shouting. They were on horses and in a hurry to catch up with us. A minute later three horses came into sight and stopped. An officer in an emblazoned surcoat was shouting orders. I had my arrow notched and ready.

"They can't be far ahead. Spread out more. I want them both killed and--"

My arrow pierced his throat and ended whatever he was about to say. I couldn't really criticize them too much. After all, they thought they were chasing a small teen-aged girl who never had any weapons training and her unarmed chaperone--neither a threat. Run them down and kill them.

My second arrow also struck the next rider in the neck. I had my third arrow notched as the third rider turned his horse to retreat. *Coward.* I tracked him through the trees got a clear bead on his horse, and put it down. I hated shooting the horse, but if the soldier got away, the enemy would know exactly where we were. They would learn that I was armed and dangerous. I edged toward the downed horse.

The officer stepped out from behind a tree and smiled. "Well, hi'Lord Varius hired a female bodyguard for his daughter, not a chaperone. You are good with that bow, but now you are facing a knight in armor. Is she worth dying for?" His sword was out, and he was smiling.

"You should ask yourself the same question, sir knight."

"I will make you a bargain, mountain-woman bodyguard. Turn over pri'Rhiannon to me, and I will spare your life. Maybe I will even give you some gold scrules if you are sweet to me." I stepped forward.

He smirked as he lunged. I flicked my hand and my throwing dagger sank into his right eye. He made a small gurgling sound, dropped to the ground, and didn't move again. I collected my knife and jogged back to Rhiannon.

"I never hurt anyone. Why do they want to kill me?" Rhiannon said, her voice quivering.

"For the power you will inherit." I took her by the arm and led her into the trees.

"Why did he offer you gold?"

"Because he valued gold and thought I would. He had no honor."

She frowned thoughtfully. "How do you know he had no honor?"

"He tried to run when his fellow knights were under attack."

"Was it honorable to throw your knife at him without warning?"

"No, Anka. It was duty."

For the rest of the day I played hit and run with the soldiers trailing us. Fortunately, we encountered them a hand or less at a time. I assumed they didn't know which direction we chose when we fled the camp. They had to spread their forces thin to search for us. They must figure they don't need more than a few troops to hunt down a girl and her chaperone. Later search patrols tracked us on foot with one officer on horseback.

An hour passed. A mounted officer with three-foot soldiers approached. I sent Rhiannon into the nearby dense brush to wait. They moved slowly, searching behind trees and in thick brush. When the mounted officer turned to answer a question from one of the soldiers, I put an arrow through his throat. A second later I shot one of the foot soldiers in the chest.

The soldier furthest away turned and ran. The other charged. Concerned about my supply of arrows, I drew my sword. He yelled, his sword raised for a downward strike to my head. I snagged my foot on a protruding root and lurched forward slightly to the left of him. I tucked my head toward the ground and rolled. He swiveled his sword to follow me. The blade sliced into my ankle. I hit the ground and sprang to my feet and spun. My injured foot gave way. He grinned and swung at my chest.

"You are not thinking of failing in your duty, Aisha Talon?" I would have sworn I heard Master Jiang's voice.

Falling backwards, I swung my feet up. I kicked his sword arm up then slammed both feet into his stomach. As I rolled, I took him with me, up and over me. He glanced off a sapling and landed on his back several feet away. I jumped to my feet. My arm flashed downward. The knife made a dull thud as it buried into his chest.

"No Master Jiang, I will not fail in my duty," I said under my breath.

One soldier had escaped. I didn't want to continue on our same track.

The next groups were more cautious. I don't know if it was from the report of the soldier who ran or the dead I left behind, but they weren't in as much of a hurry to catch up. Only the persistent prodding by their officers kept them moving ahead. I killed ten and wounded several. We would no longer be considered easy prey.

Towards evening I was worried because I was low on arrows. We had lost our pursuers, so I stopped to rest Rhiannon and think. If I couldn't change our strategy, they would triumph in the end. They outnumbered us and would eventually trap us.

Rhiannon stood up and waved. "Look, Aisha, one of my father's knights."

I sensed the Illusion Sigil. Rhiannon saw a knight in her father's colors, tall, handsome, and smiling. Our savior. What I saw was a misty illusion and an enemy knight with a menacing sneer.

"Rhiann--" echoed through the forest as he fell off his horse with my last arrow in his eye.

"No, he is here to help us!"

He fell and his illusion faded. Three soldiers appeared out of the trees. I sensed they each wore war sigils. They smiled as they fanned out in a line. Rhiannon realized her mistake and moved behind me. I edged to my right, forcing them into a line so they couldn't encircle.

The lead man wasn't worried because he trusted his sigil. His sigil didn't notify him it stopped working. He rushed in sword flashing in a figure eight. I put a throwing knife through his neck on his first step. The next soldier waited for his partner to get even with him. I shifted left to attack, putting him between his partner and me. We locked guards. I kicked hard down through his knee. Bones crunched, he screamed, and I pushed him into his partner. By the time the other shoved him out of the way, I moved in close with a knife in my hand. He tried to swing at me, but I was close and moving fast. My knife slid into his belly and up into his heart. The attacker with the broken knee crawled toward me, sword in hand, as I brought my sword down on his neck in a killing blow.

"Can you make a fire, Anka?" I collected my knives.

"Fire? They will see it and know where we are!"

"The wind is from the south. If we start a fire, it will spread back towards the soldiers following us." I plucked a handful of grass, tossed it into the air, and watched it drift on the breeze. "The wind is from the south."

"They will just go around it. They know we are headed to Dassel." Rhiannon sounded weary.

"Think! Yes, they'll go around it and assume we'll continue south after setting the fire. They will think we're headed for Dassel. And yes, they will kill us if we do what they think we'll do." I sighed at how much she had to learn so fast.

"So what do we do instead?"

"Go west?"

66

"Right. They're trying to box us in. That's why the pursuit has slowed. So instead of doing what they expect, at first, we'll follow along the line of the fire so that we end up behind them. Instead of doing what they expect, we'll go towards Jaddah to the west?" I watched Rhiannon as I talked. I needed to know if my charge would focus and obey my commands. It didn't affect my duty, but it might affect our safety.

"I'm sorry Aisha. You are right, I'm whining. I'm scared, and I'm not helping. I think I can start the fire." Rhiannon opened our kit and found the flint and char cloth. It took her a few tries but she got a small fire going.

"Very good, Anka." I lit the two torches I made while Rhiannon was starting the fire. "We are close to the road now because we have been traveling east since our last encounter. We will set a fire here and work our way to the river's edge, then backtrack and follow the fire north for an hour or two. By that time the attackers should circumvent the fire and search for us ahead of the burned-out area. We'll cross the river and head west into Jaddah. Any questions?"

"Aisha, father always said that the Jaddahan people are vicious and cruel. Will we be safe?" We trotted towards the river, trailing our torches in the brush to set fires along the way.

"Nothing we do will be safe. As for the Jaddahans, the desert nomads lead a very harsh life. That makes them appear cruel to those who live in kingdoms like Granya and Valda where life is easier. They are excellent fighters, seen as vicious by those who challenge them. Who could be more vicious than those who attacked us last night?"

Rhiannon didn't answer. My remarks were based on what I had learned at the Aerie about Jaddah and its people. Soon, we would find out the truth.

The fire line was set in about half an hour.

"Now we go back to the middle and follow the fire north." I pointed into the already burned out area. The wind had stepped up and the fire gained strength. We followed the most intense part of the fire so we wouldn't be seen; the smoke hid us, as well. After an hour we rested next to a small gully surrounded by burned out brush. We were hot, drenched with sweat, and covered with soot.

After some respite I heard men talking. Through the brush I saw ten soldiers walking along the edge of the water, about fifty paces away. I wanted to get into the river before daylight, but I needed to make sure all the soldiers were well ahead of us before we tried to cross. So we waited.

I nudged Rhiannon who had fallen asleep. *A good thing. Many hours will pass before we get to sleep again.* "Can you swim, Anka?"

"No, Aisha," Rhiannon said. She rubbed her eyes to wake up. Then she straightened. "No, but I can hang onto something."

"Good, we'll find a log or something to hang onto. I'm not a good swimmer either." I spotted a large log in the water, caught in a small inlet. It looked big enough to keep Rhiannon and me afloat.

"Anka, our ferry is waiting over there."

I helped Rhiannon into the water, tied our kit to the stub of a branch, and pushed off into the river. I kicked to maintain travel in the middle of the river until I saw a clearing on the opposite bank. We scrambled to shore and into a sparse growth of trees.

"I'm sorry we can't rest, Anka, but we must get as far as we can before it gets light. The soldiers might realize what we have done. Besides, it is best to travel at night in the desert." I felt sorry for her. I was in excellent condition and used to hardships. Rhiannon was not. This experience could build her character or destroy it.

"Lead on, my cruel chaperone. I'm so tired I think I'll be able to sleep while we walk." Rhiannon waved her hand towards the infinite sandy landscape.

With no landmarks finding our way to Zenjir would be difficult. Sand dunes prevented us from seeing long distances. I became concerned that we could travel in circles or become lost in the desert and, worse yet, run out of water, a worse death than assassination. I remembered that sailors navigate using the stars. I wasn't a navigator, but I thought I could use the moon to guide us. It would rise in about the same place each evening. So I could use it as a reference starting point for the night's journey.

Behind me was east, directly in front of me west, and the moon about a quarter of a turn to my left, about where Zenjir should be. If I was right, we should soon meet other travelers.

I slung the kit over my shoulder and started out facing the moon. In places the ground was hard as rock, walking easy, but most of the time we walked in soft sand where our going was slow and tiring.

Trudging along, I wondered whether Rhiannon's father or my instructors at the Aerie were right about Jaddah. Or were they the same view expressed in different words?

CHAPTER SEVEN

Escape into Jaddah: Encounter with warriors

I wouldn't let Rhiannon stop until well after dawn. I knew from my studies that the sun made Jaddah scorching hot. We would make better time to rest under cover until the sun went down. I found a few sparse bushes and using my sword and bow made a small lean-to with clothes from our kit. Rhiannon fell asleep almost immediately. I stood watch, listening to the sounds of the desert until I was sure any change would awaken me. I awoke as the sun began to set. The air was still hot, but it would soon be cool, if not cold.

We had another cold snack from our dwindling supply of food. I had decided on a week's supply of food when I made up the kit's contents, a week of Talon not palace meals. I might have underestimated the time we would be on the run and the difficulty of finding edible game in the desert.

We began walking even before the sun had set. Before long, the moon would be visible, so I could determine the direction of Zenjir.

"Aisha, are we going to die?" Rhiannon said.

"Eventually."

"You know what I mean, here, in the desert."

"I hope not. I'm too young."

Rhiannon walked in silence for several minutes, looking down at her feet as they sank into the soft sand. "Yes, I'm whining. I can't help it. I'm tired, hungry, and scared."

"And you're alive. Think of this as an exciting adventure."

"Adventure? Don't you ever get scared, Aisha?"

"I would if it helped, but it doesn't. In fact, when you're scared you tend to stop thinking, and you have a real reason to be scared." I laughed and soon Rhiannon joined in.

We trudged through the soft sand that dragged at our feet. At the top of each dune, I stopped to scan the distance. I hoped the soldiers figured that we had either doubled back

70

towards Livorno or fled through the forest toward the town of Borkum on the East Mystic River, 80 leagues away. Most people wouldn't flee into the desert. Moreover, the people of Jaddah wouldn't treat armed soldiers as friends, should they cross their borders.

Late that night, I saw them. I stopped; we had nowhere to run or hide. I prepared myself to fight.

"Anka, there are at least four mounted riders several hundred paces behind us. I don't know whether they are friendly or not, but, if they aren't, do you remember our practice sessions in Savona?"

"Yes, Aisha."

"Good. Stay three or four paces behind me and keep me between you and the attackers." I had only my knives and a sword, because I used all of my arrows during our flight through the forest. They had the initiative. I could do nothing but wait and see what they would do. I thought it was curious that they didn't seem to be rushing to overtake us. In fact, it appeared that they were walking their horses, content to follow us.

Ten minutes later, four Jaddahan warriors wandered in. They dismounted several paces from Rhiannon and me. Rhiannon moved behind me. They were dressed in white baggy shirts and pants, leather sandals tied up the ankle and around the bottom of their pants, dark maroon sash with two curved-black-handled daggers, and in the Keffiyeh headdress of Jaddahan warriors. The woman, who seemed to be their leader, had a longer sash striped with a vivid red. Their horses, Sangolas, were much shorter than Savona warhorses, had wide feet with no apparent hoofs, a broad chest and a shorter back than other breeds, which I had learned was to give them enormous endurance.

"Chimola, what do you think? A slave and a noble for ransom, or two slaves?" a young warrior spoke while the warrior in the lead stood and inspected us.

"They are being chased by Valdan soldiers, Kibwe. They are either criminals or nobles," Chimola said as she approached us. She was tall, dark skinned, in her thirties, with a weathered face which smiled at the moment. I also detected a strong Illusion Sigil.

71

"Kneel, so I can put collars on you. We will determine later if you are ransomed or sold. In the meantime, you are my property." Chimola drew her dagger and pointed her knife to the ground at her feet.

I drew my knife as she took a step towards us. I motioned for Rhiannon to stay where she was.

"Continue, and you will have no need of slaves or mates," I said.

Chimola stopped in surprise. Her three companions laughed.

"Chimola, I can't believe a girl has put you in your place," one warrior said.

"I'm embarrassed for you, Chimola," another said.

"Oh, the drinks this story will earn," Kibwe said, still laughing. He was younger and smaller than Chimola with an easy smile and laugh.

"Astrakan steel. A knife fighter." Chimola broadened her smile as her warriors cheered her on.

"Fight, fight! First blood wins!" they chanted.

"First blood wins. If I win, you and she are my slaves. If you win, you go free." Chimola proposed this challenge as if being a slave wasn't all that bad.

"First death wins," I answered. *Anyone could draw first blood. To the death was the only way to determine the best fighter. Besides, no Talon would ever agree to be a slave under any conditions.*

Chimola stepped back and frowned as she stared at me. Three more figures of Chimola appeared, merged as one, and then separated again. The real Chimola meant to hide in her illusion. My sigil, however, revealed that the real Chimola was second from the right. The quartet fanned out in a crescent formation and began their approach. I waited as the illusions circled me. All four rushed me simultaneously. I parried the real Chimola's stomach-level slash and ignored the other three. Surprised, Chimola stumbled backward as I pressed my attack, scoring a three inch cut across the back of her hand. I stopped and let her back out of range.

Shaking her head, she gave a signal. Her three companions dismounted, drawing their daggers, and spread out

72

in a crescent formation. I never moved except to draw a throwing knife, from my back harness, for my left hand and folded the dagger in my right so that the blade's spine lay along my wrist.

"Chimola, she's a Talon," the older warrior said.

"You're good, Talon. I don't know how you were able to pick me out of the illusion, but do you think you can win against four Jaddahan warriors?" Chimola crouched and prepared to attack.

"Ah. Perhaps what I heard about Jaddahan honor was a lie. I'm embarrassed for you. Four against one, then." I motioned with my knife. "We shall see warrior. The question is who will die first."

"I don't want you to die for me, Aisha!" Rhiannon cried out.

"There, Aisha Talon, you have an alternative to dying," Chimola said. "You can be a live slave."

"You have a choice, warrior, live or die. I have only duty." By now, I was deep in combat mode, where no emotions exist, only awareness. The slightest move would begin the killing. Death meant little to me now. I am Talon. Only duty to the Clan and the Clan's contracts mattered.

"Chimola, a Talon with duty is a bad thing," the older man said softly.

"What do you want, Aisha Talon?" Chimola asked. The tension vibrated in the air around us like angry bees.

"I would like to hire you to take us to Zenjir and to be our bodyguards until Anka is able to return home." No one moved. I could hear their breathing and sensed a subtle shifting of weight. Chimola and the older man's breathing were normal and their bodies still. Kibwe and the other warrior's breathing were fast as they shifted their weight from foot to foot.

"How long, how much?"

"One half gold each week, ten gold when Anka is returned safely."

"Two gold each week, one hundred gold when Anka is returned safely," Chimola countered.

"One gold each week, fifty gold when Anka is returned. A fair offer and final." I could hear Rhiannon shuffling closer as the deadly negotiations went on, closing the angle of exposure to the four warriors as I had taught her.

"Blood oath of Talon and Jaddah warrior," Chimola demanded.

"Blood oath," I confirmed. I relaxed as the warriors returned their knives to the sheaths in their sashes and beckoned Rhiannon to join me.

"Give me your arm, Anka," I said. I made a small cut on my arm first then hers, using my throwing knife.

She was too shocked even to flinch as I made the small, shallow cut. She stared at it and looked faint as the blood slowly oozed out. At the same time Chimola and his companions repeated the process a few paces away.

Chimola and I repeated the bargain and gripped arms touching the blood together. I pulled Rhiannon over by her arm and held it against Chimola's. We repeated the process six more times before the bargain was considered sealed.

"Are we being followed, Chimola?" I asked as we sat sharing the Jaddahan's meal of dried goat meat, flat bread, and water. Their cold food was not only different but also far tastier with its exotic spices.

"No, they searched the shore for your tracks, but couldn't find any trace, so they abandoned the river search and went inland."

"They must have been blind or lazy." I thought back to our rush to cross the river. "We must have left tracks."

"You did. We covered them." Kibwe laughed. "Not every day good slaves cross into Jaddah."

"We should leave now," Chimola said. "With only four Sangolas between us, Aisha Talon and Anka can ride one Sangola while each of us will take a turn walking."

"Chimola, you may call me Aisha. I will take my turn walking or running."

"It would have been a good fight, Talon."

* * * *

It took two more nights to travel 24 leagues to Zenjir. Except for Rhiannon, we each took our turn trotting alongside the Sangolas. I enjoyed the opportunity to run. The last several weeks had given me little chance to practice. Before dawn each day, we stopped and had our only hot meal of the day. The meal tasted strange and spicy hot, but tasty, flat bread, flavored grain, brown fruit with seeds, and goat meat with a hot and spicy milk sauce. As we sat around the fire, I asked what Chimola and her friends knew about events in Granya.

"Chimola, you said that you wiped our tracks clean, and that they were Valdan soldiers. Are you sure?"

"Oh yes," she said. "Those chasing you from the north didn't have Valdan uniforms. But the ones who backtracked came from the south and had Valdan uniforms. They knew each other and were from the same force. Strange that Valdan soldiers were on Granya soil and stranger still that they were chasing you and Anka. Did they chase you from Valda, or did they enter Granya to find you?"

I changed the subject. "What is Zenjir like?" I didn't want to talk about what had happened until I knew more about Chimola and the situation in Granya. Chimola smiled at me and didn't press further.

"It is an oasis in the desert. A great city, many people and many warriors." We learned a little about Zenjir and the Jaddahans that night as each of the warriors shared stories about their homeland and their travels. Chimola and her small group were scouts who roamed the border with Granya and sometimes Valda, watching for undefined incursions into Jaddah. Their clan paid them for their services. Chimola avoided the details.

* * * *

Magnificent! The only word I could think to describe what I saw did it no justice. The town of Zenjir shimmered in the sunlight like the grains of sand that made up the kingdom of Jaddah. The architecture radiated a beauty I never had seen, strangely designed domes and curved arches. I saw paintings as a student at the Aerie, but no picture could approach the vivid colors and majesty that lay before me.

"Is that a mirage behind the town, Chimola?" Rhiannon asked. She waved her hand toward the shimmering blue ribbon which lay beyond the city.

"No, Anka, that is the great lake Tiamat, made from the goddess Tiamat's own tears to give the Jaddahan people life." Kibwe proved the most gregarious of the warriors with an

75

opinion and comment about everything. He clearly admired his commander, Chimola.

The rectangular walls surrounding Zenjir towered ten paces high and at least two leagues long, with slender watch minaret fifteen stories high at each of the four corners. At the very top of each structure were four open arches supporting their golden domes.

Outside the walls, hundreds of open air tents formed the bazaar. Wending our way through the throng, we passed vendors crying their wares. I gasped at the designs and bright colors made lively as they moved and flapped in the warm desert breeze. As we passed the bazaar, on the way to the gates of the city, the multiple colors and exotic designs flapped in the gentle wind created a breathtaking scene that seemed alive and moving. Chimola made a signal to the guards at the entrance before she left us just inside the gate. The guards stared hard at Rhiannon and me but did not bother us.

"We will direct you to the Red Hawk, a clean inn, that our Clan owns, where you can stay until you determine where you want us to take you," Uzoma said. He appeared cordial, maybe the oldest warrior in the group, but clearly not its leader. I guessed his age in his forties. "Chimola must report to our clan leader to inform him of your presence and our contract."

"Are there any Talons in Zenjir, Uzoma?" I asked. Talon support would be welcome.

"Yes, a few. Hi'Lord Baqir employs several, and Talons are hired to guard caravans coming to Zenjir from other kingdoms. These usually stay in the city to rest and relax before returning."

"Can you get word to one of them that Aisha Talon would like to talk with him?" I failed to contain my excitement.

"Yes, Mistress Aisha." He waved to Kibwe who peeled off in another direction. We strolled down the wide streets lined by domed structures and decorated with variegated fronds and flowers. If it weren't for duty, I would have stopped and gaped at the houses, shops, and temples. Most of the buildings were white or contrasting shades of light and dark brown; the trim included intricate mosaic designs of blues, oranges, and greens. Arches were inlaid with intricate embossments and writings that I would

76

have liked to study. I forced myself to concentrate on my duty and scanned the people around us for signs of trouble.

The Red Hawk Inn was a modest two story structure with an open colonnade with tables for eating outside. Inside it was clean and bright from the multiple open arches allowing access. We paid for a room with two beds; it was clean and pleasant if austere.

"This is rather ... plain and small." Rhiannon looked around the room. "It reminds me a bit of the dungeons."

"Uzoma, Anka, and I need to shop for clothes. We didn't exactly have the chance to bring any and what we have might draw attention." I smiled at the thought. "We seem to have gotten separated from our luggage. Can you help us?"

"It is my duty to protect you while you shop," Uzoma said with a small grin. "But I'm not sure how much help I could be. The women who are warriors shop in the same places as the men, but many women prefer clothing that is more beautiful. I never shop with my wife or my daughter. They don't allow it."

I smiled. "How many children do you have, Uzoma?"

"Two sons and a daughter, Mistress."

"You must be anxious to see them after being away." I learned as much about our escorts as I could, valuable when trouble exposed its ugly fangs.

"Yes, Mistress Aisha. I would like to spend some time with my family, but we are under contract to you, which takes precedence. You have not indicated how many of us you expect to guard you while you are in Zenjir?"

"One of you, night and day. Is that acceptable?" We were far from Granya or Valda, unlikely to encounter more than an isolated assassination attempt. I could handle that myself, although back-up could be valuable. We needed most a guide and informant.

"Yes, Mistress. Very reasonable, considering what you are paying us." Uzoma grinned. "Three of us are married and would like to spend some time with our families while we are home. The fourth, Kibwe, has several women friends. He would not like them to forget him. For now, I will be outside your door while you freshen up." Uzoma closed the door as he left.

"Do you think father is alive, Aisha?" Rhiannon said.

"I think the attack was intended to kill you and your father, Anka. I saved your life at the cost of the other Talons. I hope that your father's Talon guard was able to save him too. I know they would give their lives to save him, but bravery is not always enough." I paused to consider my next remark. "You should begin to regard yourself now as hi'Lady Rhiannon. It couldn't hurt. If you are not now, you will be someday in the future."

"You think my father's dead." Rhiannon sat on the edge of one of the beds, sobbed, and covered her face with her hands. "And why do you keep calling me Anka?"

"I continue to call you Anka to protect you. Whether your father is alive or dead, you are still in danger. The longer we can hide your identity, the less likely you are to be attacked. As for your father, it is best not to assume, because, if you do, you will act on that assumption. And if the assumption is wrong, it could mean your death. Before we act, we will try to find out the truth while we are here."

"Will you stay with me, Aisha?" Rhiannon asked. "I don't know who else I can trust."

"Yes, Anka. I'm contracted for a year. At that time, you may extend the contract if you wish."

"Are you and the Talons going to seek revenge for whoever killed the Talons in the ambush?"

"Probably not. The soldiers and nobles attacked you and your father, not the Talons. It was not personal against the Raptor Clan. The Talons are professional soldiers." I knew this whole conversation would sound harsh to a young girl, but better the truth than a lie.

"So you only protect me for the money!"

"I am here for my Clan's honor, and for that honor I would give up my life to protect you. No, I do not do it for the money. But do not dismiss money. People need it to eat, to feed their families, to buy clothes, and to provide shelter for them. The poorer you are, the more important money is to your survival. You will also find that you can't buy loyalty. You must earn it by the way you rule."

"I'm confused--" Rhiannon was interrupted by a knock at the door.

"Yes?" I asked as I put my hands on my knives.

"Mistress, four Talons are here to see you," Uzoma said through the closed door.

"Let them in, Uzoma." I motioned for Rhiannon to go to the far corner of the room. Until I was sure, I would be prepared to fight.

CHAPTER EIGHT

Zenjir: Temporary safety

Our room at the inn seemed small as four men entered, and smaller yet when the last one closed the door. It was large enough for two beds, a table, and two chairs, but too small for six people. The four were Talons, donned with traditional sashes, black silk shirts and pants. They walked with a cat-like lilt, stood and watched me as I eyed them. An uneasy standoff.

I sensed that the four had War Sigils and three had additional sigils. One had an Energy Sigil, one had an Illusion Sigil, and one had the Truth Sigil. I decided not to use my Negativity Sigil since I wanted the Talon with the Truth Sigil to be able to establish the truth of my statements. My problem was determining the truth of theirs.

I didn't recognize any of them, and none showed that they knew me. A cold silence pervaded the room as if the chill of the desert night entered with them. I presumed they were waiting for me to identify myself; that was not so easily done. Talons had no identifying Clan scars or tattoos. Even our weapons, while expensive and distinctive, were not unique.

Welcome Brothers, I signed and waited. The four men, all different heights, builds, coloring, facial hair, and looks, had a stamp about them that was easy to see but difficult to describe. Two were above average in height, one medium, and one short, although at least a hand taller than me. **I'm Aisha Talon.**

Who is the girl in the corner? the oldest of the five signed. Judging by his sash, he was a Master Talon.

Anka, my duty. I signed. I didn't allow myself to relax. The fact that the older one could "battle sign" was encouraging since Clan law forbade teaching anyone the Talon's sign language. But, I had heard stories that a few rogue Talons existed, and they would know how to sign.

"When did you graduate?" the older man asked.

80

"I was called sister this year." I said aloud, hiding my smile at the test.

"Name three masters at the Aerie."

"Bakaar, Jiang, Dragos." It was now my turn. "Name their positions."

"Master Bakaar manages supplies, equipment and conducts knife training; Master Jiang is the senior trainer; and Master Dragos is the senior Talon of the Raptor Clan." The senior Talon looked back at each man, who nodded. "Have we tested each other enough, Sister Aisha?"

"Yes, Senior Brother." I didn't think rogue Talons would have current knowledge of the masters at the Aerie. Besides, I had heard rumors the rogue Talons lived in the Salda Kingdom or even further south. I had to assume that these four were Talons, although I hated to assume anything with Rhiannon's life at stake.

"Welcome, Sister Aisha. I am Anton, and these brothers are Marku, Stanko, and Vasile. Brother Cezar is the other Talon in Zenjir. He is currently on guard duty with hi'Lord Baqir. How may we help you?" The four men sat themselves on the floor in a semi-circle facing me.

"First let me introduce my duty. Her name for now is Anka. Her title, the last we knew, was pri'Rhiannon. Master Dragos contracted me to hi'Lord Varius as her bodyguard, pretending to be her chaperone." I detailed the attack on the caravan, our subsequent escape into the desert, and my existing agreement with the Jaddahan warriors. "Before I can decide what action to take next, I need information about the situation in Granya. I hoped my brothers could help me."

"Do you know the status of Anka's detail?" a younger Talon asked. "I have an old friend on that detail."

"No. To my shame, I had to leave with Anka and could not stay to help. When we fled the camp, they were greatly outnumbered, and they could not disengage since Anka still lived. They would have held to the last man to give us as much time as possible." Every time I thought back to the scene and having to leave them, bile rose in my throat. I had done the right thing, duty came before honor, but that didn't make me feel any better.

81

"Cezar, Vasile, and I are under contract to hi'Baqir. However, Marku and Stanko are not currently under duty and are free for Clan work," Anton said. "If you wish their services, Anka, you must negotiate a contract with the Talon."

"I don't know how to negotiate a contract." Rhiannon turned to me. "And I have no gold, Mistress Aisha."

I frowned, finding myself in an awkward situation. I was Clan and, therefore, could not negotiate against the Clan; yet, I was under contract to Rhiannon and responsible for her safety. Having a duty to protect both put me in a tenuous position. *Where did one end and the other begin?*

"Master Anton, you are the senior Talon here and, therefore, represent the Clan. I wish your advice as to the extent that I may assist Anka in her negotiations with you."

"You may not participate in the negotiations, but you may advise her beforehand on what resources and services she will need, and the questions she should ask the Talon."

"Anka, we need information. To get it, you must send two Talons to Granya to determine the current situation. One Talon must return to us with a report. The other should report to the Aerie, but that is Talon business and you need not pay for that. Then I would suggest we plan to meet with a representative of the Talon from the Aerie at the town of Dahab. There you and the representative can determine your next action. You must ask Anton Talon his standard rates for these types of services and negotiate a rate based upon how different your services requirements are from standard. Remember how I negotiated with the Jaddah warriors?"

"You threatened to fight them to the death!" Rhiannon half-shouted, which brought smiles to the Talons' faces.

Rhiannon was right. The threat had been part of the negotiations. I smothered a laugh at an image of Rhiannon standing, hands on hips, challenging Anton to a duel. "No matter what happens, Anka, I am your bodyguard and advisor for the year. And the four Jaddahans are also yours to command."

"Oh." Rhiannon walked over to the table and sat in the chair. "Anton Talon, what is the standard rate for a Talon to enter Granya, find out what is happening, and return to tell me?"

Rhiannon found her most noble-like voice while sitting straighter in her chair.

Anton spoke after some thought. "What you want is a general spy, someone to travel through Granya, eating and drinking at inns, and listening to the gossip. Two gold scrules each week for each Talon plus a scrule per week for their food and lodging."

"Mistress Aisha, how much did father pay for you?" Rhiannon looked at me.

I had to admit that was good thinking. I expected her to agree with Anton's price.

"Four gold scrules each week and he would provide food, lodging, and clothing." I resisted the urge to smile.

"Anton Talon, my bodyguard has saved my life twice, has risked her life several times, and has spent every hour attached to me. That seems many times harder than what I require. One scrule each week for each Talon and one scrule for their expenses." I noted several lips twitching in what would have been broad smiles on anyone except a disciplined Talon.

"Two scrules each Talon each week," Anton countered, "no food or lodging. But you must pay for a Jaddahan guide to Granya and back to Zenjir."

"Aisha, can we lend one of our Jaddahan warriors as a guide?"

"Yes, they work for you." Rhiannon took to bargaining as if she was born into a merchant's family. She matured before my eyes. The months ahead would not be easy. Her choices could make the difference between hi'Lady and dead.

"I will provide the guide to Granya and back to Zenjir," Rhiannon said. She turned back to Anton.

"That would be acceptable, Anka." He nodded agreement. Rhiannon looked at me, and I gave her a small nod.

"I agree to your terms, Anton Talon, but, I don't have any gold." She wrung her hands nervously.

"You don't need any, Anka. Your word will be sufficient. If your father is alive, he will pay the debt. If he is dead, you will be the hi'Lady of Granya and have the gold to pay your debt."

"What if I die, Anton Talon?" Rhiannon asked. I can't say I blamed her, based on the events of the last year.

"Do you want Aisha to fail in her duty?" Anton asked. It was spoiled a bit when his lip twitched.

"No, Anton Talon." A smile spread over her face. "She wouldn't allow it."

"Good, then you have a contract with the Talons."

"Do I have to cut my arm again, Aisha?" Rhiannon turned to me. Anton could not suppress a laugh.

"No, Anka, Anton Talon will write up a contract which you will sign. A Talon's signed contract is his blood oath. The Jaddahans think the blood makes the oath more binding." I paused to think about it. "Or maybe they can't read and write."

"If you would come to Zenjir Castle tomorrow morning," Anton said, "I will have the contract ready for signing, and Marku and Stanko can be on their way to Granya. Cezar, Vasile, and I train the hi'Lord's elite guards, the Fangs. We meet in the castle's training yard each morning at nine glasses. I thought perhaps Anka could benefit from some training, and you may enjoy the exercise, Sister. Some of the warriors are quite good."

Anton and the other Talons rose to leave.

"Can I, Mistress Aisha?" Rhiannon asked, reverting back to the young girl she had been weeks ago. She seemed to forget I worked for her. I guess, in truth, the lines of who was in charge blurred from time to time.

"As I have told you, we cannot teach you to be a knife fighter without years of training. However, surprise is a powerful weapon. Even with limited knowledge on how to use a knife, you could be very dangerous, as long as no one knew you had one. I have already shown you some tricks. More training would be helpful." I liked the idea of Rhiannon learning to defend herself in an emergency and would welcome the chance to practice. "Thank you, Master Anton. I am rusty from a lack of practice and would welcome the exercise."

As the Talons left the room, Uzoma entered. "Mistress Aisha, my wife sent word that you are welcome to eat with us tonight. Afterward, we will take you and Anka to the market."

I looked to Rhiannon who nodded eagerly.

"We would be honored, Warrior Uzoma. First, we need to freshen up. Is there some place we can bathe?" I hoped we didn't have to use the bowl and pitcher sitting on the table. Neither of us had the chance for a real bath in over a week.

"Yes, mistress, there is a bath house attached to the Red Hawk Inn. They will even clean your clothes while you bathe." He led us downstairs and through a long hallway that ended in an arched entrance. Inside, several women in long white robes waited to help us.

"Hala, this is Mistress Aisha and Anka. They are residents of the Red Hawk Inn and require a bath and their clothes cleaned."

"Welcome Mistress Aisha, Anka. This way please." Hala and another woman led us around a tall barrier into a second room. They stepped out of their robes. Underneath they had brief panties and narrow halters around their breasts. They stripped the two of us naked and led us into a third room, where we were doused with water, scrubbed with a perfumed soap, and rinsed clean. They led us into another room with a large pool with steaming hot water. It was glorious. My aches and pains from the previous week's activities seemed to dissolve in the pool. I could have stayed there for hours.

"Mistress Aisha, Anka," Hala said, "I'm afraid you should leave the pool. It is not good to stay in the hot water too long. After a quarter glass, some people experience problems. We can offer you a relaxing massage after you have been in the cold pools."

"Not me but I'm sure Anka would like a one," I said. If I had a massage, it would mean I couldn't watch Anka, and I would be defenseless and under someone's control. I knew I was being overly cautious, but I was not going to make it easy for someone to kill her.

We went from there into another room with another large pool filled with cold water. Surprisingly, it was invigorating. Hala and the other woman held towels ready to dry us as we stepped out. Once toweled off, we were led into a smaller room with padded tables, and they helped Anka up onto one. I stood to one side and watched.

"Aaaaah, Aisha. This is wonderful." Rhiannon moaned for what seemed like hours but was probably only a little over fifteen minutes. When Hala finished the massage, our cleaned clothes were waiting. Dressed, we met Uzoma, as we exited the baths.

* * * *

Uzoma led us down several narrow passages to a small light brown wall with decorative tiles around a wooden door. Inside the gate was a narrow garden and a small white building with a flat roof. The narrow windows were outlined with tiles which had intricate green, yellow, and orange patterns and carved sigils I didn't recognize. A heavy cloth material, not glass or wood, covered all of them. In the doorway, a small, plump woman awaited us.

"Welcome to our home, Mistress Aisha and young Anka. May your days be filled with gentle, cool winds. My name is Akinyi, and this is my daughter Nyah."

"Thank you, Akinyi. We are honored by your kind offer," I replied. Once inside, I saw a small house, two rooms separated by an arched opening with a cloth covering acting as a door. I assumed the room we entered served as kitchen, dining, family, and guest room, and that the other room was sleeping quarters. Their daughter, Nyah, looked a few years older than Rhiannon. She had her mother's features, raven black hair and a striking figure. I found the food hotly spiced and tasty. Eating with my hands became strangely relaxing.

After the meal, the five of us left for the market outside of the city gates. I sensed that most of the merchants had weak to moderate sigils that indicated amulets purchased from the Blessed ones. The most popular were Charm and Truth Sigils, although a few had Illusion Sigils. As we mingled with the shoppers, warriors passed with War or Energy Sigils and nobles, with a variety of sigils, mostly weak to moderate in strength. I wondered if the sigil holders realized the strength or weakness of their sigils. I kept my sigil off. I could just imagine the chaos if I suddenly negated all the Charm, Illusions, and Truth Sigils in my vicinity.

Akinyi led us to several stalls with ready-made clothes. These were acceptable because the styles tended to be baggy or were cloth wraps. Sizes sold as small, medium, or large. For a silver scrule or two, they could be altered in minutes. I had to chuckle at Uzoma's bemused expression as he stood aside to

86

watch us shop. Obviously, he had told the truth when he said he did not normally escort his wife and daughter. Even so, he stayed close enough to aid me if we should be attacked.

"It's so strange and wonderful at the same time," Rhiannon said as we wandered the market visiting merchants. At one stall she found a small knife with a strange animal carved into the handle. "What is this figure? What is it carved from, Mistress Akinyi?"

"There are giant animals in the Great Lake Tiamat. These figures are replicates of the animals, carved from their bones."

I purchased several outfits for Rhiannon and me and found a set of black pants and shirt that could be tailored in the Talon style.

"I hoped you found everything you needed, Mistress Aisha and young Anka," Akinyi said. We prepared to leave the market.

"Yes, we did. You and your daughter have been very helpful, and you were very generous, cooking a meal for us, Akinyi. We hope you will accept this small gift from us." Rhiannon handed her the cloth that she and her daughter had admired while we shopped.

"Thank you, Mistress Aisha, young Anka. We enjoyed your company. Feel free to call on us if you need any more help."

I turned to Uzoma, who lagged behind us after hours of shopping. "Uzoma, would you please talk to the others. I will need one of you to escort two Talons to Granya. I will give the person who goes an additional gold piece. Whoever is selected should be at the castle training yard tomorrow morning at nine glasses, ready to leave."

"I will take care of it, Mistress."

After saying goodbye to his family, Uzoma escorted us back to the Red Hawk Inn to take up his post outside the door. Once in our room, Rhiannon sat quietly on the bed as her expression grew sad. "Mistress Aisha, do you think my father is dead?"

"I don't know, Anka. Many people died that day because someone wants your father's power." I paused. Based on the size of the attack and the carnage, someone already with power wanted it badly. "I wish your father alive and well, but it would be best if you planned as if he were dead. It is like when I assumed the caravan would be attacked and planned accordingly. If I had been wrong, you and Leszek would have laughed at me. Not such a terrible thing. However, when we were attacked, we were prepared, and you survived."

"I'm not old enough to be hi'Lady," Rhiannon said, her voice rising in desperation.

"That is a wrong attitude. You are truly hi'Lady or you are not. If you are not, others will rule in your place. You need to listen to those with experience, but you must make the final decisions. I thought you were excellent today with Anton, and so did the Talons. You listened to advice and you negotiated a very good contract." I spoke the truth to Rhiannon rather than words of comfort.

"Anton Talon just felt sorry for me."

I laughed at her suggestion. "Anka, Talons never feel sorry for anyone. Negotiating the best contract he could for the clan was Anton's responsibility. Although a Talon will never cheat you, he will charge as much as he can if you are willing and able to pay it. He merely conceded to your arguments because they were valid. The risk was minimal. And the Talons need to know what happened to the others of our Clan."

I wondered whether I had gone beyond protecting my young charge to tutoring, or if tutoring was an intrinsic part of my contract in protecting her. Tomorrow I would allow Talons to teach her how to use a knife. I hoped I was doing the right thing. At times I felt so old, and at other times, like now, I felt so young and inexperienced.

CHAPTER NINE

Zenjir: A duel – Talon vs Fang

I awoke to the sound of voices outside the door to our room, footsteps fading into silence. I assumed it was our Jaddahan guard changing shifts. I would have to arrange a signal with them so I wouldn't have to assume such things. Rhiannon was sound asleep, but the room filled with the dusty light of dawn, so I rose.

"Anka, it is time to rise. They will expect us at the castle at dawn." I gave her a slight shake.

"You've gone from a cruel chaperone to a cruel advisor." She buried her head under the pillow.

"At least you know I'm not trying to get on your good side." After a few minutes, she did get out of bed. We pulled on our new outfits I had tailored for physical training, loose shirt, pants pegged at the bottom, and a narrow sash to hold up the pants.

Kibwe stood guard outside our door when Rhiannon and I stepped into the hallway.

"Would you like to break fast with us, Kibwe?" I asked.

"Yes, Mistress Aisha. Oluchi will meet us at the castle. He volunteered to guide your Talons to Granya and back. He thanks you for the extra coin." Kibwe's face lit with an easy smile. "They have a baby on the way. Their second."

Breakfast was strange but tasty, a mixture of grain, meat of some kind, and egg. Kibwe, bright and cheerful, made good company.

"Uzoma told me," Kibwe said, between bites of food, "that you and Anka are going to the castle today to work out with Baqir's 'Fangs.' They are the finest warriors in Jaddah. The castle is the oldest structure in Zenjir. It was built over two hundred years ago and the mosaics are the builder's original work. Beautiful work. Of course there have been many additions since then."

89

The trip to the castle was interesting in itself. The houses grew in size and so did the walls surrounding them as we moved closer to the castle, but the architecture seemed to remain the same. The only difference seemed to be that the mosaic designs adoring the walls and doors were bigger and more complex.

The castle walls stood five stories high, easily five paces thick. Eight massive turrets were embedded in the outer wall and another five turrets rose to a height of ten stories. Two massive gates, now open, limited the access into the castle grounds. The guards looked alert, indicating good training and discipline.

The guard gave Kibwe a quick yet thorough eye, then said, "Your reason for wanting access, Warrior."

"We have an appointment with Master Anton Talon," I said.

"One moment, I will have a guard escort you to him. He's in the training yard."

While we waited off to the side, I looked around. Very different from the castles in Granya. This one didn't seem to be made of stone. Its surface was smooth and bright white except for inlayed mosaic tiles, which adorned the walls and pillars of an arched colonnade that spanned the length of the building. The mosaic's colors and intricate designs overwhelmed my senses. I had never seen a structure so amazing. The main building, a modest three stories high, had four golden domes of various sizes that rose close to four stories, and a narrow cylinder shaped tower soaring twenty stories from one corner of the building.

When the guard arrived, he led us around the main building to a smaller dome supported by two-story pillars every ten paces, creating a large covered space out of the intense sun. Inside, some warriors paired off to practice with a variety of weapons, while others lounged around the edge, watching.

When we entered the training yard, Oluchi, Marku and Stanko were waiting. Anton joined us immediately.

"Anka, I have the contract ready for you. Please read it and sign it, if you agree." Anton handed Anka a parchment.

"Anka, you need to read the contract," I said. "I will answer any questions you have." I led Rhiannon over to some empty benches used to observe the practice area. Anka sat and began reading. Anton had made the contract short and concise, typical of Talon agreements.

"Mistress, it is what we agreed to. How should I sign it?" Rhiannon asked. I wasn't surprised. I had been calling her Anka to avoid advertising her identity, and Rhiannon didn't know whether she was Anka, the hi'Lady, or the hi'Lord's daughter. And she had never had to worry about money or signing anything.

"Sign it 'pri'Rhiannon' since, as far as you know, that is your current rank." Rhiannon signed it and we walked back to Anton. She handed it to him.

"Marku, you and Stanko now are under contract to Anka. Warrior Oluchi will guide you to Granya and wait for you in Dahab to guide one of you back." Anton dismissed them. He turned to me. "Aisha, with your permission, I would like you to work with some of the Fang warriors while Cezar helps Anka with a knife. He will not leave her alone."

"I could use the knife practice. Acting as a chaperone prohibits working out with a knife." I signed, **What is my cover?**

You are, Talon. Anka is your business. You could imply she is your daughter. Pri'Rhiannon is dangerously fond of you, Aisha.

She is feeling very vulnerable. I turned to Rhiannon. "Anka, Cezar Talon is going to show you how to use a knife while I practice." I pointed to Cezar. "It is very important that you work hard."

"Yes, Mistress." Rhiannon said, smiled, and headed towards Cezar.

"Farai, why don't you and Aisha Talon work out?" Anton said to a tall young man, dressed in a dark purple shirt and baggy pants, black calf-length boots, and a red sash. Farai went into the ring with me. Behind him, smirking, stood a young man that I heard someone call Amadi. He wore a rakish mustache and goatee. I shrugged and began my sparring with Farai.

During the morning, I sparred with ten different warriors, only one of them a woman. They were all good, but none of them could match my skill. I did learn a few new moves and eventually worked out reasonable counters. For the most part, the Fangs' techniques were basic moves taught at the Aerie. After each fight, I went over the details of the match with my opponent

"Anton, I think that is enough for me today." I felt tired after my tenth match. I would be slower and my opponents wouldn't oppose my best.

"You need a real man to fight. I'm next." Amadi approached me.

"I'm finished for today, Warrior Amadi," I continued walking over to Rhiannon.

"Are you afraid of a real fight?" Amadi yelled, but I ignored him.

"Well Cezar, how did my ward do?"

"They treated you easy because you are a woman. I think I could reduce you to tears," Amadi interrupted.

"She did well, Aisha. She worked very hard," Cezar also ignored Amadi.

"I think you are a coward and afraid to fight me!" Amadi shouted, spitting in my direction.

"If you like, Warrior Amadi, you can demonstrate how bad I am tomorrow. Right now, I'm going to go get something to eat." I steered Rhiannon towards the gate.

"Mistress, he called you a coward!" Rhiannon said indignantly as she intently watched me.

"Amadi ignored the most important rule of fighting. He got excited. Emotions make you overly aggressive, careless, hesitant, or slow because you are distracted. The thought of embarrassing me had him excited, and he could have been pushed into anger with little effort. A Talon learns early not to be pushed into an emotional reaction. Besides, a Talon has nothing to prove especially against wooden knives with stain on them. The only test of one's skill is when you are staring at someone with steel who wants to kill you." We followed Kibwe back to the inn. I noticed that he was very attentive during the walk.

Back in the room, Rhiannon showed me the techniques she had been taught. Cezar had chosen situations that relied on the element of surprise. I concurred with his choices for Rhiannon.

"But I doubt I will ever be good enough to fight with a knife, and I don't think I could stab anyone, anyway," Rhiannon said.

"The most important element in a fight is surprise, doing something your opponent doesn't expect. If no one knows you carry a weapon and know how to use it, you have the element of surprise. The next most important element, knowing where to strike. Cezar will teach you that while we are here, but without the will to use your knife, it is useless. The final choice is yours. Remember, never draw your knife unless you decide you are willing to kill someone with it. Otherwise, it will be taken away and used against you. Either fight to kill or wait for me to do your fighting for you."

"Why are you teaching me, Mistress?"

"Because people are trying to kill you, and I may not be able to get to you in time. At least this way you will keep yourself alive until I get there. But the only way to truly defend yourself in a knife fight is to kill the one who is trying to kill you."

* * * *

The next day, when we arrived at the training yard, Anton pulled Rhiannon and me aside.

"Aisha, Leszek Talon arrived last night. The healer treated his wounds, and he should recover in a few days. He had serious cuts to his arms and chest and lost a lot of blood."

"Can I see him?"

"Farai," Anton called. He joined us. "Take Aisha over to the room where Leszek Talon recovers. Cezar and I will watch Anka."

Farai laughed and said, "The warriors who brought him in last night said he was a magnificent fighter. They found him fighting twelve soldiers. They were tempted to wait and see if he would win." The room was large and could accommodate several persons, but Leszek was alone, lying in bed covered with a light blanket. I walked over and kissed him on the forehead. I was happy to see him. He opened his eyes.

"Sister Aisha. It is good to see you alive. I heard you escaped with Rhiannon." His voice sounded weak and shaky. "I'm sorry I can't get up to greet you."

93

"Don't you dare try. I convinced myself you had survived. The last time I saw you, I thought I was leaving you to die." My eyes moistened. I choked back a sob of joy.

"I probably would have, but a group of attackers got around us and entered the forest a few minutes after you did, so I disengaged to follow them. I thought I could harass them from the rear to slow down their pursuit. They split into small groups and took off in different direction, tracking where you had gone." Leszek paused, and I handed him a glass of water on the table next to his bunk. "I hunted your pursuers, killing everyone I could find. If any other Talons escaped, I didn't see them."

"I had wondered about the lapses in our pursuit." I thought about our encounters in the hours after fleeing the camp. "Your distraction helped us elude them."

"At some point in the action, they encircled me. I fled into Jaddah, but they pursued me across the border. I started towards Zenjir, and then they trapped me in a ravine an hour later. I fought. It was a losing battle. I think I may have killed three or four and wounded another two before they closed in for the kill. That was when ten Jaddah warriors descended on them. Afterward, I agreed to pay the Jaddahans to take me to Zenjir, and the rest..." He waved a hand weakly.

"Did you know they were Valdans, supporting sec'Lord Tadzio?"

"Not until yesterday. The Jaddahan told me on the way to Zenjir." Leszek paused, stared at the opposite wall with a scowl, and blinked hard as though forcing back tears. "Aisha, I'm scared." I couldn't believe what I heard.

"Why?"

"Healer Herk wants to be the Master Healer for Savona. Remember that he conspired with tri'Lady Caster. She told him he would be appointed when hi'Lord Varius was replaced."

Once more Leszek stopped and looked at me for several heartbeats before continuing. "I fear that Healer Herk knows Healer Luminita is my wife. He will want her imprisoned or killed. The hi'Lord Radulf may execute her and my son because she married a Talon." Leszek blurted in a rush as a tear ran down his cheek. I stood shocked and didn't know what to say. He had a son. He was married to Master Luminita, and he was distraught.

94

I sat down and took his hand in mine while I tried to sort out my thoughts. He looked away but squeezed my hand in his.

"Unless I'm wrong, Brother Leszek, your wife is no one's fool. She will understand the danger and take appropriate action. She won't risk herself or your child by staying in the castle. We will find her. Rhiannon and I will help."

* * * *

Rhiannon and I fell into a comfortable routine over the next eight days. Up early, breakfast with whoever stood guard outside our room, practice at the castle, dinner at the inn, and usually a stroll around one of the markets or just sightseeing. Leszek was now well enough to be up and spent time in the training grounds. Though he hid it well, I could tell his mind was elsewhere.

Warrior Amadi fought me several times during the week. He would have been a good fighter even without his War Sigil. With it, he had excellent reflexes, a smooth rhythm, and used a variety of complex techniques. I chose not to use my sigil, testing my skill and limits. We were about evenly matched, equal in the number of killing blows. Few fighters, even exceptional ones, can match a fully trained Talon.

Whenever Amadi won, he always made a big speech afterwards about the inferiority of women or about being better than Talons and would never allow me to critique the match. If he lost, he stormed out of the training yard. Today was no different.

Most of the Jaddahan warriors respected the few women warriors among them, but I soon realized that Amadi had something to prove in besting a woman. He often glared at Chimola. I suspected she had gained her position of leadership at his expense.

On this day, Amadi scored what would have been a killing blow and walked around the yard preening. "See my friends, the hi'Lord's Fangs are great, and I am the greatest. We are the equal of the Talon, and the Talon women would die at our feet in a real fight. Do you finally admit it, Aisha Talon?" Amadi added 'Talon' with emphasis, which he had omitted since we met.

"You are an excellent fighter in the practice ring as are all of the hi'Lord's elite guards. But the training ring is meant to learn, not to show off. That diminishes the purpose behind training and serves no one well." I hoped to draw him into a meaningful discussion of training. He was good and could be helpful to his comrades. As it was, they were afraid of him and learned nothing from matches with him.

"Get your knives and I will teach you respect. First blood." He smirked as he surveyed the warriors still in the training area.

"I must decline, Warrior Amadi. Talons do not fight first blood matches, only first death, and I have no reason to want you dead."

"You coward!"

"Enough, Amadi!" Anton stalked into the ring. "Leave this ring and do not return until you have regained your self control." Amadi left with several of his friends. I worked with Anton a half hour, and then finished the hour watching Rhiannon train. She had progressed well in the short time she had been practicing. Cezar emphasized deception and surprise, and showed her striking areas that would kill or maim. I hoped Rhiannon never would use these skills.

Chimola was our escort today as we began our walk back to the inn. When we reached the castle gate, Amadi and seven other warriors blocked the gate exit. Amadi had his knives drawn.

"Well, if it isn't Aisha, the coward," he shouted over laughs from his audience. Most were enjoying Amadi's bravado, but a few looked nervous. Chimola immediately drew her knife.

"Put it away, Chimola, unless the cowards attack Anka," I said.

"You are the coward." Amadi sneered, pointing at me. I knew I wasn't going to be able to distract Amadi from a fight. He had committed himself in front of his friends and couldn't back down or even give the appearance of backing down. I couldn't avoid the fight so I went on the offensive. I wanted him mad, blind with rage.

"I don't need seven men to help me. You are a little boy sulking because you didn't get your way, Amadi, a little boy trying to prove you are a man. Your mother is going to be very disappointed when she finds out." I snapped on my sigil and dropped into battle mode, no fear, hate, or exhilaration, just awareness.

Amadi charged towards me before I had finished. Enraged, he slashed at me with both knives. I parried his initial flurry and circled, light on my feet. He managed to give me a shallow cut, about a hand long, on my left arm that dripped blood down onto my hand. I could see his excitement at the sight of my blood. He pressed his attack with intricate patterns rather than going for the kill. Since he had the longer reach, I was content to wait for an opening. He scored again. This time a slightly deeper cut on my upper right arm, slightly longer than the first. I moved in close, keeping him from blocking my counter slice to his thigh. He had the advantage of reach, so I kept going in close. He didn't seem to realize he should worry about attacks to his lower body. I slashed his leg again, missing the leg artery, but I had produced a deep three inch gash. Blood ran down his leg, dripping onto the ground.

"No wood and stain. Real steel and real blood. Real death," I said in a soft tone.

His excitement turned to fear. He knew the loser would die. As he attacked again, I felt the jerkiness of the moves. He thought through each move and counter move, a bad sign, for him. I could smell the fear as sweat trickled down his cheeks and soaked through his tunic. I heard his ragged breathing, saw the trembling in the limbs.

He lunged at me. I twisted, dodging to the side, cutting his throat with my right hand and stabbing him in the kidneys with my left as he stumbled past me. He dropped to the ground with a groan. I kicked the knives away from his hands, and nudged his still body over with my foot. Seeing he was dead, I nodded to myself.

My knives covered in blood, I turned to his friends and met each of their eyes one by one until they looked away. I knew without looking that Anton had arrived and stood to my right.

"It is a shame," Anton snapped, "that warrior Amadi did not pay attention to Aisha Talon's instruction at training today. The training yard is to learn, not to show off. I think we will

97

make that tomorrow's lesson. You had best be about your business now." They gave me one more look, then looked down and avoided my eyes as they turned and walked away.

"Chimola, I need to stop at an Alchemist on the way to buy some herbs and cloth for my cuts," I said as we entered the gate.

"You need a healer, Mistress," Rhiannon replied. "You are bleeding from those three cuts."

"No, they aren't serious. We learned at the Aerie how to dress minor cuts like these. You can help me, Anka. It will be a good lesson for you."

Chimola led us to a small house with elaborate tiles, adorned with fescues of leaves, flowers, and plants. Inside, the shelves were lined with hundreds of jars.

"How may I help you mistresses?" A small, rotund man met us, his white robe and hands splotched with stains.

"Do you have tea tree, myrtle leaves, lemon grass, and witch hazel?" I asked, looking around the little shop.

"Yes, and I have aloe vera gel, also." His eyes darted to my wounds. "And cloth to wrap your cuts."

The herbalist and I spent the next few minutes negotiating prices. I think he gave me a good price because I was dripping blood on his floor.

I hurried back to our room because, although the cuts were not serious, losing blood would weaken me. I showed Rhiannon how to sew up my cuts and how to grind up the leaves, soak, and make a poultice to wrap them.

"Not something you are likely to need, Anka. But all knowledge can be helpful sooner or later," I said as she finished. "This poultice will keep the cuts from becoming infected as well as help them heal faster."

"Weren't you afraid, Aisha? I thought he was going to win." Rhiannon ducked her head and looked embarrassed.

"No, Anka. Amadi was a skilled fighter, but not as skilled as I am, and he was ruled by his emotions. His excitement made him over confident and careless. His anger made him too aggressive. But his fear is what killed him. The training yard made him prideful, excited by the thought that he could kill me. My taunting made him angry. When I cut him, he became afraid. His moves became measured and he grew desperate to end the fight quickly, even though he might have won. The golden rule, emotions kill." I lay down on the bed and closed my eyes.

* * * *

When Rhiannon and I arrived at the castle training yard the next morning, Anton and two Jaddahan Fang Warriors stood in the middle of the practice yard waiting for me.

"The hi'Lord Baqir has requested you attend him this morning. These two warriors will escort you to him." Anton motioned towards the warriors.

It was his nephew you killed, Sister Aisha.

CHAPTER TEN

Zenjir: A Jaddah proposal of safety

Rhiannon and I followed the guards into the main building through a large arched opening adorned with intricate carved columns. We entered a huge vestibule with a semicircular staircase at least five paces wide. Upstairs, we followed through a magnificent colonnade, a hundred paces long, with doors on both sides. Halfway down the hallway, we stopped at a door with two guards and a man dressed in gold with a bright maroon tabard and keffiyeh. He disappeared through the door and returned several minutes later.

"You may enter the reception room, Aisha Talon," he said, ignoring Rhiannon. The four-story ceiling of the room had a gold cloth pulled up at the center to look like the top of a large tent. Tapestry containing hundreds of scenes of desert life hung on the walls, enhancing the impression of a tent. I realized that it told the history of Jaddah that spanned hundreds of years. Light streamed in from windows slits two stories off the ground level. The hi'Lord's throne sat on a raised platform, thirty paces into the massive room, with a red carpet leading from the door to the throne. Ten of his elite Fang Warriors flanked the carpet, at least twenty soldiers on both sides of the hall, half of them armed with crossbows.

He's not taking any chances. I mused and calmed myself for whatever was to come.

I whispered instructions to Rhiannon as we approached the throne. "I hope there won't be any trouble, Anka, but the floor would be a good place for you if something does happen."

"Yes, Mistress." Her voice trembled. She darted quick looks around the room and paled.

"Hi'Lord Baqir, we are honored." I stopped several paces short of the platform. The warriors surrounding the hi'Lord eased their white-knuckled grip on their weapons.

A tall captain stepped forward to within a pace of me, looked me over and asked, "Are you armed?" He had a strong War Sigil and appeared readied for action.

"Captain, I am a Talon," I said. *Stupid man.* He might as well ask me if I had teeth inside my mouth.

"Give me your weapons." He stretched his hand out towards me. I wondered at the game being played here. Was this the Captain's idea or Baqir's, and what was the purpose?

"Thirty soldiers afraid of one small woman and a girl? I thought better of the Fang," I said.

"I can force you to give up your weapons."

"Of course you can, Captain, which is why you don't need them." Baqir and his Captain were playing a game of wits, but I had to be careful not to let it get out of hand. "Besides, it wouldn't be in keeping with your customs to ask a woman to undress in front of all these men."

The Captain looked over his shoulder at Baqir and then turned to walk back to stand next to the smiling hi'Lord.

Baqir leaned forward as if to get a better look at me, inspecting me from head to foot. "You're a typical, arrogant Talon, but you don't look like someone who could have killed my nephew in a fair knife fight." I detected two strong sigils, Illusion and Truth. I decided against using my sigil. For now, I had no reason to lie.

I raised my eyebrows. "Can you tell me how a knife fight can ever be fair, hi'Lord?" I asked, curious as to what Baqir considered fair.

"You must know what 'fair' means?" Baqir scowled at me.

"No, hi'Lord, I don't. Knife fights are never fair, not even with a referee. One fighter always has more experience, or is better trained or has more skill." I paused. Hopefully, I had made my point.

"And which was it in his case?"

"I am a Talon. No one is better trained. But your nephew's anger and fear killed him, hi'Lord. He was filled with anger and resentment."

"That would seem an advantage." Baqir sat back in his chair.

"That depends on who you are fighting. It could be an advantage if you are fighting someone unskilled. If you're fighting someone who is a skilled knife fighter, it's a disadvantage."

A man and woman stood off to the side, watching me. The man was dressed in a plain white robe with maroon trim, a seal of office around his neck. The woman in a similar robe, but simpler and without the trim. I could see the tension in their bodies and the anger in their eyes. The man bore a resemblance to Warrior Amadi, silver-gray hair, stocky, and a little overweight, and the other, a female in her forties, black-haired and slender.

"What would happen if his father or brother would seek revenge, Aisha Talon?" The hi'Lord didn't look towards the two.

I shrugged. "They would have to live with the consequences, hi'Lord." I wondered what kind of an answer he was looking for, and whether Rhiannon's and my fate depended upon my answers.

"And what would that be, Aisha Talon?"

"I am no seer, hi'Lord. A son loses a father, or a father loses a son. Or I am assassinated and Anka loses my protection and the fate of kingdoms is uncertain. Choices have consequences, many unintended." I kept my face bland and expressionless.

Baqir nodded. "What say you, Third Buziba?" Baqir turned towards the old man.

"I, my son, and my wife wish her dead. However, everyone I've talked to agrees my son gave her no option and the fight was…fair. It is sad to think my son died because he had strong emotions." Buziba glared at me. "But she is right. Revenge against a Talon will only bring more grief."

"Thank you, tri'Buziba. You have always been the voice of reason in my council. Go with my good will, and thanks." Baqir turned back to Anka and me and waited as Buziba and his wife left the room.

"I have a proposition for you, Aisha Talon, and for the heir to Granya. First, let me tell you what is on the winds. You, Aisha Talon, were pri'Rhiannon's chaperone in a caravan escorting her and her father to the kingdom of Valda for talks of

102

an alliance. It is claimed that Jaddahan warriors attacked the caravan, but most believe or suspect hi'Lord Radulf plotted the attack. Regardless, sec'Tadzio has usurped the position of hi'Lord of Granya and claimed hi'Varius and his daughter were killed. All the Talons, including you, were said to have been killed." Baqir paused, watching us.

"My father's dead?" Rhiannon asked, just above a whisper. A tear crept down her cheek. I pulled her close to me, putting an arm around her shoulder. I had assumed him dead because of the ferocity of the attack, but now it was confirmed. The information about the Talons, however, was new and a shock. Usually, when the contracted person dies the Talons stop fighting, because the contract is void. If the Talons were not allowed to stop fighting, Radulf or Tadzio must have wanted them all dead.

"Yes, you are now the rightful hi'Lady of Granya, but sec'Tadzio claims to be hi'Lord and has the support of hi'Radulf as well as a substantial part of his army." Baqir watched Rhiannon. "I am willing to give you asylum in Jaddah. I will provide a suite in the castle, a generous allowance, and the respect due royalty. For my generosity, I would have you release Aisha Talon from her contract so that I may negotiate a contract with her. I could use a Talon of her talent."

He looked from Rhiannon to me. "I have heard many stories of your adventures in saving your duty, killing twenty-five of your pursuers, and I am impressed. You just killed Warrior Amadi, one of the best knife fighters in the Fangs. I would pay well, Aisha Talon."

I patted Rhiannon's back as she continued to sob on my shoulder.

"Your offer to pri'Rhiannon is very generous, hi'Lord Baqir, but now is not a time for her to make such a decision. Also, she has yet to hear from her Talon scouts, although I believe your information is accurate, except for the twenty-five kills. I didn't count, but it was less." I needed to get Rhiannon out of here so she could have time to regain her composure and make a calm decision. The Clan would decide my options. My duty remained to Rhiannon until then.

"I understand. I'll await your decision, hi'Lady Rhiannon," Baqir said. His guards were definitely more relaxed as we exited the room, as was I.

"What should I do, Aisha?" Rhiannon asked between hiccupping sobs.

"Only you can make that decision, hi'Lady Rhiannon." With the secret out, no purpose would be served by calling her Anka. "But this is not the time. Give yourself a few days to grieve for your father. By the time you hear what your Talon scouts report about the situation in Granya, you'll be better able to make a decision. There is no reason to rush into something you could regret for the rest of your life."

* * * *

Marku Talon and Warrior Oluchi returned two days later to find us breaking our fast at the Red Hawk Inn.

"Hi'Lady Rhiannon," I said, "I know you are anxious for the news, but I would like Anton Talon present. He has more experience than I do. His advice could help you in making your decision." Rhiannon did not seem in a hurry to hear Marku's news.

"I trust you, Aisha. If you think Anton will help, I can wait. I've reconciled myself to my father's death. Maybe hi'Baqir's offer is the best I can hope for, and you could do well working for the hi'Lord," Rhiannon said with tears in her eyes and resignation in her tone. The past two days had been difficult ones. Rhiannon tried hard not to show her grief, but she was young and left with no one. I understood the tears that she couldn't help shedding.

"Hi'Lady Rhiannon, I already work for a hi'Lady now and will do so until such time as you no longer need or want me. This is a decision that will affect your entire life. I want you to have all of the facts and the best advice we can give you before you make a decision." Although I knew that I shouldn't, I had become fond of Rhiannon. I felt almost as though she were a younger sister. I wanted desperately to tell her to fight for what was hers, but that would have been wrong. She must decide for herself.

Anton arrived an hour later, and they followed Rhiannon and me to our room.

"You made good time, Marku," I said as we sat down. I had thought it would take a week or two more to ascertain the current situation and the fate of the caravan.

"Actually, collecting information was simple. Every inn, market, and group of two or more people talked about it. I knew you would want my report fast, even if unverified, rather than waiting weeks for me to verify the obvious." Marku paused before continuing. "I'm sorry to tell you hi'Lady Rhiannon that your father, hi'Lord Varius, died in the attack on the caravan."

"Thank you, Marku Talon for your concern, but you're not the first to tell me of my father's death. Hi'Lord Baqir told me two days ago that he had information my father had died," Rhiannon said.

"According to the talk, every man and woman in the caravan was killed, including you and your chaperone." Marku paused before he continued. "And almost every Talon was killed. The Valda soldiers wouldn't let the Talons stop fighting after hi'Varius was killed. We know because two escaped -- Taras and Leszek Talon."

"Brother Leszek arrived here right after we did, but I did not know of Taras' escape. I believed he had died as well." Relief flooded over me. I had grown to respect Brother Taras, glad he escaped the slaughter.

Marku continued. "It seems clear hi'Radulf's soldiers attacked you. His soldiers now occupy all the major cities -- Livorno, Terni, and Savona. They claim to support sec'Tadzio and bring order in this time of chaos. Hi'Radulf and sec'Tadzio took up residence at Savona. We learned that hi'Radulf attempted to kill the Talon guards under contract in Valda because they refused to participate in the ambush of hi'Varius's caravan. Only five of the twenty Talons escaped."

I frowned, hoping that Healer Luminita had news soon enough to get away. Leszek might well be right that she would be a target, but I could think of no way of finding out what had happened to her.

"Master Dragos is enraged at their treachery. He has ordered the Clan to war and ordered all Talons to meet in Dahab. I've sent word with Sanko Talon that you and hi'Lady Rhiannon are alive and in Zenjir."

"Oluchi, did you hear anything while you were in Dahab?" The town of Dahab was close to the border of Granya and traded with the towns of Terni and Livorno, the three towns forming a triangle, each separated by thirty leagues.

"The same general rumors. The town is being flooded with soldiers and others loyal to hi'Varius. I talked and actually drank with quite a few soldiers. I told them that I had heard the rumor that pri'Rhiannon had escaped the attack on the caravan. Almost all of them said they would fight for her. I hope I didn't do anything wrong."

"What do you think, Master Anton?" I asked. I had an idea forming but wanted the opinion of someone with more experience.

"Master Dragos will destroy hi'Radulf," Anton said so quietly he might have been talking to himself. "That is the reason he is calling the Clan to war and ordering all Talons to Dahab."

"How can he do that, Master Anton? Many of us have contracts." I didn't think the Clan would ever break a contract unless the other party violated its terms. Yet, his recall required us all to break our contracts.

"Master Dragos will be forced to demonstrate to all four kingdoms that targeting Talons has consequences to be feared. Hi'Radulf, sec'Tadzio, and all their supporters are dead men." Anton shook his head. "They will be an object lesson for the next hundred years."

"How can the Talons win, Anton Talon?" Rhiannon said. "I didn't think you had that many fighters."

"My dear hi'Lady, the Talons are the best assassins in the four kingdoms. We will not fight army to army. We will kill in the shadows. No one who supports hi'Radulf will be safe, neither in the kingdom of Granya nor in Valda." Anton actually laughed.

Rhiannon squared her shoulders and lifted her chin. "I don't know what I'll do if you leave. But if you must, I'll manage somehow."

I was Talon and would obey the Clan. They were my family, my life, but I was Rhiannon's bodyguard and under Clan contract. How could I desert her? Yet, Anton was right. Master Dragos had declared war on Radulf, and all Talons would answer the call. It tore at my heart to desert Rhiannon, especially since Baqir's offer seemed conditional that I accept a contract to him. Desperately, I tried to think of a way to satisfy the Clan without breaking my contract.

A glum silence descended on the room, broken only by the sound of Rhiannon's soft sobs. Earlier an idea had started growing, one that I hesitated to even mention. Yet, if I was going to solve this dilemma, my idea might be the only way.

"Perhaps I have an idea," I said. "Let's see if you can do this."

Rhiannon face brightened as she listened to my plan. "The hi'Baqir has three sons. You could propose a marriage between you and one of his sons with the understanding that you would rule in Granya, not the son. It would be a tempting offer for one of his younger sons. I believe you can raise a small army from those who have fled to Dahab and those still in Granya who supported your father. I also believe Master Dragos would support you since your interests are similar." I stopped to look at Anton who neither agreed nor disagreed. A good sign, I thought.

I got up to pace back and forth across the room, which helped me think as I spoke. "And if hi'Baqir agrees, he will support you for his son's sake. The idea should appeal to him as his grandson or granddaughter will eventually rule Granya. If you rebuilt the Granyan army, you and hi'Baqir could attack Valda and defeat hi'Radulf. You could agree to support Jaddah and give the kingdom to one of his sons to rule. Hi'Baqir's family then would rule three of the four kingdoms, not a minor matter from his point of view. "

I looked at Rhiannon. She stared at me. I couldn't tell if her look was one of approval or horror.

"You aren't betrothed. A marriage of convenience..." I let the rest go unspoken.

Rhiannon shrugged, sighing. "That is what a marriage always is in a noble family for men and for women. If you're lucky, it's someone you can like and respect."

"What do you think, Anton?"

I waited for Anton's reaction. My suggestion was presumptuous in the extreme, involving a hi'Lord and a hi'Lady as well as the leader of the Raptor Clan. I hoped he wouldn't laugh.

"I like it," Oluchi said.

"If it works, it is worthy of our Master, Sister," Marku said.

"If hi'Lady Rhiannon agrees, I will support your proposal," Anton said.

I turned towards Rhiannon who frowned at the floor. She put her hand on my arm and looked straight into my eyes. "Only if you remain my bodyguard ... and adviser."

"Do you support such a contract, Anton?" I asked. I didn't want to violate my Clan oath, but this couldn't wait for Master Dragos to approve it. It had to be made conditional on a betrothal of Rhiannon and one of Baqir's sons.

"If hi'Baqir agrees," Anton said "as a member of the Clan Council, I will witness a blood oath and declare it made in the Clan's interest. I will prepare a contract stipulating the terms."

"Now all we need is hi'Lord Baqir's agreement." Oluchi laughed.

CHAPTER ELEVEN

Zenjir: A counter proposal, the Plan

We stayed up late discussing various aspects of the proposal including possible counter offers from hi'Lord Baqir. Master Anton spoke for the Talons. I found out that he served on the Raptor Clan Council. I spent the final hours throwing questions at Rhiannon, since she would negotiate with Baqir.

"What is your pitch to hi'Baqir, Rhiannon?" I asked.

"I will propose a marriage alliance between the Granya and Jaddah houses."

"Why?"

"So I can retake Granya."

"Not enough. There must be mutual benefits from the alliance."

"He helps me take Granya, and I will help him take Valda."

"Better. Don't forget that your children will be his grandchildren and eventually inherit your rule. What do you bring to the table?"

"I can raise an army of Granyans and I have the support of the Talons." Rhiannon paused. "How do I know that the Talons will support me?"

"Because it is in our best interest, hi'Lady," Anton said. "We must punish sec'Tadzio and hi'Radulf. They violated their contracts with the Talons and violated long established rules. Every ruler will think they have the right to life or death over the Raptor Clan, if the Clan allows them to get away with this. We must eliminate sec'Tadzio and hi'Radulf and everyone who supports them. If you have an army, and you are intent on punishing them, then our objectives are the same, and we will support you. If not, we will do it on our own."

"How can you do it on your own, Anton Talon?" Rhiannon asked.

"We are trained assassins. We will kill them one at a time until they are afraid to leave their houses, their castles. And then we will kill them in their homes and castles. Their punishment will take time, but we are patient."

"You said they broke their contracts and the rules. What rules?"

Master Anton cleared his throat and gave Rhiannon a piercing look. "Rules go back a hundred years, since the last time the Talons had to remind rulers that we were not their subjects. One, if we are hired to guard you, we will give our lives to defend yours, but if you are killed we will stop fighting, because our contract is void. Two, we have no interest in avenging your death. We are not your kin—we are hired help. For those reasons we expect our opponents to stop fighting. Hi'Radulf and sec'Tadzio broke the rule when their soldiers would not let your father's Talons quit fighting after your father was killed. Everyone understands these rules, and these rules benefit both parties."

Rhiannon tilted her head, giving Anton a long look. "I didn't. How do they benefit me?"

"If you hire a Talon, you know you will not be attacked by Talons someone else hires. And if you kill or hire a non-Talon, to kill a person a Talon is guarding, you know no Talon will seek revenge."

"Are there any other rules?"

"Yes. Talons are not under the rules of any kingdom in which we are employed." Anton smiled. "Remember when the rumor was that Aisha would get whipped? The Talons wouldn't allow it. If a Talon needs punishment, the Raptor Clan will intervene. Hi'Radulf had Talons killed as punishment because they would not attack your father, who had Talons guarding him."

"It sounds so cold."

"These rules make us dependable. Those who hire us know exactly what to expect. We are predictable. Most mercenaries for hire have no rules. Not so the Talons of the Raptor Clan, which is one of the reasons we are in demand. But we must enforce our rules."

* * * *

110

The next morning Rhiannon sent word to Baqir, requesting a meeting. Near sunset a messenger returned to the Inn to find us outside, drinking a spicy beverage made with yellow leaves, hot water, and sweet syrup.

"Hi'Lady Rhiannon, hi'Lord Baqir has agreed to receive you and Aisha Talon tomorrow at ten turns of the glass." He read from a parchment document.

"Thank you. Please tell hi'Lord Baqir we will be there," Rhiannon said. "Aisha, I think I could learn to like it here in Zenjir if I accept hi'Baqir's offer."

"Yes, it would be an easy life with few worries." I masked my thoughts, not difficult since I didn't know what Rhiannon would face here. Her life seemed linked to mine. Baqir's deal linked to me. Rhiannon's betrothal linked me contractually to her. Though I fought it off, somehow I cared. I could hear Master Jiang lecturing me about emotions.

"What would you advise, Aisha?" Rhiannon put her hand on mine. "Please?"

"I can tell you what I wanted at eight, I no longer want at eighteen. I suspect what you want today will not be what you want ten years from now. I can only tell you that whatever you decide to do, don't do it to avenge your father. Do it for yourself or for your people." Somehow my words made me feel old.

"You are going to fight sec'Tadzio and hi'Radulf for revenge?" Rhiannon watched me intently.

"No, Rhiannon. I will do it to protect my Clan, not for my own feelings of anger or need for revenge." I nodded, feeling the truth of the statement.

"Thank you, Aisha...advisor to the hi'Lady."

* * * *

The next day Rhiannon and I arrived at the castle gate a quarter glass early. We were escorted to a small private room where Baqir and Anton waited. Baqir stood as we entered. He appeared anxious to hear an answer to his offer.

"Please make yourselves comfortable, hi'Lady Rhiannon and Aisha Talon." Baqir motioned for us to sit. The walls of the room were lined with a hundred cushions of different shapes and sizes. As soon as Rhiannon sat, servants entered with trays of hot drinks.

111

"Hi'Lady Rhiannon, I assume your scouts verified the information that the winds carried and that you recognize the benefits of my offer?" I stood next to Rhiannon as Anton stood next to Baqir. It was Rhiannon's place to negotiate with the hi'Lord, not mine. By now, she understood her options, but even I didn't know what decision she had made. She had listened to Anton's and my advice but was going to make her own decision.

"Yes, hi'Lord. My scouts report that hi'Radulf's troops attacked the caravan, that my father was killed and all his Talons executed, that sec'Tadzio claims to be hi'Lord of Granya and that he is supported by hi'Radulf's and his soldiers. In addition, hi'Radulf had the Talons in Valda killed for refusing to participate in the ambush." Rhiannon paused and took a sip of her drink.

"Hi'Radulf had Talons killed?" Baqir shook his head. "He is a bigger fool than I had been led to believe."

"Your offer was more than generous, hi'Lord Baqir. However, I have a counter proposal for you." Rhiannon's breath came fast but she clasped her hands in front of her and pressed on. "I propose a marriage between my house and yours. I can raise a small army and will have the support of the Talons. With your help, I can reclaim Granya. In a year or so, I can build a large army. Between you, me, and the Talons, we can crush hi'Radulf's army. Afterward, I will support whichever of your children you want to appoint as hi'Lord to the kingdom of Valda. Under our alliance, your blood will rule three of the four kingdoms."

Baqir roared with laughter, slapping the cushions next to him. "I thought the winds had brought me a small honey bird. Now I find I was mistaken. They have brought me a bird of prey. Do you believe you can win without my support?"

Rhiannon looked toward me, so I put in, "I have been told that all Talons are being recalled for war against sec'Tadzio and hi'Radulf."

"Including mine? That will be a breach of contract." Baqir voice rose slightly and his eyes narrowed.

"All Talons. The Raptor Clan can't ignore this treacherous breach of contract against us. All must know that there are rules in dealing with Talons. Hi'Radulf and sec'Tadzio have violated those rules. We will make their blood line extinct," I said. Hi'Baqir looked up at Anton who nodded his assent.

Rhiannon continued. "Yes, hi'Lord. It will take longer without you, maybe years, but we will win. I will join forces with the Talon, and together we will avenge our dead and rid the kingdoms of hi'Radulf and all who support or follow him. In that case, I will decide who rules Valda."

"Talons seeking revenge...a frightening thought. Please stay for a midday meal, while I discuss the issue with my wife and children. My aide, Chima, will escort you to the garden. My family and I will join you shortly."

Chima led Rhiannon and me out of the room and down the colonnade through a small arch with a single warrior guard. We entered a walled garden, grassy with a white pebble walk threaded through flowering shrubs. The walls of the garden were white, barely visible behind the tall fronds of the palms lining them. The castle shielded the courtyard from the heat of the scorching midday sun. A double hand of fountains scattered about sprayed water skyward and cooled the air.

"Please make yourselves comfortable," Chima said, stepping aside at the top of the steps off the colonnade.

I took a deep breath of the scented air and walked toward one of the fountains, appreciating the coolness.

Rhiannon followed at my side. When Chima left and was out of sight, she asked, "What do you think the hi'Lord will do, Aisha?"

"You did well, hi'Lady." I acknowledged Rhiannon's no nonsense approach and refusal to be cowed by the older leader. I hoped the Clan would let me continue to guard and advise her. "I think the idea appeals to his ego as well as the obvious benefits of having three kingdoms aligned with him. He will discuss it with his family to work through the details. He has three sons and two daughters. He must decide who will be his heir, who will lead the army that supports you, who will marry you, and who will be appointed hi'Lord of Valda. He probably already knows, but he has to pretend to discuss it with them."

Chima returned with several servants carrying plates of food served in individual small bowls. He led us toward the only table in the courtyard, a large one made of light wood. The table was set about with green-cushioned chairs surrounded by palm trees."

I found the strange, spicy food delicious, and once again I enjoyed eating with my hands. Rhiannon also seemed to enjoy her food as well as the break from the tension. We had finished our meal, the servants had cleaned up the dishes, and we had been served cool foamy drinks, when Baqir and his family entered the courtyard.

"Hi'Lady Rhiannon, I have gathered my family here to discuss the details of your proposal and to introduce you to them. I will dispense with titles as it seems you will soon be family."

I stood to one side and scanned everyone as the introductions took place. I was not one to relax while on duty.

"My honored wife, Sauda," Baqir said with a proud smile.

Baqir's wife smiled at Rhiannon. With her almond shaped eyes and high arched brows and black hair pulled back into elaborate braids, she was a beautiful woman in spite of having grown sons.

"Welcome," she said, nodding to both of us.

"My oldest, Tafadzwa. He grows weary of waiting for me to die, so we decided he will lead the Jaddahan army and will be the new hi'Lord of Valda." His son stepped forward, a man of middling height, but he had a muscular build and moved with the smooth grace of a trained warrior. A dark moustache drooped around his lips and his dark eyes sparkled.

"Rhiannon, if you weren't so young, I'd marry you myself. Your idea is pure genius," Tafadzwa said with a small bow. "Instead, I will help you make it a reality, sister."

"Thank you, brother Tafadzwa. I look forward to you being the new hi'Lord of Valda."

"My next oldest and heir to Jaddah, Kamau." He gestured to a slightly younger son to his side.

"Rhiannon, welcome to the Baqir family, and thank you for getting rid of my older brother. Being second is worse than waiting to be hi'Lord," Kamau said with a warm smile.

"You are welcome, Kamau."

"My third son, Awotwi, and your future consort. He will also accompany you to war. The experience will be good for him since he will eventually command your army or that of one of his brothers."

"Welcome, Rhiannon, my betrothed. May the Goddess bless our union," Awotwi said with a somewhat shy looking smile. Awotwi looked to be about Rhiannon's age, and I thought that Baqir made a wise choice in the betrothal.

"Welcome Awotwi, my betrothed. May our union strengthen the ties between our kingdoms and produce heirs worthy of our fathers and mothers," Rhiannon said. Her cheeks flushed but her voice flowed steady, an heir doing her duty to her kingdom as I was doing my duty to my Clan.

"My forth child, Isooba," Baqir said as a small girl stepped forward uncertainly.

"Welcome Rhiannon. May the sands bless your reign …you're pretty--" Isooba blurted out to everyone's amusement.

"And my fifth child, Emerka."

"Welcome, Sister Rhiannon," Emerka said. The girl tilted her head and looked Rhiannon up and down. "You look different than anyone I've ever seen before."

"Welcome, Emerka. Yes, my people are somewhat different. Perhaps you can come visit us someday." Rhiannon beamed a warm smile.

"Rhiannon," Baqir said, "a betrothal contract will be drawn up today for you and me to sign. If you stay for dinner, we could sign it afterward."

"Excuse me, hi'Lord Baqir and hi'Lady Rhiannon," I interrupted. "Could we hold a war council afterward? I would like your sons, Tafadzwa and Awotwi, and Anton Talon to attend. I would like to set everything in motion as soon as possible. I think we have the element of surprise for a couple of weeks and would like to take advantage of it."

"Of course. That is an excellent idea." Baqir nodded agreement as he looked from me to Rhiannon.

Dinner was a quiet affair with only Anton and me as guards. Afterward, Baqir said he was ready for the war council. He motioned for Tafadzwa and Awotwi to join us. The six of us followed Baqir down to a small study where more of the hot yellow drinks were served.

"Hi'Lord Baqir, with your permission I would like my advisor, Aisha Talon, to begin the discussion. She planned a campaign we should consider."

I had discussed my plan with her earlier, but she had been reluctant to present it on her own. Baqir merely nodded to me to continue.

"I believe we have the element of surprise at the moment, and the enemies' weak points are the towns at Terni, Livorno, and Dassel."

"Dassel." Baqir, Tafadzwa, and Anton all repeated it in shock. Awotwi just sat there with his mouth open.

"You want to attack Dassel? They would laugh at us from their walls," Tafadzwa said finally.

"Yes, I want you to take three hundred warriors to Dassel and blockade them. Stay well away from the city and turn back anyone trying to deliver anything. If you operate in small groups, Dassel's commander will send out small patrols to track you down. Ambush them and he'll send out a larger force. You will ambush them. You will fight in the shadows." I reviewed a sheet of notes I had in front of me. "The commander at Dassel can't have much more than two hundred fighters or so left in the castle. He will have to send to hi'Radulf in Savona for reinforcements if you succeed. When he does, the combined armies, you, hi'Rhiannon, and the Talons, will ambush them on the road to Valda. Many may desert, and we will soon reduce his army to a few hundred."

"What do you think, Anton Talon?" Tafadzwa asked, still staring at me. His dark eyes swept me from head to foot. I stared at the paper in front of me determined not to blush at his stare.

"The Talons are taught to be assassins," Anton answered, "and fight in the shadows, although most think of us only as elite guards. Shadow fighting would be the best way to cripple hi'Radulf's army without serious losses to our own forces. We weaken our enemy while we build up our own forces. The Jaddah are excellent at knife fighting and with bows, the perfect weapons for ambushes and fighting in the forests. I could provide you with a few Talons to help."

116

Anton paused for a moment, looking at me. "Think of it, Tafadzwa. Over fifty soldiers were chasing Aisha and Rhiannon in the forest. She and Rhiannon not only escaped, but Aisha killed fifteen or more of them in the process. A Talon with duty is a fearful thing."

"I like it, and hi'Radulf isn't expecting it," Tafadzwa said with a warm smile in my direction. Tafadzwa stared at me for a few moments, and I felt myself coloring. "Shadow fighting."

"And ..." Baqir prompted.

I took a sip of my warm drink to moisten my throat before I continued. I didn't want anyone to know how nervous making all of these plans in front of everyone and Tafadzwa's looks had me. "Awotwi will accompany hi'Lady Rhiannon with a hundred warriors to Dahab where she can begin recruiting her Granyan army and join with the Talons gathering there. If they haven't arrived yet, we would go on to Terni. The castle should be poorly defended since sec'Tadzio pulled most of his troops to Savona. Only a token force remains, at best, maybe twenty-five Granyans and possibly another twenty-five Valdans."

"And ..." Baqir said, this time with a laugh.

"That should require sec'Tadzio to send reinforcements to Terni. By then hi'Rhiannon's army and the Talons will be in a position to ambush the reinforcements," I said and shrugged. "After that hi'Rhiannon and the Talons will join you in Dassel awaiting hi'Radulf's reinforcements."

The plan seemed obvious to me as I had scribbled the numbers down. Radulf must have taken at least five hundred fighters with him into Granya, leaving only two hundred or so to defend Dassel, if the numbers of his army I had read in the past were correct. He must have lost at least a quarter of his force when he ambushed the caravan, considering the ferocity of the fighting and that Varius and his Talon guard were prepared for an attack.

"Sec'Tadzio couldn't have more than one hundred fifty fighters available at Terni. So with the Valdan's fighters and one hundred from Livorno, hi'Radulf probably has over five hundred combined. When we consider desertions or killing those loyal to hi'Lord Varius, Terni and Livorno can't have more than fifty soldiers defending them, even if hi'Radulf left a small contingent at each." I felt sure that Terni, Livorno, and Dassel were under-defended, and if they were attacked quickly, Radulf and Tadzio would have to rush to defend them.

"I thought this would take years, but, if your plan works, hi'Lord Radulf and his allies could be dealt a death blow in months. What do you think Anton Talon?" Baqir asked.

"I think Aisha's strategy is good. We need to review her estimates of the enemy forces and work out the details. The success of her plan depends upon moving quickly."

Tafadzwa hadn't said any more, but his eyes had never left me during the entire war counsel. I glanced at him out of the corner of my eye, hoping he wouldn't notice as we rose to leave. But his eye caught mine. With his back to the others, he winked at me, and I felt myself blush. I couldn't help the smile that twitched at my lips.

I hope you haven't interfered in Raptor Father's plans, Raptor Sister. Anton signed.

As do I, Raptor Brother.

118

CHAPTER TWELVE

Jaddahan warriors to Dassel: Shadow tactics

Two days later Anton Talon rode alongside Warrior Tafadzwa, who commanded the three hundred Jaddahan warriors, toward the city of Dassel. Sweat rolled down Anton's face and the back of his neck. He squinted against the glare of the blazing sun as they rode along the meandering track that passed for a road in the desert. Dust rose from every clop of the horses' hooves. With an envious glance at Tafadzwa's protective headdress, he wiped his wet forehead with his sleeve and sighed. They were only a few leagues from the gates of the city but already he was sweat-soaked and grimy.

"Anton, is your Sister Aisha a normal woman Talon?" Tafadzwa said. Anton glanced at him out of the corner of his eye in surprise.

"It is difficult to say, fir'Warrior." Tafadzwa was no longer heir to the Jaddah kingdom; therefore, he no longer deserved the formal title 'pri.' However, he was now commanding a Jaddahan army and had the rank of First Warrior. "In the past twenty years, I'm only aware of five women having graduated to become Talons. I've met each of them but did not work with all of them. They tend to be more like their brother Talons--they survived by being strong, aggressive, and excellent fighters. Aisha is a fine fighter, like any Talon, far beyond any you will normally meet. On the other hand, she seems to survive almost as much by her wits. Warrior Amadi was an even match for Aisha, but she killed him. Why? Because she understood his weakness, his emotions, and used it against him."

Tafadzwa turned in his saddle to look at Anton. "When we were planning the campaign, I could almost see her mind working. She amazed me."

Anton nodded and paused to think over what he had seen of Aisha over the past days. "It is interesting to watch her and other Talons in a room. I can easily see the difference. Every Talon is observant watching every person for signs of trouble.

119

Aisha not only watches every person but also seems to be constructing "what if" scenarios. What if five soldiers burst through the door? What if third lord so-and-so attacked her charge? What if--"

"Don't other Talons plan ahead for what might happen?"

"Of course we do, but she is better at it and does it more. She escaped hi'Radulf's attack on hi'Varius' caravan because she had planned for any possible type of attack. She escaped the bands of soldiers searching for her by doing the unexpected. She out thinks her opponents. No, fir'Warrior, she is not typical of our Talons, either women or men."

"But are all Talon women as beautiful as she is?"

Anton's mouth dropped open. "Aisha Talon is my Talon Sister. Besides, she's very young." He choked out his answer.

"She's not too young to marry, and I think she is very beautiful. Would she marry me, do you think, Anton?" Tafadzwa wore a slightly sheepish smile. "I can't stop thinking about her."

"Fir'Warrior, you are a brave man. Give me a docile woman who wants nothing more than a good provider and ten children." Anton interspersed his opinion with snorts of laughter. "Aisha is twenty years younger than me, and I'm riding to war at her bidding. The thought of being married to her frightens me."

"I'm a hard man to frighten." Tafadzwa waved that idea away. "You obviously think her plan is doable, Anton. I do too, but I'm not sure I understand the tactics."

"There are only four main accesses to Dassel. Your father has already ordered a stop to any shipments or caravans leaving Zenjir for Dassel. That leaves three routes to guard." Anton paused until Tafadzwa nodded. "The road from Livorno in the north, from Borkum in the east, and from Soumiri in the south."

Anton stared at Tafadzwa to be sure he was following the idea. "We will stop the traffic on those routes into Dassel, but we will give the impression we are only a few bandits. In response, the commander at Dassel will send out troops to open the roads. We will ambush them. If we can get him mad enough, he may send out a large group. We must kill enough soldiers to make him send to Savona for help. If hi'Radulf feels his castle is in jeopardy, he will send a large force which we ambush with help from the Talons and hi'Rhiannon's Granyans."

They rode along in silence for a few minutes. "Anton, I would like to develop specific plans for my sec'Warriors, those second in command. We have four nights before we reach the Valda border. I want to spend the time working out the details of the campaign. My warriors are experienced in a different kind of fighting."

Anton agreed. He had been taught "shadow fighting" strategies at the Aerie, but he had never had to implement them. Anton's career had progressed normally, from guard to small group leader to senior Talon guarding hi'Lords. He was appointed recently to the Raptor Clan Council. He had been contracted to assassinate a thief and had led an attack against a rebel group, but he had never fought a shadow war. He wondered if Aisha had conceived the idea, because she was fresh out of training, or it was her natural way of viewing problems. *Probably the latter*, he decided.

The dinner that night was hot and spicy, simple, and good. After the meal, the area was cleaned and readied for an early departure. Tafadzwa called his senior Warriors to conference, and Anton included his three Talons since they would advise the Jaddahans. He was sure they knew the theory, but, like him, they had no actual experience. When everyone had settled down, Tafadzwa began.

"For the next few nights we will train in the Talon's shadow fighting. Master Anton will demonstrate and we will learn. "

"We are going to learn together," Anton said. "Neither my Talon brothers nor I have actually been involved in a shadow war. We have the theory, but it must be adapted to the situation at hand, so your participation in this advanced warfare will be necessary. You will implement the plan." He wanted leaders not puppets.

"The theory of shadow fighting is easy. Like an assassin in the night, you find a target, kill, and fade back into the night. Our objective is to force the commander at Valda to send out a large force and destroy the bandits harassing his citizens. We need to act and look like a small groups of bandits." Anton

121

stopped when he noticed one of the third ranked warriors frowning at him.

"You mean we aren't going to attack the castle? We have hundreds of warriors."

"We will not attack directly, tri'Warrior. We aren't strong enough. Even if we succeeded, our losses would be great. No, we are going to set up traps and ambushes where we have the advantage."

Anton looked around the group and made sure he had their full attention. "We will rob the travelers to and from Dassel in small groups, give the appearance of bandits or Jaddahan raiders. We want to accomplish two things, reduce the number of soldiers guarding Dassel and force the commander to send to hi'Radulf for reinforcements. When hi'Radulf sends guards to the rescue, we will waylay them on the road. Ambush tactics favor us. We are not looking for a fair fight. We will kill ten for every one warrior we lose."

The Warrior continued to frown at him. "I don't understand."

Anton looked around the tent to be sure all of them were concentrating on him and went on to explain in detail how they would go about cutting off trade and forcing a fight on their terms. He concluded, "If Aisha is right, hi'Radulf left Dassel severely under-defended."

Tafadzwa laughed. "You're right, Anton. Aisha would be more of a challenge than most men could handle." But Anton wasn't quite sure he knew what the young warrior meant by that comment.

After going over the details twice, Anton was sure that the others understood their goal.

"Let me think about what you've told us, Anton." Tafadzwa stood and signaled the end of the meeting.

Tafadzwa called an end to the day's march at dawn, much to Anton's relief. The cool morning air was a relief to the intense heat they rode through for most of the previous day. Sunrise in the desert was glorious, tinted pink, purple and gold in the eastern sky. Anton knew he should enjoy the cool while it lasted.

As he rode near the head of the column of warriors, Tafadzwa trotted up on his bay steed to ride beside him. "I thought much about what you told us last night, Anton."

"I was sure you would, fir'Warrior. You're an experienced leader, and I have full confidence in your abilities."

The warriors mouth quirked at the compliment. "Thank you. It seems to me we will need to split our forces up. I don't like to do that for a battle, but I see no other way to gain our goal."

Anton nodded. "Go on."

"I'll split the force into three units. Each one commanded by one of my sec'Warriors. They will set up a blockade a few leagues out of Dassel. I'd like you to explain to them the best way to set their traps and strategies to deal with a large force sent from Dassel. While waiting, they will stop anyone attempting to enter Dassel. What do you think, Anton?"

Anton nodded. "It's a good plan. They can make their camp well back from the roads and use small groups for the blockade to give the illusion of small bands of disorganized bandits. They'll need to keep a close watch out for when the Commander sends out troops against them. And he will."

* * * *

Three days after leaving Zenjir, Anton and Tafadzwa with their one hundred Jaddahan warriors watched as their force crossed the West Mystic River and entered Valda about seven leagues north of Dassel. In a valley a half league from the broad dirt road from Livorno, Anton and Tafadzwa would set up a blockade.

Cezar Talon and the other hundred warriors under a sec'Warrior continued east and south to blockade the road from Borkum and Adorf. At the same time, another sec'Warrior, Vasile Talon, and one hundred more warriors rode to take up a position seven leagues south of Dassel and blockaded the routes from Salda.

* * * *

"What now, Anton?" Tafadzwa asked, as the last of the warriors rode out of sight around a distant bend in the road.

"We scout the land for places to setup ambushes. Most of the warriors will make our camp their base. Next, you can

123

designate several small groups who will patrol the roads and the river. Then we begin our harassment of Dassel."

* * * *

Anton and Tafadzwa led a band of twenty, organized by groups of five, and blockaded the road. The Jaddahans had changed from their traditional garb to plain studded leather armor that any bandit would wear. Tafadzwa divided their force into two, and they waited on each side of the road in the forest. The copse of trees on each side of the road gave them a good view from the top of a hill down a long slope in each direction. Several hours later they spotted a small caravan, two merchants, a string of eight mules, and six guards.

Anton and one group moved onto the road. "Stop! Your mules and the merchandise are ours. You may pass unharmed without them." The six guards charged, but, as they did, the Jaddahan on both sides of the road opened fire with their bows. Four died instantly. The remaining two died when they reached Anton and the five warriors.

"Well, merchants, my offer still stands," Anton repeated. "You may pass unharmed without your mules."

"Hi'Radulf will have you hunted down and killed!" A thin merchant snarled his threat as he passed. "Leave us our mules and we won't report you."

Anton barked with laughter, deep into his role as a bandit. "Go while I'm still in a good mood." The two merchants kicked their horses into a gallop and headed for Dassel.

"What do you think, Anton? Will it work?" Tafadzwa asked.

"I think we got lucky. The commander will be under great pressure to find us since we robbed wealthy and probably influential merchants."

Anton sent two of the men to clear away the bodies. He regretted the deaths, but the traitorous lords had forced this war on them. They resumed their positions.

Early morning the next day two farmers and their wives and children pushed barrows full of vegetables towards the city.

"Stop," Anton said. The two families were armed with swords, old and not well maintained, weapons to discourage a single robber or two.

"We are protected by the armies of hi'Radulf," the older man said. "The last robbers were hanged."

"What are you selling, old man?" Anton asked.

"Selling? … Potatoes, carrots, mushrooms, and some rabbits. You want to buy something?" the old man's eyes widened with astonishment.

"How much for all? Consider, you don't have to go all the way to Dassel. You can sell it all without haggling with hundreds of people."

"All?" The old man huddled with the others for several minutes. "One gold."

"Sold," Anton said as he produced one gold piece and flipped it to the old man. "Unload it here, and leave."

"We could have gotten the food cheaper, Anton." Tafadzwa said, scratching his chin.

"We could have taken it, and they knew it. But these people may someday be your subjects. Your rule will be easier if they don't all hate you. Besides, we need food and our farmers will be back as soon as they can."

Tafadzwa laughed and nodded his understanding.

The next day was much of the same. The group Tafadzwa had sent to blockade the river managed to stop several river boats, sinking one of them. Several more farmers sold their produce and went away happy.

The next morning dawned cool with a damp breeze off the river. Anton sat next to the fire with a cup of a hot drink steaming in his hands when Tafadzwa strode up.

"My scouts just got back. They spotted three patrols on the roads. One patrol is two leagues north of our warrior's base, the second is a league from the city, and the third patrol is in our area and escorting two groups of farmers. Do we take them all?"

"No, fir'Warrior. Let's take the patrol with the farmers. We want the commander to send out a large group after us. We still want to appear to be a small but a well-armed group of bandits."

When Anton and his ten warriors reached the farmers and their Valdan escort it was two hours after sunrise and the group was less than two leagues from the city. There were eight soldiers. Hidden within the trees, Anton waved a signal for the

Jaddahans to open fire with their bows. The Jaddahans were expert at firing from horseback. He listened to the steady thwap of the bows behind him as, one by one, five soldiers fell. The farmers panicked and ran for the side of the road while the soldiers milled around, then charged toward the trees where Anton had his men.

"Charge," Anton yelled. They burst from the trees at a gallop. The exchange was over in a few minutes. Eight soldiers lay dead in the dirt. One of the women the soldiers had been escorting knelt, holding her clasped hands up toward Anton.

"Please! Please! Don't hurt us. We'll give you what we have."

Anton laughed. "No need, since we'll buy it from you."

The woman's mouth dropped open for a few seconds before she spoke. "My neighbor told me the bandits bought food from them, but I didn't believe it." The transaction went quickly and the Jaddahans were gone before a second Valda patrol encountered the farmers.

As Anton and Tafadzwa sat breaking their fast at the campfire, two scouts came in with the news that the road was swarming with large groups of Valdan soldiers.

"Well Anton, what do you think?" Tafadzwa asked with a grin, his dark eyes sparkling.

"Hit and run ambushes, fir'Warrior. Draw them into the woods if they will come. Be ready for an all-out assault, but try to avoid it."

Six groups worked the roads, killing small groups when they could find them. Anton went with one group. They ran across a patrol of about twenty. He looked them over and decided his group could take them. The first volley took down five, and they faded back into the forest with the Valdans following. Hidden in the trees they took almost half down with short bows as they charged. It turned to one-on-one fighting. In spite of the Valdans' advantages with their long swords and crossbows, the short bows and knives Jaddahans favor were perfect for their hit-and-run tactics. Long swords were best in open spaces and crossbows took time to load.

Anton backed against a small ravine, luring three fighters after him. As they ran at him, he snapped his throwing knives into the throat of one and then another. The last one reached him and screamed with rage. Anton caught the fighter's blade on his, twisting his own to slash across the man's throat. In the meantime his group had cleaned up the few remaining Valdans.

For the next two days, nothing happened. Reports from the other two groups revealed less action but they had still killed some fifteen soldiers. Anton and Tafadzwa talked it over around the campfire after dusk fell and decided they needed to change their tactics. They took fifty from the south and fifty from the east and moved them to the Livorno group in the north. Opening the road to Livorno was clearly the commander's priority.

Two days later, Tafadzwa found Anton watching the road leading to their blockade.

"Anton, this is what we were looking for. My scouts just came back. They tell me close to one hundred fifty soldiers are hunting us. They are only about a league away."

"Good. I'll send these twenty warriors down on the road. When they are seen, they will run, using the road, until they reach our ambush area. There they will disappear into the forest. Not too fast, we need the Valdans to follow."

Anton and Tafadzwa joined the bait group on the road. They rode at a walk with scouts, ten to twenty paces in the forest on each side. Anton made sure the army had seen them, and then he ordered a retreat. He brought up the rear to make sure that the Valdan army followed, pacing to let the army keep them within sight. A little over a league later, he signed to turn to the north and enter the forest. The ambush was set about three hundred paces from the road. Two hundred warriors waited with bows.

"Watch for the traps! Make sure and go around where we set them." Anton pointed to the far edge of the killing zone and his men edged around it.

The Valdans followed.

"Fire!" Tafadzwa shouted to his archers. They rained down arrows on the oncoming Valdans. Anton heard the Valdan commander shout an order to charge. Anton shook his head over the stupidity of charging the archers. Over half of the Valdans died before the bloody hand-to-hand fighting began.

Anton could never tell how long a battle lasted. They seemed to last forever and yet be over in an instant. He wiped

127

the sweat that dripped down his forehead as he held up his hand to stop. The ground around them was littered with Valdan bodies. A few Jaddahan's lay moaning among them. He watched as a handful of Valdans, still alive, rode back toward the road.

"Why let them go, Anton? We could catch them easily." Tafadzwa stood, his clothes covered in blood, his face flush with color.

"No, fir'Warrior. Those were no more than ten, and they will convince the castle commander that we have an army out here and are preparing to attack the castle. Now he will have to send messengers to hi'Radulf who will say Dassel is under attack. It will take a messenger at least seven days to reach Savona. Keep the blockade for now, but send messengers to Zenjir, Terni, and Dahab with news of our success. I don't believe the commander will send out any more soldiers. We wait for the next phase of the war."

"What about Valdans troops from Borkum and Adorf? They are both Valda cities. The commander may ask for reinforcements from those. They could have a hundred each."

"I don't believe they will send anyone. At best, they could send only fifty or so and even that small a number would weaken their castles. No, I believe Aisha's plan has delivered Dassel to you."

Anton motioned toward the bodies around them. "Let's see to our own men. We have a few dead, perhaps twenty-five or thirty, it looks like, and the wounded have to be seen to."

CHAPTER THIRTEEN

Dahab: Talons called to war

The sun streaked the western sky with gold as it dropped below the horizon. The day's heat eased. I had requested an early halt. We rested before our approach to Dahab the next day. Awotwi had dispersed ten scouts beyond the camp to detect intruders so that we had plenty of warning in case of attack. We had traveled for four days and should reach Dahab the same time Master Anton and Tafadzwa should reach the area around Valda.

We pitched camp, an informal sprawl of small cooking fires and tents. Rhiannon, Awotwi, and I sat on the ground in a circle around a fire built between our two tents. We all ate a simple dinner of grain and bits of meat. I felt more comfortable with this dinner than dining at the lavish feasts put on by the nobles at Savona, Terni, and Livorno.

"Fir'Warrior, how far are we from Dahab?" I asked.

"We are about eight leagues from Dahab. I would expect to reach the city around noon tomorrow. I have sent a warrior ahead to alert Second Lord Faddei that we come by order of hi'Baqir, so he does not think they are under attack and can arrange for our comfort."

"Your family would be proud of you, fir'Warrior Awotwi. You will make a fine leader of an army someday." The young man seemed much older in his ways than some of the nobles' sons I had encountered. I liked the Jaddahan people and their way of life, probably because it mirrored my life at the Aerie.

"You changed much for us, Aisha Talon. Third sons like me, and fourth and fifth daughters like Isooba and Emerka, had little to look forward to. At best, sec'Warriors. Now with Tafadzwa off to run a kingdom, I will be a consort to another kingdom and can expect to command either the army in Granya. Emerka and Isooba can command another if they want or take a more peaceful path." Awotwi smiled. "This war under your

129

leadership will do much to give me the experience I will need to command wisely."

"I don't think you will be following me. Master Dragos will probably determine our strategy, and hi'Rhiannon is in command." *Children leading children. Awotwi is only sixteen, Rhiannon sixteen, and I'm only nineteen.*

"I may be the hi'Lady of Savona, but you will lead, Aisha. I trust you and your plan," Rhiannon said.

"Thank you, hi'Lady Rhiannon. Tomorrow we will know more." I stood to retire for the night.

* * * *

We broke camp with only a sliver of light on the horizon, hoping to reach Dahab before the worst of the heat. As we approached the city, two riders rode toward us. Awotwi held up his hand for a stop, and we waited to see who approached. When they got close, I recognized one of the riders from the Aerie, one of the few women Talons.

"Good morning, Master Bakaar," I said as they slowed their horse to a stop in front of me.

"Good morning, Aisha Talon. Master Dragos wants to see you, immediately."

"Fir'Warrior Awotwi and I will accompany you, Bakaar Talon."

"Your contract with Aisha Talon has been terminated, and your presence is not required." Bakaar waved for me to join her.

"My betrothed, I want to go," Rhiannon said with a smile at Awotwi.

"Warriors, to me!" Awotwi shouted, and a hundred knives flashed into the light of day and a hundred warriors surrounded the two Talons.

"Aisha, this does not help you," Bakaar said.

"Bakaar Talon, although I would not advise the action hi'Lady Rhiannon has taken, she has an interest in the upcoming war and has information Master Dragos needs. That being said, I do not command the hi'Lady, nor do I command the son of hi'Baqir. And based on what has happened in the past several weeks, I don't believe they are bluffing." I spoke without emotion, but I felt sick knowing what she said was true, and my duty would be to defend the two Talons in a fight.

"Alright hi'Lady Rhiannon, but I can not guarantee how Master Dragos will react to your aggression." Bakaar pursed her lips slightly as she looked Rhiannon up and down.

"Aisha, are you still my bodyguard?" Rhiannon asked. I was impressed with Rhiannon assertiveness, but she had just put me in a very dangerous situation. If I said yes, I would defy the Clan's call to war, to assemble and break all contracts. If I said no, I might jeopardize the alliance which would benefit the Clan's war on hi'Radulf. It came down to what was more important, her or the Clan?

"Yes, hi'Lady Rhiannon, I am your personal bodyguard although I may not be for long."

"Then fir'Warrior and I will accompany you to see Master Dragos." Rhiannon gave an imperious tilt with her head.

"Sec'Warrior, take the troop to the Jaddah compound and get them settled," Awotwi ordered, readying himself to accompany Rhiannon and me.

You have made a great mistake, Aisha. Bakaar signed as she and the other Talons turned their horses. We proceeded towards the city, Rhiannon, Awotwi, and me following. Dahab was smaller than Zenjir, but it seemed to spread out for several leagues in every direction and had more tents than permanent structures, such like I had never seen before. Each tent was the size of a small house, bright with colors, designs, and multiple pendants for their many poles. A canopy shaded the front area of the tents where men and women sat and ate, conversing on beautiful crafted rugs.

"Fir'Warrior, why all the tents?" I asked.

"They are nomads," Awotwi said. "They come to Dahab and negotiate contracts for their caravans, buy and sell merchandise, and exchange information with friends. They spend many months each year traveling the sands to the cities of Atusei and Enurta on the Great Mother Sea." An hour later, they entered the city and were led to a large inn, The Cool Sands. I recognized Talons everywhere I looked, and, as I dismounted, Master Dragos stalked out of the main entrance.

"Bakaar, who authorized these persons to accompany Aisha?" Dragos asked.

"No one, Master Dragos. They insisted, and we were too out-numbered to resist," Bakaar replied.

"And now?"

"We could eject them, but I believe Aisha would object," Bakaar said.

Bakaar remained relaxed, but I knew she would act instantly at Dragos's slightest gesture.

"Would you, Aisha Talon?"

"Yes, Master Dragos. I am sworn, by contract, to protect hi'Lady Rhiannon," I said, although I knew the Talons were no threat to her.

"In violation of the Clan call to war, a call that terminates all contracts. Are you Clan or not?"

"I am Clan, Master Dragos, and I have answered the Clan's call to war. I stand ready to be judged by the Clan's council."

"And if they chose to banish you from the Clan?"

"I have acted in what I thought was the Clan's interest. If the council disagrees with me, then I deserve banishment and death." I knew this to be true. My only thoughts had been to aid the Clan in destroying Radulf in revenge for my brothers' deaths. If I had been wrong, I was not fit to be Clan.

"NO! You can come with me, Aisha," Rhiannon shouted.

"If I have dishonored the Clan, I will cut my throat. It is our way, hi'Lady Rhiannon. Be patient. The Clan will give me a fair hearing." I looked at Dragos.

"Yes, Aisha Talon. You are Talon and entitled to a hearing before the full council. I guarantee hi'Lady Rhiannon that you will get a fair hearing," Dragos replied then turned back to me. "Do you know where Anton Talon is? I thought he was in Zenjir with Cezar, Vasile, and Marku."

I reached inside my blouse and pulled out a rolled up parchment which I handed to Dragos and waited as he opened it. Before he could react, I added, "I believe hi'Lady Rhiannon and fir'Warrior Awotwi need to be there. They have information the council will want."

"We will meet here in two hours. That will give time for the three of you to rest and refresh yourselves. The meeting will be held outside the city where we can talk without being overheard or interrupted."

And one new female Talon can be punished without a fuss, I thought.

* * * *

Rhiannon and I got a room at the Cool Sands Inn. This time we had to freshen up with the pitcher and bowl in the room.

"Why can't you come with me, Aisha, if the Raptor Clan no longer wants you? I want you. You can be my minister and advisor and bodyguard." Rhiannon rambled on as I washed.

"I am Clan, as you are Granyan. You agreed to a marriage to someone you didn't even know to save your land, your people. Should I do any less?" What I chose not to say was that one did not just leave the Clan, especially when they had you here for judgment. I had acted in what I thought was the Clan interest. Now I would have to answer for my decisions.

"But you said they would kill you. I will have fir'Warrior Awotwi protect you."

"No. That would undo all you have set in motion. It would wreck the alliance and ruin your chance of regaining your place as hi'Lady. What is done is done. We will hope I have done the right thing, and the Clan sees it that way."

* * * *

Rhiannon and I walked out of the inn, where Awotwi waited with two Talons and our horses. We rode back past all the tents and into the desert. After about a league we came to a huge white tent standing alone with no identifying marks. One of the Talon guards took our horses' reins as we dismounted.

Inside, Master Dragos and five Talons sat dressed in black silk. Each shirt had a silver Raptor embroidered on the sleeve and sashes with two, four-talon foot of a Raptor around each waist. Rhiannon and Awotwi were also wearing silk; Awotwi all white with gold crossed sabers, of the house of Baqir, and a maroon sash. Rhiannon wore a matching light blue outfit with a darker zigzag pattern and a white sash. After everyone was seated, I slowly removed my outer clothing to reveal my knives which I removed and staked in front of me. I then redressed in my black silks with the embroidered Raptor and single four-talon foot on my sash as befit my rank and sat.

"Our sister, has given us an interesting problem, brothers. She violated the call to war by not breaking her contract. She has insisted that non-Clan members attend her judgment, and has taken actions without the approval of the council. In her defense, she returned on her own and submits herself to our judgment. Ironically, council member, Anton Talon, gave her his place on the council. She is, therefore, both a council member and the accused." Dragos paused for questions or comments.

When the council remained silent, he continued. "Aisha Talon, you have heard the charges. What do you have to say in your defense?"

I stood. "First, let me introduce the two non-Clan members. This is the hi'Lady Rhiannon, of Granya, and this is fir'Warrior Awotwi, third son to the hi'Lord of Jaddah and betrothed to the hi'Lady. The reason I have ask for them to be included will become apparent soon."

They each stood and made a slight bow toward the Council as I introduced them before reseating themselves.

"For you to understand my actions I need to start at the beginning. Master Dragos assigned me to be a bodyguard for pri'Rhiannon but posing as a mountain-woman chaperone ... " I went on to explain the cyanide poison, identifying Third Lady Castor's involvement, enlisting Ferox as a spy, and Ferox's warning of a possible attack on the trip to Valda. I told of my warning to hi'Lord Varius and Master Taras and the attack on the caravan.

"How many attacked, Aisha?" Master Jiang asked when I paused for breath.

"I believe they must have had at least three hundred fighters based on what I saw and the way they overwhelmed the caravan even though the Granyans and Talons were prepared for an attack."

"How many attackers were killed," Jiang asked.

"I don't know. Their losses had to have been heavy. Maybe half."

"How did you escape?" Jiang asked.

"At the cost of the lives of the detail guarding pri'Rhiannon. Leszek and his guard were on high alert, and I had prepared a kit for both pri'Rhiannon and myself. When the attacked started, Leszek and I could see that they could not hold. I slipped out the back of the tent while the detail held off the attackers. I fled with pri'Rhiannon into the forest." I continued my explanation of the subsequence chase, the fire, and my decision to cross into Jaddah.

"Twice clever, Raptor Sister," Jiang said to nods from the others.

I continued to tell about my encounter with the four warriors and our trip in to Zenjir. Then concluded with my killing of Baqir's cousin and his proposal to Rhiannon.

"I think hi'Lady Rhiannon should continue as this is her story."

"Thank you, Aisha. First, I would like you to know I owe my life to the Talons, specifically to Aisha Talon who saved my life at least twice. She advised me to propose to hi'Baqir an alliance." Rhiannon then explained the marriage proposal and the alliance to overthrow hi'Radulf and his supporters and create a family triad of Jaddah, Granya, and Valda. She concluded with Aisha's plan of attacking Dassel.

"Your reasoning, Aisha?" an older member, I did not recognize, asked.

"They had to be over-extended, Master..."

"Master Syasya, Sister."

"The kingdoms maintain about nine hundred fighters each. Hi'Lord Radulf would have had seven hundred of those at Dassel. I believe he sent about five hundred to attack Granya. That left Dassel vulnerable with only around two hundred fighters. With Anton Talon's help, if they could lure a hundred or so out and ambush them, the Valda commander would be forced to call on hi'Radulf for reinforcements which we could ambush--"

"Shadow tactics," Syasya interrupted.

"Yes, senior Brother. Sec'Tadzio would feel safe withdrawing his fighters from Terni leaving it vulnerable. If we attacked Terni and killed the nobles and remaining fighters, Tadzio would have to reinforce his home. Again, the fighters

135

would be open to ambush. Livorno is also vulnerable because it was loyal to hi'Varius, so hi'Radulf would have had to leave a small guard there. I thought a combined force of Talon, Jaddah, and Granya would be able to reduce the enemy to no more than three to four hundred with few losses using shadow tactics. That would be too few to defend Valda or Granya."

"And that is why you refused to break your contract with hi'Lady Rhiannon?" Dragos asked.

"She wanted an alliance with the Talon to avenge her father and the Talons who died defending them. I thought it was in the best interest of the Raptor Clan to keep her safe until you could consider her proposal. When I proposed this to Anton, as a member of the Council he agreed. The hi'Lady's goals are in line with those of the Clan, we thought. Perhaps the best way to gain both goals is to work together."

"And sending Anton Talon to Dassel?" Syasya asked.

I nodded to Awotwi who stood up. "My father, hi'Lord Baqir, agreed to support hi'Lady Rhiannon based on the betrothal between her and me. Anton Talon and my older brother discussed Aisha Talon's idea to attack Dassel with him. Everyone agreed with Aisha Talon's belief that it was vulnerable, and the shadow fighting approach gave them a huge advantage." Awotwi finished and sat back down.

I stood again. "Anton Talon thought it was in the Raptor Clan interest to help the Granya Jaddah alliance."

Master Dragos rose. "If you, hi'Lady Rhiannon, and fir'Warrior Awotwi would step outside for a moment, the council needs to decide the issue of Aisha and Anton's actions." He waited until they left.

"Aisha, Anton has given you his vote, how do you vote?" Dragos said with a slight smile.

"I refrain from voting for me or Anton. I will only say that both of us acted in what we thought was the best interest of the Raptor Clan's call to war. I stand ready to do the will of the council." I sat.

"Jiang?" Dragos asked.

"I say Aisha and Anton have already taken the war to the Clan's enemies while we only sit around and talk. I declare them

136

Raptor Sister and Raptor Brother," Jiang said and looked around the room to general nods of agreement.

"Does anyone else have anything to add?" Dragos continued when no one spoke. "Aisha, my sister, you continue to amaze me. I would have thought you were the least likely to survive to become a member of the Clan. In fact, I was not alone in that assumption. Yet, you survived. I thought yesterday that you had exceeded your authority and violated Clan law. Again, I find I was wrong. We, the Raptor Clan council, not only find you innocent of breaking Clan law, but this council holds your actions in high esteem. Now, let's bring our allies back in and plan the destruction of our mutual enemy."

I didn't know whether to cry or jump up and scream with joy. I decided neither would be held in high esteem.

CHAPTER FOURTEEN

Dahab: Raising an army

The council resumed a few minutes later, when Rhiannon and Awotwi rejoined the meeting.

Master Dragos motioned to Master Jiang to address the council. "Well, Aisha, I would like to hear what action you think we should take next. As I remember your ten years at the Aerie, you were not the strongest student nor the fastest nor the best with weapons. Yet, you survived against all odds. My impression was that you were the best planner. Your opponents relied upon their speed and strength, on pure skill, to their peril. It is, therefore, not surprising that we, the senior Talons, discussed a plan to rush off to Granya to confront the hi'Radulf without seeking any alliances. You see, Sister, we are again relying on our speed, strength, and skill to win."

"The advantage of not having great speed or strength," I said, "is that I don't learn to rely on them. I anticipate the actions of others and play to their weaknesses, which my masters advocated. Hi'Radulf and sec'Tadzio have also relied too much on speed and strength to take Granya. They created a weakness which we can take advantage of with our allies." I nodded to Rhiannon and Awotwi.

"Which is?" Jiang prodded with a smile.

"Dassel and Terni, for the same reasons. They left them undermanned and vulnerable. As soon as sec'Tadzio and hi'Radulf realize that, with our help, they will have to send fighters to support those cities, exposing themselves on the road. We have already attacked Dassel. We should attack Terni as soon as we can, and should consider Livorno. This will weaken their hold on Savona, where their real strength lies." For the next two hours we worked out the details of the attack on Terni and Dassel. The first part of the plan sent Rhiannon to Dahab to be seen recruiting a retaliatory Granyan army. At my insistence, Rhiannon would be escorted by a group of Talons, Awotwi, and his warriors. The objective was to gather enough support for an attack on Terni. The attack on Livorno would wait until the Granyan army was larger. Awotwi kept one hundred of Dahab's warriors to supplement his force and Rhiannon's Granyan force for the planned ambushes.

* * * *

When I stepped outside of the tent with Rhiannon and Awotwi, Leszek was waiting.

"Hi'Lady Rhiannon. I am so glad to see you again and well." Leszek bowed. "I heard you are now engaged to a son of hi'Lord Baqir. Congratulations."

"Thank you, Leszek. I am pleased to see you again."

"With your approval, I have been assigned to head your guard."

"Yes, Leszek Talon. I would be delighted to have you in charge of my detail. Together, we shall avenge our dead." Rhiannon turned to her betrothed. "Leszek Talon, this is fir'Warrior Awotwi, third son of hi'Lord Baqir."

"Greeting fir'Warrior Awotwi." Leszek bowed to Awotwi, showing respect.

"Greeting Leszek Talon," Awotwi replied. "I have heard how you helped save my future wife in the Hazwood forest. Thank you."

"Leszek, have you heard word of Healer Luminita?" I asked.

The muscles of his jaw knotted. "No. I can't search for her and my son with the Clan at war."

"Since you are accompanying hi'Rhiannon, you may be in luck. I think we will be going to Terni shortly, and maybe Livorno."

"That is beyond what I could have hoped for." He kept his face calm, but knowing him as I had come to, I could guess at his feelings.

"Leszek, have you picked a detail? We need to tour the city for the next two days, announce hi'Rhiannon's presence, and recruit Granyan fighters for her army."

"Yes, eight Talons are ready now." He motioned with his arms to his right and left where Talons stood.

I waved them closer.

"Talons, this is hi'Lady Rhiannon. We are going to be touring the city for the next two days. People will need access to her, but we need to control who is allowed next to her. Watch Leszek and me for direction. This is fir'Warrior Awotwi who is part of hi'Rhiannon's party. He will also have a number of personal guards which he will identify," I said. "Let's be off."

Awotwi was very helpful in identifying inns around Dahab where we would most likely find refugees from Granya. In addition, he sent out runners to spread the word that the hi'Rhiannon was in Dahab gathering a Granyan army.

The next day as they broke fast, the lift of dawn still faint in the sky, an older man in a Granyan captain's uniform approached slowly. When he was near Rhiannon, he dropped down on one knee in front of her.

"Hi'Lady Rhiannon, I thank the gods that you are alive."

She smiled. "I'm more grateful than I can tell you to find so many of my people loyal to my father and me."

"I am Captain Symon. We were told you had been killed, along with your father, by the Jaddahans, who sec'Tadzio defeated. He claimed to have asked for hi'Radulf's support in keeping the peace in case more Jaddahans crossed the border. When sec'Tadzio started replacing Livorno nobles faithful to your father, many of us decided it was time to leave. Many more will join you when they find out sec'Tadzio lied and you are alive. My men and I acknowledge you as the rightful ruler of Granya and pledge our loyalty to you." The man bowed his head to the ground.

"Rise, Captain Symon, and join us. We have much to discuss. This is fir'Warrior Awotwi, an ally of Granya and mine. This is Aisha, my ... advisor, and Leszek Talon, senior Talon of my guard."

"Captain, do you know approximately how many loyal Granyan troops are in Dahab?" I asked.

"I've been recruiting since that Jaddahan warrior, Kibwe, told me that you survived the attack. We have as many as 140 fighters, knights, and nobles. Most are bivouacked at a temporary camp to the north of the city."

"You were stationed at Livorno, Captain?" I asked. We needed as much information as we could get. The Captain may have first-hand information.

"Yes, Aisha Talon." He pulled out a chair and seated himself at the table with us.

"What is the situation there?"

"When the others and I left Livorno, hi'Radulf had added some fifty Valdan troops to supplement the twenty five Granyan who remained."

"Hi'Lady, it would be good for you to visit the camp," I suggested. We could tour the city today and make sure everyone knows of your miraculous return from death, then visit the camp tomorrow." Raising a small army might be easier than I had anticipated.

Dahab had eight inns and three markets. At the first inn, Rhiannon talked with a few ex-Granyan fighters. They gathered around her, kneeling to pledge their loyalty and exclaiming over her return. At each subsequent inn, the number grew as the rumor spread that the heir to the Granya kingdom was alive and in Dahab. Rhiannon met with nobles, knights, and common fighters. The markets buzzed with talk about the alliance between Granya and Jaddah.

"I never knew it took so much effort to talk," Rhiannon said when we returned to the Cool Sands Inn later that evening. "I'm exhausted."

"You did well, hi'Lady," I said. She had been natural, which endeared her to everyone who stopped to talk. "You accomplished a lot today. Everyone knows you are alive and about the meeting tomorrow. Beside, many have had a chance to get to know you and will spread the word."

"Do you think they liked me?" Rhiannon showed concern on her face.

"I think they like the fact that you were real and natural. The real question is whether they will follow you into war. I think they will." Liking Rhiannon wasn't enough. They would need a reason, and the reason was likely different for each person.

* * * *

141

Although young, Rhiannon looked the part of a hi'Lady as she approached the camp with ten Talons and another ten Jaddah warriors. Awotwi had brought a large open tent that his warriors set up. Rhiannon sat under the tent's awning on a large rug woven with a mosaic design of greens, maroons, and yellows.

The nobles seemed to have organized this meeting. One by one, they approached Rhiannon, introduced themselves, and pledged their allegiance. Then the two captains took their turns.

"Aisha, what now?" Rhiannon whispered to me when the last captain finished and everyone seemed to be waiting for her to say something.

"These men and women are pledging to die for you, hi'Lady Rhiannon. It would be nice if you recognized their sacrifice. That will make you someone they know personally. It will make them clan." I didn't understand kingdoms or nobles, but I did understand clan allegiance.

Rhiannon rose and took a couple of steps towards the crowd of fighters. "I am the only surviving heir of hi'Lord Varius. In their greed, men from Valda along with sec'Tadzio killed, no slaughtered, our country men, our fathers, mothers, brothers, sisters, relatives, and friends. I pledge to you that I will see them pay for their evil against Granya and her people. Are you with me?"

I thought the roar could be heard across Dahab. Everyone stood as Rhiannon continued.

"Thank you. I would ask each of you to come forward, one at a time, give me your name and position, and your pledge to me and to Granya." When Rhiannon finished, everyone remained in silence. Then one person approached, kneeled, and pledged his loyalty. The rest followed. Rhiannon spent a few minutes with each one. Even in the shade of the canopy, sweat dripped down Rhiannon's face because of the noonday heat, but she received all of them in turn.

"Thank you, Aisha. I didn't know what to do, but that felt right, and it was very interesting." Rhiannon stood and turned towards the nobles and captains, who waited off to the side.

"Hi'Lady Rhiannon, we are proud to follow you. Your father would be proud of you this day. Those fighters will follow you anywhere." Second Lord Lucjan spoke with the nods of the others. "What do we do now hi'Lady?"

"Advisor Aisha?"

"Hi'Lady, sec'Lucjan will need to organize these men and women into a fighting company, find a leader for each group, and assign men to them. Time is short, but some training will be necessary. Your Jaddahan warrior allies and 25 Talons will join them. Master Jiang agreed to lead the attack on your behalf while you are in Granya, raising additional support. In the meantime, we must keep your enemies off balance." I faced Rhiannon but made sure I spoke loudly enough to be heard by everyone.

"It is unusual for the Talons to be leading. They are usually guards." Lucjan objected. The sigils I sensed were what I expected, mostly war and endurance. No one had a sigil of illusion and I relaxed somewhat. Mine must stay unused. I smothered a smile at imagining the chaos that would ensue if I did.

"Under normal circumstances, you are right, sec'Lucjan," I said directly to sec'Lucjan and, loud enough, to the others. "Right now, Granya has too few fighters to harass hi'Radulf and sec'Tadzio. Hi'Rhiannon has built an alliance with the hi'Lord of Jaddah and the Master of the Talons. Even so, she doesn't have enough troops to storm the castles in Granya and win. But the Talons have effective war strategies. We will deal with hi'Radulf and his alliance with minimum losses to hi'Lady Rhiannon's forces."

"Sec'Lucjan, I need your loyalty and leadership. We can not win without the allies I have made," Rhiannon added.

Sec'Lucjan kneeled. "I am yours to command, hi'Lady Rhiannon."

* * * *

The next day Rhiannon and I sought out Master Dragos. We found him outside the city at the same tent where we had the council meeting.

"Master Dragos, hi'Rhiannon has secured the loyalty of her Granya army and Awotwi has allocated an additional one hundred Jaddahan warriors that are stationed in Dahab. Both will accept your leadership." Rhiannon sat quietly beside me and

143

Master Jiang sat aside her and listened. "The Granya force will need a couple of days to get organized, but should be ready to move after that."

"Hi'Lady Rhiannon," Dragos asked, "wouldn't you feel safer staying here in Dahab?" His face showed little emotion.

"Yes, I am not a fighter. But I am the leader of the Granyans. Aisha feels we should be with the group who liberates Terni. I cannot, in good conscience, sit here while my country men, Talons, and Jaddahans are dying to free my kingdom. Besides, I may actually be of value in helping to gain the support and confidence of my people." Rhiannon maintained eye contact with Dragos. I was proud of my charge. She was afraid, but she wasn't letting it dominate her.

"Very good, hi'Lady. I am sending forty Talons with you. Leszek and his group are there to ensure you are protected. The others will help liberate Terni. Master Jiang will lead them," Dragos turned to me. "Sister Aisha, you and Jiang will run the operation. It is your plan, and he has experience you lack." I was surprised. I had assumed that Master Dragos would go or assign a senior Talon to lead the Talons and the operation. Rhiannon and Awotwi were too young, without experience, and I was neither senior nor experienced.

"Thank you, Senior Brother," I said, bowing low with respect. I recognized the honor he had given me. "Master Jiang, I hope that--"

Jiang interrupted me as we left the room. "I recommended we share the responsibility. I was impressed by you at the Aerie and even more at the council meeting. Most of the Talon today are excellent at following orders, but you have always been one to look beyond your orders to your duty."

CHAPTER FIFTEEN

Army moves into Granya: Implementing the Plan

I looked around the small, crowded room at Rhiannon's war council: Master Jiang for the Talons, sec'Lucjan for the Granya soldiers, and Awotwi for the Jaddahan warriors. Leszek was present as her private guard.

"Master Jiang and I have worked out the initial strategy for our entrance into Granya and hi'Rhiannon has reviewed and approved it. I have already worked with each of you individually on your part of the plan. Sec'Lucjan and Captain Symon have organized the Granyan soldiers in three attack groups. Captain Symon has been promoted to Senior Captain and second to sec'Lucjan in command. He will lead group one. Senior Sergeants Calix and Helier were promoted to Captain to lead groups two and three. The three groups have trained as units for the past two days. Today, I want to reiterate our plans with all of you to ensure we each know what the others are doing." I nodded to Awotwi to continue.

"Last night I sent twenty Jaddahan warriors accompanied by five Granyan soldiers and five Talons to scout the area ahead of the army and keep us informed. They will detain anyone they find until we can interview them. They will also look for the safest way to enter Granya and seek information about the situation in Terni." Awotwi finished and looked back to me.

I nodded and looked to sec'Lucjan, who stood. "Tonight Senior Captain Symon and Captain Helier will leave with group three, about fifty Granyan soldiers, fifty Jaddahan warriors, and five Talons. They will support the scouts and establish a safe staging area, in the Hazwood Forest near Terni, for the rest of the army."

"Four hours later," I said, "hi'Rhiannon and her war council, accompanied by the remaining Talons, Captain Calix and group two, and fifty Jaddahan warriors, will depart. And tomorrow evening group three and the remaining troops will follow. Our objective, the castle at Terni. For now, stealth, not speed, is most important. Our entire strategy depends upon slipping into Granya unnoticed." I hoped that everyone understood that the ideal was deception, not a clash of force.

"What about after we arrive?" Sec'Lucjan asked, looking at Master Jiang. "Do we have enough force to re-take the castle at Terni?"

"No. Even though it appears the castle is under strength," Jiang replied, "they could most likely survive a siege long enough to get support from Savona. Even if we could take the castle, the cost would be more than we can afford. At present, we number a little over three hundred, whereas sec'Tadzio and hi'Radulf number over six hundred and have the advantage of fortresses. They can afford heavy losses. We cannot. Our specific attack strategy will be formulated after we arrive in Granya and determine the situation. Right now, we are going on assumptions. In the end, we anticipate using stealth and deception rather than force, sec'Lucjan."

"Hi'Lady Rhiannon," I said.

"I value every life, Granyan, Jaddahan, and Talon." Rhiannon looked from one to another, gazing for a moment into each of their eyes as she spoke. "I wish none of you had to die for me, for Granya, but I know that is not possible. I, therefore, want our enemies to pay dearly for each life. We will fight a Talon war -- from the shadows. Go with my thanks."

If she lived, I thought, she might make a great ruler. But first we had to win.

* * * *

I was up at sunset with Rhiannon, Awotwi, and Lucjan to see Senior Captain Symon and Second Warrior Martrius lead their troops off. I encouraged Rhiannon to reinforce their orders.

"Captain Symon, sec'Warrior Martrius, remember that your objective is to sneak into Granya and to establish a safe area for the rest of the army. You are to avoid any confrontations if you can. Is that clear?" Rhiannon asked. When they nodded she continued, "May the goddess protect you."

Rhiannon's war council left four hours later, surrounded by Leszek and Rhiannon's personal guard, more loosely by over a hundred Talons, Granyans, and Jaddahans. Tomorrow at dusk, the remaining Granyans and Jaddahans would follow.

146

We stopped as dawn appeared on the horizon. Time enough to set up shelters and prepare a meal before the midday sun turned the desert into a furnace. An hour later two scouts appeared from the direction of Granya. Both were Jaddahan warriors, with weather beaten faces and looking used to traveling the desert. The war council assembled to hear their report.

"Hi'Lady Rhiannon," the smaller of the two scouts began, "we have encountered one small caravan and two civilians who appear suspicious. Captain Symon detained them at our present camp, awaiting your arrival and according to your orders. If that is not acceptable, we will return with your instructions." Rhiannon looked to me, then Master Jiang.

Jiang deferred to me with a smile. I didn't know how to take it. He should be in charge and making the decision, but he seemed content to let me. Was he testing me, I wondered? Well, you don't argue with a master Talon.

"No, stay here and rest. We may need scouts later on," I said. Our concern had been that anyone seeing the army moving towards Granya might report to the enemy and give them warning.

We ate in silence, each immersed in our own thoughts. I led Master Jiang aside after we finished the meal and served hot drinks laced with herbs. "Master Jiang, you should be leading the expedition.

"The rest of us seem to have forgotten those lessons. Besides, hi'Rhiannon trusts you and considers you her adviser. I am content to watch. If I believe you are wrong, I will tell you. If I know a better way, I will suggest it. Consider this training for your future role in the Clan." Jiang turned to Rhiannon.

"Hi'Lady Rhiannon, why don't you and Aisha retire to your tent? You have been up for more than a day. I will take care of setting the guard and settling the camp," Jiang offered. I could have kissed him. Exhausted, not so much physically, but mentally, I felt the strain not only as a member of Rhiannon's war council, but also making life or death decisions. It felt like I prepared for a seventh Ordeal, one encounter with hundreds of lives in the balance. I made sure Rhiannon was ready for bed, assured she was prepared to flee in an emergency, and settled down myself. After the attack outside Livorno, Rhiannon no longer resisted my diligence. I lay and listened to the camp sounds that led me into sleep.

Rested, the next day I felt alive. No longer pretending to be a servant, I was Talon for the world to see for the first time. In addition, I had Clan around me, and my contract was alive and well. Actually, I had become fond of Rhiannon, which worried me, since I didn't know whether that was good or bad. I needed advice.

"Good morn, Master Jiang," I said, joining him at a small fire where a group prepared a gruel of grains and spices. It smelled delicious.

"Sister Aisha, you seem to be in a very good mood. Sit and eat. You never know when you will be able to eat or sleep again."

"I am. I finally have someone to share my burden with." I drew a smile. "And since I do, I need to ask you a question, Master Jiang. I've become very fond of hi'Lady Rhiannon. Is that wrong?" I felt concerned and confused. Jiang had always stressed that emotions killed.

"No, Aisha. We Talons are human and have emotions. We love, hate, worry, feel sorrow and joy like everyone else. What we teach and hope you learn is to dampen those emotions and to avoid extremes. In battle mode, you learn to dump them entirely, since they distract you and can get you killed." Jiang paused as he looked me in the eyes. "When it comes to your contract, extremes are bad. If you hate your contract, you are unlikely to risk your life for them. But if you love them, you are more likely to martyr yourself for them. Neither benefits you, your contract, or the Clan."

"Thank you, Master Jiang. I love being Clan and the work, but I miss having senior Clan around." Events had happen so quickly I didn't have time to think about them and had pushed many questions to the back of my mind. "I'm thankful to have you here."

"From what I have seen and heard, you have exceeded what we should expect from a new Clan sister. Follow your instincts, Aisha. They have served you well. The Clan is pleased with you."

Jiang's reply astonished me. I felt like dancing around the fire, but that wouldn't please Master Jiang, so I bowed my head in acknowledgement instead.

* * * *

We rested until dusk. The sun tinted the western sky with pinks and purples at the time we broke camp.

"Aisha, I'm scared," Rhiannon whispered to me as we rode. In the quiet desert with only the moon for light, the shifting shadows made for an eerie ride.

"As you should be. You are not a soldier and weren't trained to fight like the sons or even some daughters of most nobles, especially heirs. After all, you were a younger daughter. You weren't raised for this. But you are brave, and that is more important. Doubly brave, because you chose to come along, even though you are scared."

"Thank you, my advisor."

We reached the small camp that detained the caravan and the two civilians. I let the caravan go, sending two warriors with them to ensure they went on to Zenjir, their indicated destination. While I talked with the caravan leaders, Rhiannon and Jiang met the two civilians. I joined them after dismissing the caravan. Walking toward the four of them, I could sense strong Charm Sigils.

"Aisha," Rhiannon said as I approached, "these two men are running from sec'Tadzio. This man's brother was killed. I've asked them to join us and explained were we are going." I looked to Jiang who nodded agreement. I realized I had a problem. If I negated the Charm Sigils, everyone standing here would realize what happen and who caused it.

"Do these men have sigils?" I asked Leszek, who shrugged. "Search them."

Leszek moved forward and conducted a thorough search. "No sigils, Aisha."

"Aisha, why are you doing this? They are on our side," Rhiannon said.

"Leszek, remove their shirts."

Rhiannon frowned as she put her hands on her hips. She was getting ready to argue.

149

"They have Charm Sigils on their backs," Leszek said before Rhiannon could object. That confirmed the strength of the sigils I had sensed. Master Jiang smiled at me; only the goddess knew why.

"I'd like to talk to them with guards who haven't been influenced already. Fir'Warrior and a couple of warriors, I think." Getting no argument, I pointed to the men to follow me away from the camp. Awotwi and four guards joined me minutes later.

"Aisha Talon, you wanted me?" he asked.

"Yes, fir'Warrior, these two men intend to kill hi'Rhiannon. What do you think we should do with them?" I had invoked my sigil so that Awotwi and his guards would not be affected by the Charm Sigil. I also knew Awotwi had a Truth Sigil.

"We aren't spies or assassins," one of the men said.

"He is lying. I think they are spies," Awotwi snapped, eyes narrowing.

"Do you think your warriors could find out?"

"Yes. We could stake them. Two days in the sun with their eyes pinned open should do it. Of course, they will be blind."

"Wait! We're just scouts. Sec'Tadzio sent us out to see what the soldiers were doing in Dahab and see if we could find out anything about pri'Rhiannon," one of the men shouted. "I'm Fifth Lord Rollo. That is Captain Tycho. Sec'Tadzio will have revenge if you dare harm us."

"Scouts don't need Charm Sigils. Of course, they are spies. Hi'Lady Rhiannon must decide their punishment." Awotwi nodded. "Have the guards keep them here. I don't want them near the hi'Lady, but I would like you to accompany me, fir'Warrior."

The guards grabbed the arms of the two men. Awotwi followed as I strode back to where Rhiannon and Jiang waited. "Well Sister Aisha. What did you find?"

I glanced at Awotwi. "What did we find?"

"One is a noble, fif'Rollo, and the other a Captain Tycho. Sec'Tadzio sent them to Dahab to spy, probably as assassins," he said, glancing at Rhiannon, his brow furrowed.

She paled.

"Hi'Lady, their punishment is for you to decide. But there is only one possible for spies and assassins." I knew this was a hard step for her, and I felt sorry to push her. As a ruler, this was her duty and nothing could make it easier.

Her voice was low but steady. "My betrothed, have your men execute them. But I don't want them to suffer more than they must." She turned away, and I thought her shoulders shook. I let her walk to the tent by herself. Some pains no one can help with.

"Someday I would like to find out how you knew they had Charm Sigils," Jiang said.

"You and hi'Lady Rhiannon liked them too much."

* * * *

We reached the West Mystic River a few hours before dawn. The scouts led us to a shallow river crossing where we traversed with no problems, wet but safe. The army camped about five leagues south of Terni, deep in the dense pine forest. The cool darkness of the forest refreshed us from the searing heat of the desert. Trees soared high overhead, and the camp was spread out among trunks so large two men couldn't reach around them. It occupied a square league with guards stationed another quarter league in every direction. We were informed that the advanced troops had encountered several people and had taken them prisoner.

"Master Jiang, I would like to talk to the prisoners," I said. "They could provide valuable information about Terni and what has happened since the attack on hi'Lord Varius and his daughter."

"I agree. Are you taking hi'Lady Rhiannon?" Jiang looked at her and back to me.

"I would like to go," Rhiannon said.

"An excellent idea. They are far more likely to cooperate if they see you are alive. Sec'Tadzio would like everyone to believe you are dead." I continued to struggle with the contradictory needs, keeping her safe and at the same time visible. As was apparent in Dahab, her presence could help raise her people to action and win their loyalty.

151

A scout led us deeper into the forest to where the first group of Granyans camped. Six men and two women sat around a small fire and ate. Four guards stood watch.

I motioned for Rhiannon to wait with Leszek and his guards while I entered the small circle alone.

"I am Aisha Talon. Identify yourselves." I sat on an empty log.

"I demand to know why we are being held captive," a big, muscular man with a thick beard and mustache said as he stood and turned towards me. He had several bruises on his face which attested to his resistance.

"The good news is you're still alive, and will probably stay that way, so long as you don't do anything foolish." I couldn't help a small smile at his attempt to intimidate me in the middle of an armed camp. "Now, who are you?"

"I'm Johana. I work the forest for logs, firewood, and wild game. Who are you and them?" He waved toward the guards.

"Thank you, Johana. And you?" I asked gesturing to the remaining seven.

"I'm Victar and these are my two sons, my daughter, and my son's wife. We were on our way back to our farm when your soldiers detained us." He looked around and wrung his hands.

"You haven't been hurt, have you?"

"No, mistress."

"And you?" I asked, looking at the two men. One was lean and young, the other older and slightly overweight.

"I'm Janus, a messenger on my way to Terni."

"I'm a merchant returning from a visit to Livorno to see my son."

"Hi'Lady Rhiannon and her army need information--"

"She's dead!" Johana shouted, his face red with rage. "The Jaddahan sand vipers you're with killed her and her father."

"Hi'Lady Rhiannon." I stood as she approached the fire with Leszek and several guards.

"She could be," Johana said. He took one step toward her but stopped as knives appeared.

"Pri'Rhiannon," the messenger shouted and went down on one knee with head bent. "I was one of your father's messengers. I've seen you many times at Savona. I'm yours to command, hi'Lady Rhiannon."

With that, the others rose and went down on one knee along with Johana.

"Please rise." Rhiannon approached them and took a seat on the log I had been sitting on. I stood near her. "As Aisha Talon said, we need information. I have been pursued by these usurpers for several weeks and am unaware of what has been happening in Granya."

"The story is that hi'Radulf and his army pursued the Jaddahan army who has been raiding Valda. He caught up with them after they had killed you and your father. Sec'Tadzio, asked him to stay until he could establish order and ensure no more Jaddahan warriors were on Granyan soil."

"That's interesting. Now we have two different versions of who destroyed the Jaddahan warriors. Probably because there weren't any. What is the situation in Terni?"

"Sec'Tadzio left a little over three weeks ago," the messenger added, "with hi'Radulf, to Savona. He took most of his troops. Only a few are left at the castle. Maybe fifty. Half Granyan and half Valdan. I was ordered to ride to Livorno with a sealed message for Third Paulus."

"The town folks are nervous. They don't like the Valdan troops. They are arrogant and have no respect for our women," one of the sons scowled.

"Can we go then, hi'Lady Rhiannon?" the older woman asked.

"That is up to Aisha and Jiang Talon," Rhiannon said, "but I can promise you that all will be treated well while you are with us, and no harm will come to you."

"Master Jiang, I think we need a war council," I said as we walked away. "I would like to send a few Granyan soldiers into Terni to see what they can discover about the castles garrison and the mood of the citizens. We should infiltrate the castle, but we can't do so without more information."

CHAPTER SIXTEEN

Terni: Liberated

Late the next day the five Granyan soldiers returned from Terni. I was anxious to know what they found but restrained myself as I assembled everyone for a council meeting. The cool fragrance of pine drifted over our forest as the sun set. The five soldiers stood shifting from foot to foot as we took our places around the fire.

I looked to Master Jiang to start the meeting, but he showed me a bland smile. He didn't seem to want to take the lead, content to watch. I doubt he missed a thing. I felt like a student being judged on my performance.

"Well, what did you find out?"

"The town is nervous. Valdan soldiers are in town every night, acting more like occupiers than visitors. The Granyan soldiers aren't seen much, and the city guards keep a low profile." The soldier paused and looked at his comrades, who nodded.

"The castle has fifty or so soldiers," another soldier said. "At least thirty are Valdan troops. Most of sec'Tadzio's family is in Terni, his wife, a young son and daughter, two cousins, also two nobles, a forth and a third. A Valdan, a Third noble, is in charge, and a Captain commands the troops."

Another soldier spoke. "Security at the castle is very tight. They always have a couple of soldiers at the gate and on the walls. Storming the castle would be hard."

"It sounds impossible," Rhiannon said and frowned. "I don't want to see a lot of men killed just to take Terni. It would not be worth it."

"Master Jiang, what do you think?" I hoped Jiang would have a magic solution.

"The Talons may be able to get into the castle," Jiang replied, "depending how alert the night guard stays. Once done, we should be able to open the gate."

"The guards are alert," the first soldier said. "They are worried about the unrest in Terni. The people resent the Valdan soldiers, and a lot of Granyan soldiers chose to leave or were dismissed."

"We need to poke the tiger. Make it mad." I saw a solution take shape. "We need to kill a couple of Valdan soldiers each night, make it look like one person, maybe two, working together."

"Why?" Awotwi asked. "We can't kill them all. Eventually they will stop going into town or go in large numbers. Oh, you want to weaken them for an assault on the castle."

"No, she wants to use the front gate!" Jiang laughed. The others looked at him in bewilderment. "Very good, Sister. While we are all looking for a bigger sword to slay the enemy, she is looking to have them slay themselves."

"I don't understand," Lucjan said. All nodded in agreement.

"Aisha?" Jiang said, nodding for me to explain.

"Our response depends upon how the castle responds, but they must respond. If we can force an emotional response, anger or hate or fear, they will give us the opening we need."

* * * *

Three Talons left that night dressed in everyday working clothes. They were told to start slowly, one or two kills.

"Do you think this will work, Aisha?" Rhiannon pulled her tunic over her head and reached for her nightgown.

"The Talon teaches that in a fight or war, emotions are a liability." I yawned. "When you become emotional, you lose your judgment and leave yourself vulnerable. I hope whoever is in charge will overreact and give us an advantage."

I think we all had trouble sleeping that night. I wanted to help in town, but I knew my place was with Rhiannon. But tonight was only the beginning. Many nights would pass before we could expect the response we needed.

The ambushes went on for six nights. The Talons killed eleven soldiers, eight Valdans and three Granyans. Our soldiers reported that, at first, the Valdans ordered their men to go out in

155

pairs and in triples. The fourth night they ordered a curfew. Last night they offered a reward of one hundred gold scrules.

"Time to move," I said. "The front door is open."

"How?" Rhiannon asked. "They still have forty or more soldiers."

"We will catch the murderer!" I replied, "and turn him over to the castle guard." Master Jiang laughed. I glanced at Master Bakaar, standing nearby. "I suspect the murderer is a woman."

It took another two hours to work out the details.

* * * *

The next night Jiang, Bakaar, and I stood in the shadows and prepared for our gambit. Jiang made a small cut on the top of Bakaar's head. Blood ran down the side of her head and face. She applied a little pressure to stop the bleeding, and we waited for the blood to dry. We then tied Bakaar's feet to the old horse's saddle we had purchased earlier in the day. We stepped out into the street and walked slowly up to the castle gate, a pretty threesome, Jiang with his long gray hair and uncombed goatee flying about in the wind, Bakaar on the ground, filthy as the horse dragged her down the street, her face covered with blood, and me, clothed as a beggar.

"We got her," I said to the gate guards. "We captured the one who's been killing the soldiers. I banged her in the head and my grandfather tied her up. She wounded another soldier who just arrived in town. He's at the healer. We want our hundred scrules."

"Go take a look, Vollo. I'll wait here," the sergeant ordered as he stood by the inner iron gate. Vollo opened the outer gate and approached Bakaar, looking Jiang and me up and down, then looked away.

"Sergeant Aeson, this woman they captured is a Talon, judging by her clothes. Get a few of the guards on the wall to help me get her inside." Vollo shook his head.

"When do I get my money?" I danced from one foot to another. "A hundred scrules, the reward said."

"Sergeant, let her through the gate. The Captain will want to talk to her. He has your reward." He sneered at Jiang. "You stay here, old man."

I skipped through the two gates. The guard at the other end grabbed my arm and pulled me over to him. He was Valdan.

"Hello, sweet thing," he said with a leer as the other hand groped at my breast. Reaching behind me, I found the small blade I had woven into my hair and pulled it. I smiled as he pulled me face to face with him, and I cut his throat. I could see a captain and two soldiers rush across the courtyard. I was covered in his blood. I held the body upright and watched them approach. The Captain, a Valdan, pulled a tabard over his head as he walked. I released the dead guard and, in the same motion, grabbed the sword out of his scabbard. I had no other weapons on me for fear I might be searched. The sword weighed more than my Astrakan sword, not well balanced, but it would have to do. I held it low, pretended I didn't know how to hold it, shifted my feet, and tried to look frightened. The captain strutted out in front of the two soldiers with a smirk on his face. I shuffled a step back toward the gate, acting frightened. As he got close, he lunged. I twisted sideways as his sword passed an inch past my stomach, then I slashed across his neck. The impact of the blow threw the captain back between the two soldiers. The nearest soldier sliced downward at my head. I parried, twisting my sword up and into his neck. I saw the sergeant's blade swing at my head. I dropped to the ground, rolling away. Coming to my feet in one motion, I sliced under his blade, slitting his belly open. He dropped his sword and grabbed his stomach. As I reversed my motion upward, my sword crashed into his head. Blood and bone exploded.

An arrow tore through my shoulder, tearing cloth and leaving a nasty gash. Blood dripped down my arm. I stepped back and saw four Talons dash into the courtyard, shooting arrows into the few guards on the ramparts. Talons seldom missed. The guards fell dead.

Granyan and Jaddahan troops poured through the gates and headed for the garrison where Valdan and Tadzio's Granyan soldiers emerged. Stuffing a cloth atop the gash on my shoulder, I bound toward the castle.

"Do you mind if we join you, Sister?" Bakaar ran up beside me, the four Talon brothers with their bows behind her.

"No. I decided to tour the castle."

"Jiang asked me to give you these." Bakaar handed me my sword, my sash, and several throwing knives. I wound the sash around my waist and tucked my knives into it. No one met us at the main entrance to the castle. We started down a long corridor lit by a few flickering torches. Halfway down, two guards turned a corner, running down the hall toward us, shouting something as they ran. Bakaar stepped in front. With a couple of lightning-quick motions, she blocked and killed both guards. I had to smile as we moved forward, kicking bodies out of the way. I knew I was good, but watching a true master in motion was humbling.

We went through the first floor, Bakaar and I with swords in our main-hands and knives in our off-hands, the Talons with arrows notched in their bows. Once we were sure it was clear, Bakaar motioned to the stairs with her chin. We walked up on full alert, expecting a counter-attack. The first hallway was empty. As we turned a corner, a man stepped out of a niche to swing at my back. I caught his sword on mine, our hilts locking as I slid my knife under his ribs and into his heart. At his shout, another charged out of his room, dying on Bakaar's blade in an instant.

Towards the end of the hallway, a woman opened the door with two young children and peeked out. "I would stay in your room for now. You and your children could get hurt in the hallways." She slammed the door shut in my face. We passed by as the door opened again.

I turned as a tall Valdan noble stepped into the hallway, sword drawn. He attacked with a hard backhand stroke. My shoulder throbbed now from the arrow I'd taken, and I felt light headed, but I parried his stroke. I took a step backward. He realized his mistake as two arrows went through his chest, and he fell backward from the force.

"Thank you, Brothers," I mumbled. Everything went black.

* * * *

"Will she live?" I heard Rhiannon say in a whisper.

"Yes, hi'Lady Rhiannon," Jiang replied. "The wound is not serious. The arrow ripped through the upper part of her arm. It's deep but not life threatening. Had she stopped and had it taken care of, she would have been fine. But she chose to continue fighting, and the loss of blood caused her to pass out."

I opened my eyes to find it was evening, so I hadn't been unconscious long. I tried to lift myself on my elbow, but my head spun and I collapsed on the bed. Obviously, I had been out long enough for them to move me to one of the castle's bed chambers.

"How do you feel, Aisha?" Rhiannon looked pale and sounded worried. Master Jiang was standing next to her.

"A little tired," I said. I cleared my throat when my voice sounded raspy. I probably needed a good night's sleep, even though the room had stopped spinning.

"You have been unconscious nearly a full day, Aisha." Rhiannon put her hands on her hips, looking angry.

"A full day," I repeated. I vaguely remember passing out in the hallway and waking up a minute ago -- in bed. Loss of blood, I had heard Jiang say. Oh, that damn arrow. It didn't seem to hurt at the time. I moved my arm and felt a deep twinge.

"She needs some food, and she will be all right." A stranger in healer robes raised me into a sitting position against some pillows.

"Bring the food over here. Eat." Rhiannon ordered.

Two maids carried over a platter. I sniffed at the scent of a roasted chicken. The food smelled wonderful, and I was ravenous. I pulled some meat off the chicken, sighing with pleasure as I stuffed it in my mouth.

"What has happened since I passed out?"

"I talked to Master Jiang, and he agrees. You are in violation of your contract."

"I am?" I managed not to choke on the mouthful of chicken.

"Yes. You went into town with your friends for a night of partying and were unable to perform you duties as my bodyguard today. Master Jiang had to fill in for you."

I sat there speechless. Rhiannon still had a scowl on her face, but I saw the corner of Jiang's mouth twitch.

"Yes. I will forgive you this time if you promise not to let it happen again. You scared me to death, Aisha!" Rhiannon shouted, hugging me until I sucked in my breath from the pain in my slashed shoulder. "Sorry."

"I am sorry, hi'Lady Rhiannon, that I worried you. I will try to be more careful in the future," I didn't mean it the way Rhiannon would probably take it. One cannot be careful in war or combat. I meant I would try not to worry her more than necessary. I was very fond of my charge -- more than I had realized.

"It's been a busy day, Aisha," Rhiannon said. She was now all smiles and her color was coming back. "Merchants, store owners, and nobles have been coming in to see me and swear allegiance. And they brought gold scrules to help me pay for our campaign against sec'Tadzio and hi'Radulf."

"You are the rightful heir to your father's kingdom, hi'Lady Rhiannon, but..." I faltered, hating to say what I was thinking but knowing I needed to.

"Yes, my terrible advisor, Master Jiang has already pointed out that while they may prefer to see me on the throne, they are hedging their position in case I win, although most don't think I will." Rhiannon laughed. "But I will."

"Yes, you will, and you will make a fine ruler." I pulled a leg off the chicken and took a big bite.

"Yes, the merchants and others are not fighters," Jiang said, "and do not want to anger whoever becomes the winner in this battle, so they must cater to both. Most believe you are the rightful successor but doubt that you can win against sec'Tadzio and Valda, especially when they only see a small number of Granyan soldiers supporting you. They feel caught in the middle."

"I understand, Master Jiang. Aisha has explained the problems with being in power, although I didn't want to hear it at the time. I do not hold it against them. As you say, they are caught in the middle." Rhiannon wrinkled her face in thought. "What now, my war advisors?"

"I would propose," I said, "that you and I stay in Terni another day and take a tour of the town. You need the support of the common people in the streets for when you do win. Besides, you may find more volunteers for your army." I swallowed another mouthful of food. Licking my fingers, I imagined a big

160

clan rather than a kingdom. Rhiannon needed to build a feeling of clan among her people. Anyway, I understood clan, not kingdom. "Master Jiang should join your troops in the Hazwood forest and help organize the ambush. I will stay with you, so that I don't violate my contract anymore."

"Master Jiang?" Rhiannon looked towards him.

"It is dangerous, but I believe Sister Aisha is correct. Support of the common people is more important than most rulers realize. But we only have another day or two before troops come from Savona to retaliate. Aisha needs to stay with you, and I need to organize our response. Sister, I will leave another ten Talons with you and Leszek to ensure hi'Lady Rhiannon's safety. Do not wait longer than another day to join us."

* * * *

Master Jiang left that night. The next day after we broke fast early in the smallest of the castle dining chambers, I pulled Leszek aside. "Leszek, send several Granyan soldiers into town to look for your wife and son. She shouldn't be hard to find if she is here. Even if they can't find her, maybe they can find information about her."

"Thank you, Sister. I couldn't bring myself to ask you to spare anyone. And as terrified as I am, I can't desert my duty."

I left him to organize a search while I organized a procession for Rhiannon in the castle courtyard. Leszek and his guard would be responsible for Rhiannon's immediate safety and form a loose circle around her, with me next to her. Another twenty Granyan troops and ten Talons would form an honor guard to the front and rear of us. It would be impressive and an effective fighting force if necessary.

"Any advice, advisor Aisha?" Rhiannon asked as we started out the castle gate and into the town.

"Be accessible, be relaxed like you were unconcerned about anything, keep the Talons around you, and you will be all right." I said a silent prayer to Yun, goddess of Charm and Luck.

The tour went well. We stopped at merchant's stalls where Rhiannon purchased a scarf from one merchant. She stopped to talk to a carpenter, buying a tiny chest from him. She bought some fruit to eat and talked small talk with everyone she met. We worked our way to the dock where she talked to the

161

boat owners and fishermen. It was obvious the crowds who followed us about the streets were fascinated with the young hi'Lady. Late in the day, we finally hit the wealthier neighborhoods and shops when Rhiannon spotted a small knife shop and entered.

"Hi'Lady Rhiannon, welcome to my shop. How may I help you?" The owner was a thin, elderly man.

"I'm looking for a small knife of good quality and a sheath for it," Rhiannon replied. The owner spent the next thirty minutes showing her knives, explaining where they had been made, the difference in steel, tempering, and balance.

"I'll take this one. You have been most helpful, and I have enjoyed the education you provided in helping me to select." One of the Talons collected the knife and sheath from the merchant.

As we exited the small shop, three nobles stepped out of a doorway a few paces away.

"Tri'Livius, do you want to be ruled by a woman…no, a girl, pretending to be our better?" the older one said as he drew back his arm to throw a knife he had concealed behind his friend's back.

I jerked Rhiannon's arm, stepping partly in front of her and sent her flying. I swatted at the knife with my free hand, deflecting its spin. I let go of Rhiannon as she landed against Leszek. Turning, I reached for my daggers and let both daggers fly while reaching for two more. One landed in the knife thrower and the other in his friend. At the same time, six other Astrakan knives landed in the three noble's chests and thirty swords were bared.

In dead silence, I searched the bystanders for suspicious movement. Everyone on the street had frozen or found shelter.

"You're bleeding, Aisha," Rhiannon said as she untangled herself from Leszek who looked a bit embarrassed.

I examined my hand. It was a shallow cut. Wiggling my fingers, they moved all right.

"At least this time, hi'Lady Rhiannon, you were partying with me," I said as I wrapped the cut with a cloth Leszek handed me.

* * * *

Early the next morning shortly after dawn, we left the castle and headed for the rendezvous in Hazwood Forest, leaving seventy-five Granyan soldiers to defend the castle. I signaled Leszek closer.

"Did you find out anything about your wife and son?" Leszek just shook his head as he gazed into the distance.

CHAPTER SEVENTEEN

Jaddahan warriors in Dassel: Eagles arrive

Three days later, deep in the forest, Anton Talon and Tafadzwa ate dinner around a small fire. They finished an excellent meal, skewered meats and vegetables grilled over the fire, thanks to the farmers who sold them supplies. The scent of wood smoke and roasting meat hung in the air.

"We're not living too badly for being at war," Anton said, leaning back against a large tree near their tent with a satisfied sigh. In his youth, he had fought in a war. He remembered the excitement as he and his fellow Talons charged the enemy. The opposing army had been poorly matched against Talons, who had spent years learning the art of war. Back then, the heat of battle had been exhilarating. Today, he preferred bodyguard assignments, monotonous work except for the occasional assassin.

"True, Anton. But I never imagined that war could be so boring." Tafadzwa gazed around at his warriors. The full moon showed through the dense foliage of the trees, lighting the camp alive with men and fires and the undertone of conversations.

The men gathered in small groups around the fires talking and eating and occasionally singing. Weapons were in neat stacks and on the edge of the camp. And beyond that the picket line where the horses were staked.

"Shadow fighting does tend to be minutes of intense danger which, if you survive, is followed by days of boredom." Anton smiled. "And I think it is going to get even more boring over the next few weeks. The Dassel commander is unlikely to send out any of his reduced force. He will wait until he gets reinforcements from Savona."

"I thought being heir to Jaddah was boring. Are you sure there isn't something we could be doing, like attack the castle?" Tafadzwa laughed. Anton knew he wasn't serious, but he'd watch to ensure Tafadzwa's craving for action didn't result in a premature response that compromised their position and jeopardize the overall strategy.

"Patience Warrior, we will do plenty of fighting when the reinforcements arrive."

A commotion at the edge of the camp cut off their idle banter. Tafadzwa stood and faced the direction of the disturbance. Anton stayed where he was to observe as a sentry appeared from among the trees followed by another warrior. One of Tafadzwa's sec'Warriors met them. He waved the sentry back to his post and, after a short conversation, turned to stride toward the two commanders.

"Fir'Warrior, a messenger," Warrior Rafimiz said. He approached the fire with a Jaddahan warrior following behind.

Dripping sweat and disheveled, the warrior bowed to his commander. "Fir'Warrior, five hundred Salda soldiers are marching on Dassel."

When Tafadzwa looked toward him, Anton stood and smiled to himself. *The game has a new player. One Aisha failed to anticipate.*

"Did your commander have any other specifics?" Tafadzwa asked.

"No, sir. Sec'Warrior Arlind said to tell you he thought they might have learned of Dassel's depleted forces and think they can take the city. But he said that was only a guess."

. "Messenger, were Talons riding along with the Salda force?" Anton asked. *Talon trained* he revised. *That would further complicate the situation.* The stakes had escalated, Talons killing Talons for the first time in their history.

"No...not exactly, but about twenty men and women at the head of the main force wore sashes like you do, but different, red, tied in front rather than on the side. Their Tabards were richly embroidered with large birds."

"Eagles," Anton murmured. *As Aisha had seen the vulnerability of Dassel, so had they.*

"You know them, Anton?" Tafadzwa asked, frowning in puzzlement.

"I do." Anton rubbed his chin. "This will change things. We need to discuss it, fir'Warrior." He turned back to the messenger. "Did your commander send any other news?"

165

"No, sir. He just said to get that information to you as fast as I could ride."

Anton nodded and went back to sit down as he considered the new players in this very serious game.

"Get yourself something to eat, Warrior. You did well," Tafadzwa said, waving the man away.

"Do you need me, fir'Warrior?" Warrior Rafimiz asked.

"No, that will be all."

Tafadzwa stared into the fire for a while. "I don't believe Aisha counted on Salda attacking Dassel. This complicates the situation. What do you think we should do, Anton?"

"We don't have enough troops to take on the Salda or enough time to set up an ambush if we had. Besides a major confrontation with the Salda force, if we won, would deplete our forces. We can let them take on hi'Radulf's reinforcements from Savona. I think it is another case of sit and see what happens."

"Anton, you didn't answer my question about these Eagles."

"It wasn't something I wanted to discuss in front of the messenger. You see, Eagles are Talons who went rogue some fifteen years ago. About twenty under contract to Salda renewed their contracts yearly. After some time, Master Dragos decided to rotate those in Salda with other Talons. We always return Talons on long contracts to the Aerie for a rest and a change of assignment. They refused to return and betrayed the Raptor Clan." Anton paused. The betrayal had been painful and was rarely discussed. "They are under a Fatwa because they broke their oaths, but the Clan has never attempted to enforce it. I think the time has come."

"You want us to attack them for you?" Tafadzwa asked, giving Anton a hard stare.

"No, fir'Warrior. They are our problem, not yours. Besides, their force is too large so I think we sit and watch what happens. We may have it all wrong. The Saldans may be here to help the Valdans." Anton shrugged. "The castle forces are depleted, thanks to us, but it still would not be easy to take. You know that a battle for it is likely to be costly. If the Saldans take the castle, we can keep them blockaded just as we have the Valdans."

166

"More waiting. I wonder what is happening up north with Aisha and my brother Awotwi." Tafadzwa seemed distracted, looking into the fire as both men descended into silence.

"I do, too," Anton replied after several minutes as if there had been no lapse. "I suspect that the Talons would have met them in Dahab. If so, Master Dragos convened a meeting of the senior Talons to consider Aisha's and my actions. She and I ignored Master Dragos's recall order which is a serious breach of Raptor Clan law. The Clan could have us both executed for that." He couldn't help but note the irony between the rouge Eagles, and he and Aisha.

"What? What did she or you do that is so serious as to justify your death?" Tafadzwa's mouth dropped open in shock.

"Talons are subject to the Clan laws. She and I both broke the letter of our Clan's laws by not returning to the Aerie or, in this case, Dahab when Master Dragos ordered it. Aisha and I will claim we acted in the Clan's interest as we understood it at the time. But the Clan may not agree even though I, a senior Clan member, authorized Aisha's actions. Also Aisha presumed to make decisions that only Master Dragos or the council can authorize." Anton stared into the fire. "I don't know what the Clan will decide."

"What decision is that?"

"That the Talon would fight with hi'Lady Rhiannon to regain her throne."

"Won't they?" Tafadzwa straightened up and faced Anton. "Isn't it in their best interest?"

"They could choose revenge rather than war." Anton picked up a stick off the ground and poked at the fire. The Talon believed in quick and direct action. They may not want to align themselves with a Kingdom for any number of reasons. "The council may not care who sits on the throne of Granya."

"You make your Clan sound hard, yet I have found you and the Talons loyal and friendly."

"The Clan is loyal to its contracts, and we make friends, but a Talon's first loyalty is always to the Raptor Clan. The Clan doesn't tolerate dissention. They don't allow fully trained Talons free to wander the land. Too many secrets and too dangerous." Anton looked up at Tafadzwa. "Aisha creates scenarios and acts

167

on them in an independent manner. At Savona, she assumed the role of a mountain-woman chaperone for then pri'Rhiannon. She was the talk of the castle, and had pri'Rhiannon and hi'Varius mad enough to threaten her with a whipping. Even I thought she had gone too far with her act. But because of her chaperone act, she saved pri'Rhiannon's life, at least twice. The senior members may see her independence as threatening the Clan's way. Even I'm doing her bidding. I think the Clan must kill her or support her. She has gone too far for any other option." And that included him. He would accept the consequences as would Aisha. They were clan not rouges.

"Which do you think, Anton? You're talking about my future wife." Anton stared at Tafadzwa. The lord's face was serious with no hint of a smile. The man doesn't realize the ramifications of marrying Aisha. She was Talon. The clan would not allow her to leave. She could marry but she would be assigned where the clan needed her. At best, he could expect to see her for short periods once every year or two. Anton shuddered. What would happen to the alliance if the clan decided to execute her? How would hi'Baqir, hi'Rhiannon and the future hi'Tafadzwa respond? The thought gave him a headache.

"I am on the council and I support her. I went so far as to give her my vote, but that's no guarantee. I can only hope the Clan agrees with me and Aisha and chooses to support hi'Lady Rhiannon."

"Come to think of it, I supported Aisha. What a hi'Lady that woman would make." Tafadzwa whispered his remark, but Anton heard it. Aisha is a first year Talon, yet so much depended on her actions, the fate of Kingdoms and possibly the Talon. Hi'Blessed Tasilaba pronounced Aisha hi'Blessed. He didn't understand but he knew Aisha would need the gods support.

"A dangerous woman, fir'Warrior Tafadzwa. She would certainly keep you alert. What is your famous curse? Oh yes, may the winds bring you interesting times. Maybe we should change it to, may the winds bring you Aisha." Anton laughed so hard he choked.

"The question is, Anton, what kind of a woman does a ruler of a kingdom need? One who is placid or one who is your equal. I assure you my mother is no placid woman, even though she is no warrior. And what kind of a woman is the equal of someone who rules a kingdom?" Tafadzwa eyes were unfocused as he talked as if thinking aloud. "Besides, who better to protect my back?"

"I think you're suicidal." Anton looked at Tafadzwa with some amazement. He had seen the young lord's attraction to his raptor sister, but the extent escaped him. For everyone's sake, he hoped Aisha wouldn't marry him or that his fascination with her faded.

"Wonderful thoughts, but back to our problem. What do you suggest we do about the Salda?"

"Patience. Let us wait and watch. When we are sure what the Saldans intend, then we will determine our next action. Besides why should we take losses unnecessarily? Let the Saldans and the Valdans kill each other off, if they'll cooperate." Anton grinned. We seem to be a little short on cooperation.

"Do you think they will?"

Anton poked at the fire again. "Think about it, fir'Warrior. We haven't attacked because of the strength of the castle, walls thirty paces high and several paces thick, well designed with murder holes and every possible defense, and inside a formidable keep. If Salda attacks the castle, their losses will be substantial."

Tafadzwa nodded thoughtfully.

"I suggest we send word to your father and Master Dragos. We need to work in concert with the forces in Dahab. They need to know what is happening in Dassel and we need to know what is happening in Granya." Be good to know if Aisha is alive and if there is a fatwa on him.

* * * *

For the next two weeks, messengers went back and forth between the three Jaddah forces on a daily basis. Anton had spies sent into the city to monitor the action. Every night messengers brought the latest news to Tafadzwa and Anton.

The Salda forces penetrated the city easily as the commander at Dassel had insufficient troops to man the walls, and guards were not equipped to defend them. The residents didn't resist since they really didn't care who ruled. Their lives

169

wouldn't change. Once the Saldans had the city, they still had the castle to take. Salda forces spent ten days of bitter fighting to gain entrance. On the tenth day, a messenger brought the news that Salda had finally breached the castle gate.

Early that morning one of their spies, a warrior with family ties to Dassel so that he could pass for a citizen, slipped away from the city to bring them the news.

"fir'Warrior, Salda has defeated the Valdan force. They now command all of Dassel."

Tafadzwa and Anton exchanged a glance. This was what Anton had expected.

"Were you able to find out how many warriors Salda lost in the fighting?" Anton asked.

"The castle garrison was killed to the last man and woman. I found an inn where some of the Salda soldiers were drinking. After I bought a few rounds of ale, they started talking, complaining bitterly about how many were killed. From the stories they told and what I was able to see, they must have lost about half of their force."

"You did well, warrior." Tafadzwa waved the man away. He turned to Anton. "Ironically, we appear to be in the same position we were in four weeks ago, Anton. The only difference now is that we oppose two hundred fifty Salda soldiers instead of Valdan soldiers."

"I suggest we start over again," Anton said with a wry smile.

"Not quite start over. Our blockade is still in piace. So that's what we'll do, even though it's boring." Tafadzwa threw back his head and laughed.

CHAPTER EIGHTEEN

Hazwood Forrest: The Plan needs revising

When Rhiannon, Awotwi, and I left the Terni Castle for Hazwood Forest, we knew that Tadzio would soon learn of his castle's capture. He could no longer pretend he was replacing the previous hi'Lord because there was no heir. He must relinquish his claim on the throne or declare himself a usurper. In the latter case, he would send an army to retake the castle, rescue his wife and family, and kill Rhiannon. *But what does Radulf gain for his part in the overthrow of hi'Lord Varius?*

The bright light of midday shone through the dense branches of the forest as we rode into the valley where our camp with our guards included an additional thirty-five recruits. I glanced around the camp and the configuration of the sentries, who were well placed out from the camp so no one could approach unseen. Two sentries saluted as we passed. The tents were scattered in no particular order but close together. Horses were picketed to the right near the supply wagons.

We rode down the hillside. Our horses' hooves trod with little sound over the thick cover of pine needles. I saw Jiang step out from one of the larger central command tents and watch our approach. We dismounted and soldiers led our horses away.

Jiang smiled at Rhiannon. "I see you brought troops from Terni. You must have done well."

She beamed. "I hope so. I think so."

"She did very well. Hi'Lady Rhiannon is a fine leader." I was proud of her.

Jiang motioned to a table and chairs set up between the tents, where Awotwi awaited us. "How long until you think they'll attack?" Awotwi asked as we seated ourselves and the guards dispersed. I sensed Awotwi was disappointed with his service at the castle and anxious to prove himself in battle.

Jiang looked into the distance, then said, "That's hard to say. He'll have several decisions to make before he attacks."

I nodded. "He'll need to decide the size of his army to bring for one thing. There are about six hundred soldiers in Savona now. One hundred fifty of sec'Tadzio's soldiers, four hundred of hi'Radulf's, and say another fifty of hi'Varius's old garrison. They can't afford to send them all for fear of an uprising in Savona."

"He has to send enough to take a castle," Jiang said, "now held with about 70 soldiers. We must show only Granyan soldiers and keep the count in that range. I think he will send between 200 and 300."

"But he doesn't have 300 Granyan soldiers to send. If he sent 200, there would be only be Valda soldiers remaining in Savona." Rhiannon pursed her lips like she had eaten something sour. I liked the way Rhiannon participated, no longer depending on others to do her thinking.

"Very true, hi'Lady. I think sec'Tadzio would want to keep most of his soldiers in Savona. If that is true, maybe he will send 100, half of them expected to return with his family after they retake the castle." Jiang paused. "Then hi'Radulf will have to supplement sec'Tadzio's force with around 200 soldiers."

I couldn't suppress a smile. Everything lined up with our plan. "So the question is, what happens when hi'Radulf finds out that Dassel is under attack? How many soldiers does he send to Dassel and how many does he keep in Granya to maintain control with sec'Tadzio as ruler?"

Jiang moved a dagger that he used as a paperweight on some messages, picked a sheet up, and handed it to Rhiannon. "This arrived late yesterday afternoon by messenger."

Rhiannon read the message and passed it to me. The message from Anton reported that he and Tafadzwa had wiped out one hundred and forty of Dassel's soldiers. He expected the commander to send word back to hi'Radulf. I blew out a long breath and gave the message to Awotwi. "Well, we'll soon find out what he'll do."

"If I were hi'Radulf, I would want at least 200 soldiers to remain in Granya. But when he realizes Dassel is under attack, I think he will have to reduce them to 100," Jiang said. "I believe he'll bring between 300 and 400 troops, depending upon the timing, when sec'Tadzio hears about Terni and hi'Radulf hears about Dassel."

"What if their force is larger?" I asked. Timing could present us with the worse possible scenario. I hadn't considered that when I talked Anton into going to Dassel. I couldn't sit still any more, so I rose and paced between the tents. I had never realized until now how many things had to be considered.

"It will depend upon how they respond to a raid. If they split their force equally, say 200 to chase the ambush and keep 200 to attack, we will have to rely on hit and run tactics, where we should have a good advantage. The Jaddahan warriors are good with bow and knife, but the Granyan and Valdan troops depend more on swords."

I realized he was watching me as I paced and felt myself blush. I stopped pacing and sat down. "Will they stop to attack the Terni Castle, continue on to Dassel, or split their forces again?" Jiang had always stressed that plans had to be flexible, because they seldom include all contingencies in the first encounter with the enemy.

"We won't know until we know, Sister." I felt Jiang's eyes probing me. I kept my face bland.

"Fir'Warrior Awotwi, you, your sec'Warriors, and the Granyan captains need to meet with us here tonight. Everyone needs to understand exactly what they need to do. There can be no confusion, once the fighting starts. We need to understand where and when we will rendezvous, in the event we are separated. In a shadow war, each warrior must understand how he fits in with the rest. It will appear to be chaos when the action starts. That is our advantage. The enemy must be confused, not us," I said.

"I'm not sure I understand our strategy," Awotwi said in a whining tone.

"It's like this," I said. "A group will attack the convoy, then flee. If they're pursued, the other groups waiting will attack them from the rear and both flanks. But we'll hold some soldiers in reserve to defend hi'Lady Rhiannon and against unforeseen needs."

Awotwi nodded. "Tonight I'll meet with my sec'Warriors and go over the details of the plan."

* * * *

The light of early morning broke through the dense forest cover as a scout galloped in on a lathered horse and leapt off in front of the command tents in a panic. I stepped out. "A large force… only three leagues behind me, on the road to Terni!"

Awotwi ran up from where he had been talking to one of his sec'Warriors. "How large?"

Rhiannon, Bakaar, and Jiang joined us as the scout, bent from the waist to catch his breath, straightened and continued. "At least 400, possibly more."

"Our chance to try out our strategy!" Awotwi ran to gather his men. He would lead the decoy group and lure Radulf's force into our trap. In a few minutes, the clatter of their horses' hooves marked their departure from the camp. The rest of us moved into place.

Master Jiang had left with the unit that would circle behind to prevent their retreat. I would lead the unit from the left flank and Bakaar the unit from the right. Rhiannon scowled in front of her tent, strongly objecting to my leading one of the units, but she finally had to give in to the argument that we needed all the fighting force we could muster.

I walked beside the sec'Warrior as we led the fifty Jaddahan warriors into the thick tree cover. The huge pines towered overhead as we moved silently through their huge trunks over the thick bed of dead needles. In the distance, a squirrel chattered. Otherwise, the forest was silent. We reached our assigned position on a small ridge overlooking the route Awotwi's unit would retreat. I pulled my bow and strung it as I checked around me to be sure that the sec'Warrior had all of the men well hidden in the thick cover of the trees.

I motioned him over. "Any questions, sec'Warrior?"

"No, Aisha Talon. They're set for the attack."

I nodded. Now it was a waiting game. With everyone still and quiet, a few birds returned to the trees. Soon I could hear the chatter of magpies overhead. Below a squirrel skittered up the bole of a tree. We had been in place for about half a glass when Awotwi's warriors thundered by below us, too fast for me to see whether he had taken any losses in the hit and run attack.

Only a couple of horse lengths behind, the pursuers galloped between the trees on heavy warhorses wearing chain mail armor glinting in the shafts of sunlight through the branches.

I lifted my arm and brought it down in a sharp motion. The twang of bowstrings filled the air. Sighting down, I concentrated on the warrior in the lead. My first arrow took his horse in the neck, my second arrow hitting the rider as he leapt from his falling steed. A steady rain of arrows fell from all three sides. Screams and shouts below echoed in the trees as the warriors realized they were trapped. One turned his horse and made it halfway up the slope before my arrow took him in the neck.

Then it was quiet. I held up my hand. The firing stopped as Awotwi led his unit back into the little vale below us. He bent over his horse's withers as he rode, examining the downed enemies.

I signaled and the sec'Warrior joined me as I walked down to see how many we had killed. We counted around 50 dead, not even close to the entire force. Radulf had not taken our bait.

* * * *

We returned to the camp to find Rhiannon pacing. "What happened?"

"We only lost six men. But Radulf ignored our bait. We only lured away a few." Awotwi shrugged, but I could see that he was pleased at his success. "They're dead."

"A messenger came while you were gone, from Anton," Rhiannon said, waving a letter in her hand. "Salda has attacked Dassel. They captured the castle."

We looked at each other in shock. "What do we do now?" Awotwi said.

"I never anticipated this complication." I grew frustrated by the collapse of what I had thought was an excellent plan.

"That is why plans have to be flexible," Jiang replied with a smile, "and commanders have to be willing to adapt to new circumstances. What now, advisor Aisha?"

"Me?" Heat rose to my face. I sounded like a little girl. Jiang was the Master here, not me.

175

"Yes, you, advisor Aisha. We still follow your original plan. It obviously needs adjusting."

I stood and walked away. Rhiannon followed. "Savona has very few soldiers defending it." Rhiannon started a discussion. "Couldn't we take it and kill sec'Tadzio at the same time?"

"I would think sec'Tadzio has about 200 warriors. Do you think we could attack the Savona castle with the three hundred we have?"

"Could we trick our way in like we did here in Terni?"

"Maybe. But won't we be losing sight of the real enemy, hi'Radulf? And what about your commitment to the Jaddahans who are helping you?"

"Aren't you supposed to agree with me?" Rhiannon shook her head with a small smile. "You were a terrible chaperone, and you are a terrible advisor. I want sec'Tadzio to pay for his treachery."

"I know, hi'Lady, and he will. But his real power comes from hi'Radulf. Without his support, sec'Tadzio will be easy to defeat. At least half of the 200 at Savona are Valdan warriors." The situation began to crystallize in my mind. Rhiannon had helped me to see the real issues. "I think we need to join Anton Talon."

"How does that help?"

"If we can take Dassel, I think the rest will fall into our laps." I had my answer for Master Jiang.

CHAPTER NINETEEN

Livorno: Liberated

For two days the Jaddahan scouts followed the Valdan troops as they rode towards Livorno.

"Hi'Lady Rhiannon, hi'Radulf has stopped in Livorno. He and his commanders occupy the castle; his army camped on the outskirts of the city." The scout reported to the whole group seated around a small fire, although he addressed Rhiannon, the highest ranking person.

"Thank you warrior," Rhiannon answered. "Master Jiang, why do you think he stopped at Livorno?"

"I would guess he intends to collect his soldiers. There must be fifty or more holding the castle along with a small number of Granyan soldiers."

"Sec'Lucjan, if he does withdraw the Valdan soldiers," I asked, "how many Granyan soldiers do you believe that will leave to guard the castle?" My estimate put the number at less than 50. The total strength before the takeover was less than 200.

"I doubt it is more than 40, more likely 25 to 30," Lucjan said. "More than 50 left with me when we retreated to Dahab. Over 100 were killed in the fighting and others deserted."

"Who would be in charge?"

"If hi'Radulf withdraws his troops, I would think two young cousins of tri'Lady Castor."

"If that is the case, I would like to stay here and recapture Livorno, Master Jiang. You could proceed to Dassel and join up with Master Anton. I don't think we would be more than a few days."

"Not without me!" Rhiannon cried.

"Yes, hi'Lady, with you." I couldn't suppress a small smile. "If you tour the city and show yourself to all of the people, the young nobles will either have to recognize you as the legitimate hi'Lady or attempt assassination. If we do it right, we won't have to attack the castle. They will come to us."

"A good plan, but it would put hi'Lady Rhiannon at risk." Jiang said what we all knew.

"I will take Aisha's advice. I am at risk as long as any resistance exists in Granya. I trust her to keep me as safe as possible."

"Master Jiang," I said, "I will need ten Talons in addition to Leszek and hi'Lady Rhiannon's normal guard, as well as twenty five Granyan soldiers."

"And what do you plan to do with them?" Jiang looked at me with the usual twitch of his lips.

"I will disguise Leszek and our Talons as Granyan soldiers and the Granyan soldiers as commoners with sec'Lucjan hidden among them. We will tour the town announcing that hi'Lady Rhiannon is alive and well." I paused until Jiang nodded. "If the nobles are loyal they will come to pledge their allegiance to hi'Rhiannon. If not, they can't afford to do anything else but try to kill her. In either case I will have 40 soldiers ready to meet them, half of them Talons."

"Sounds a reasonable plan, so long as hi'Lady Rhiannon is willing to take the risk," Jiang said as Lucjan nodded agreement.

"If I had been the oldest," Rhiannon said, "I would have been reared and trained to fight with the soldiers, to lead them into battle, as was my older sister. The very least I can do is to risk my life with you, I don't deserve to rule if I am not willing to do that for my kingdom."

* * * *

At noon the next day two scouts returned. "Hi'Lady Rhiannon," one scout reported, "hi'Radulf has left the castle with 70 soldiers to join his army. They broke camp when we left to report. Four scouts will follow them. As ordered, they will keep you informed on the army's movements."

"Thank you, Warrior. Get yourself something to eat before you return," Awotwi said.

"I suggest," Jiang said, "we wait until tomorrow to move out. That will put their army several leagues ahead of us. We don't want them to know we're behind them until we're ready. I have sent messengers to Master Anton telling him we are coming and for him to let the Valdans pass unmolested."

178

"Why?" Awotwi asked. "Aren't we going to ambush them?"

"Not yet, fir'Warrior Awotwi," Jiang answered. "It is likely they will attack the castle in an attempt to displace the Salda force. Or they will siege the castle, forcing the Salda soldiers to attack them. In either case, if we let them weaken each other first, we will have fewer to fight."

"Interesting. I had always imagined these great battles on an open field where the two armies met in a bloody clash. It seemed so heroic."

"War is seldom heroic. Mostly, there are losers, the dead, the crippled, destroyed property, and poisoned land. War is heroic only in the history parchments."

"But you are warriors!" Awotwi raised his eyebrows.

"That is the difference, fir'Warrior. We are not after glory. We don't expect to be hailed as heroes. It is merely our Clan's profession, and we know the consequences of war. Both sides, winner and loser, will pay a price." Jiang paused. "Look at the current war. Sec'Tadzio thought he could be hi'Lord by killing the heirs to the Granya kingdom. When he failed, he teamed with hi'Radulf, who seized the opportunity to expand his power. Jaddah was pulled into an alliance with Granya, and Salda has tried to exploit the situation by invading Valda. Four kingdoms have a wild cat by the tail and can't hold on or let go."

I went to sleep that night thinking about what Master Jiang had said. I had to agree with him. The greedy, the power hungry, or the ideologues never considered the consequences of war, except for themselves, and never understood the inevitable realities. I never considered that Salda would attack Valda if we weakened it, which makes me one of them.

* * * *

The next morning Master Jiang began moving our army of 250 troops south, behind the Valdan force, while hi'Lady Rhiannon and I rode into Livorno. I kept the entourage around Rhiannon small. Ten Talons dressed like Granyan soldiers. I wore the uniform of a Granyan officer. The other 32 drifted into town in two and threes and mingled with the crowds.

We started in the town center where we stopped, setting up a small stand. I mounted it and waited to be noticed. Soon a small crowd assembled to hear what I was going to say.

"Citizens of Livorno, I am Captain Aisha here to dispel the lies being spread by the killers of hi'Lord Varius." Several people in the small crowd began looking nervous and kept watching behind them. "Yes, hi'Lord Varius was killed, but not by Jaddahan soldiers crossing our borders. They were killed by Valdan soldiers."

"How do you know?" An old man asked this in a loud voice as the crowd began to grow.

"How, you ask? Because I was there. I was there when they snuck up in the early morning to kill our men, your sons, your daughters, your husbands, and friends. They slaughtered maids, cooks, and servants, in addition to our soldiers."

The crowd was growing now. I had their attention.

"And why were the Valdan soldiers in Granya? Because sec'Tadzio invited them in to rule you." I shouted. "Sec'Tadzio was responsible for killing hi'Lady Varius and her oldest daughter and son. And when he failed to kill pri'Rhiannon and hi'Varius, he invited hi'Radulf to help him gain power."

"What can we do about it? He has killed all the Varius line," a woman shouted.

"But he hasn't. I present to you, hi'Lady Rhiannon, your rightful hi'Lady. A lady who loves you and Granya." I pointed to Rhiannon. Stunned silence descended on the square as Rhiannon stepped up on the stand next to me with two Talons.

"Pri'Rhiannon was killed, they say," a couple of people in the crowd shouted.

"They tried, and they will wish they had before we are through with them," I shouted as Rhiannon raised her hands. The crowd fell silent.

"Citizens of Granya, a great injustice has been done to you and to me. Many of our people have died for the greed of a few, a few who already had a privileged life. All of us will suffer if hi'Radulf gains control of Granya. Sec'Tadzio is nothing but a puppet. Hi'Radulf has no love of us and will rob and pillage our land for his own greed. He must be stopped."

"What can we do? We aren't soldiers." Many nodded in agreement with the woman who spoke up.

"I would ask the young and the fit to join me in opposing Valda. The rest of you, I would only ask your support, your best wishes, and your lack of cooperation with the enemies of Granya."

"Rhiannon, Rhiannon..." the crowd chanted as she stepped down and began walking up the road into the market district. Varius had been well liked by the general population and so Rhiannon was given the benefit of the doubt. Besides, they liked her little speech.

Rhiannon stopped frequently to talk with vendors, shop keepers, and people milling around. She listened genuinely interested in their lives, their work, and their families. It only took two hours when 26 men rode into the street where Rhiannon had wandered.

"Halt in the name of for'Alair. You are under arrest for treason against hi'Lord Tadzio!" A young noble shouted as he and his men dismounted. I detected for'Alair's moderate War Sigil and the strong one of the man next to him. Another man a few paces away had a strong Illusion Sigil.

I stepped forward, noting the Talons uncloaking their bows to string them, and notched arrows. The Granyans moved in closer.

"Kneel in the presence of hi'Lady Rhiannon, or die," I proclaimed as I cupped two throwing daggers.

"I don't kneel to commoners. Rhiannon will be hanged for treason against the people of Granya. Arrest her," he said to an officer next to him.

"Sergeant, you heard for'Alair, arrest her and her soldiers," the captain said. At the same time, Alair's soldiers seemed to double as the officer with the Illusion Sigil activated.

"So be it," I said and activated my Negation Sigil. The illusion failed. I signed and eighteen arrows left their bows. Ten of the soldiers died. All of our guards pulled their swords as the sound of steel echoed in the square. People screamed, ducked, and ran in a moment of mayhem. Alair and his Captain kicked their horses into motion, charging Rhiannon and me with their swords raised. I realized they were on warhorses so just killing

181

the men wasn't going to be enough. I threw my knives at the horses' eye. They struck when the horses were still several paces away. Once more arrows flew, and the two men fell dead. The horses stumbled and fell with their two dead riders. When the panic stopped, all of the castle soldiers were dead.

"Leszek, the castle, I think," I said. In a minute, all the arrows, except one, were removed from the young noble who was strapped to one of the horses. Four Talons supporting the dead for'Alair and dressed as Granyan soldiers, rode towards the castle.

We followed slowly several minutes later. By the time we arrived the Talons had entered the castle, killed, or captured the remaining soldiers. I ordered the women who were not soldiers and children put in the giant reception room.

As we entered the room, full of women and children, some shouting, some crying, and some huddled in small groups, one woman dashed at Rhiannon with a dagger that she had managed to hide. I grabbed her from behind. I would have slit her throat, but she dropped the dagger. I nodded to two of the guards. They dragged her out of the room as she screamed, "No! No!" It might have been kinder to kill her, since she was guilty of treason, attacking her sovereign lady. I shook my head.

When Rhiannon seated herself on the raised platform, she looked to me.

"Aisha, what do you suggest I do to them?"

"You have several choices, hi'Lady Rhiannon," I said loudly. The room fell quiet once the woman's screaming died into the distance. "First you could have them all put to death. That would avoid any possible thoughts of revenge." Looking around the room, I saw that most of the women shook with terror, and with good reason. The adults probably deserved the death I had threatened them with and might consider that a kinder fate. "Or you could just confiscate their goods and lands and throw them out of the castle."

Rhiannon did nothing for several minutes while everyone held their breath and awaited her decision. Finally, she shook her head. "No, I don't want to punish any who are innocent of treason against my father and me."

"You can be overly generous and give them the chance to prove that they are innocent of treason and murder," I said.

"Yes, that is my decree. They are to be held here and given a chance to prove that they didn't take any active part in the treason. If they are innocent, they may reclaim their lands. If they are guilty, the lands will be given over to me to distribute to my loyal followers, and they will share the fate of the other traitors."

A woman in the back of the room sobbed. The rest were dead quiet. Rhiannon stood. "I would remind everyone that sec'Tadzio and hi'Radulf and their followers have killed nobles, hundreds of Granyan soldiers, maids, cooks and others who did nothing to harm them. sec'Tadzio, hi'Radulf, and their supporters have committed treason. I vow to you and to them, they are dead men." Rhiannon rose and exited the room.

"Leszek, you are free until tomorrow morning. Take a couple of Granyan soldiers and search for your wife and son," I said. His face brightened and he hurried off. I knew that Rhiannon had decided to stay the night and that Leszek would be distracted, thinking about Luminita and whether she and their son were in Livorno.

Rhiannon left Lucjan in charge and 25 Granya soldiers for support. He promised to raise a small army while we were gone. Rhiannon promised him a reward when she again had control of Granya. We left at dawn the next day. Leszek spoke little as we rode away, but I knew he had failed to find any trace of Luminita and their son.

CHAPTER TWENTY

Dassel: Eagles challenge Talons

We reached the outskirts of Dassel and had no trouble finding Anton and Jiang. Their warriors stopped us on the road about two leagues outside the city.

"Halt, this road is closed to travel!" A Jaddahan warrior sat on his horse next to five others. I noticed several more on each side of the road, more hidden among the trees.

"Warrior, I'm Aisha Talon. I'm here to see Anton Talon." I hoped that would identify us.

"Follow us, Aisha Talon. We were ordered to look out for you." The warriors turned and headed into the forest. We followed them for an hour until we arrived at the main camp, their tents scattered among the trees with lookouts, which I spotted, and a line of horses picketed to one side.

"I see you were successful, hi'Lady Rhiannon," Jiang said as we seated ourselves around a small fire.

"Yes Master Jiang, it was almost too easy and yet very painful. Your Talons are very efficient," Rhiannon replied. She walked over to Tafadzwa and kissed him on each cheek. "Greetings, my future brother."

"I am delighted to see you in good health, future sister. My brother is far more fortunate than he realizes." Tafadzwa held Rhiannon at arms length and surveyed her, then grinned at his brother over her shoulder.

"It is nice to see you well, Master Anton." Rhiannon turned toward where he stood.

"Thank you, hi'Lady Rhiannon," Anton said. "You have been very busy since we last talked. Terni and now Livorno are back under Granya control. And I see that the council didn't censure you, Sister Aisha. In fact, I understand you share joint command with Master Jiang. Very impressive."

"It seemed so easy back in Zenjir, Master Anton," I said.

"That is true, Sister Aisha. You can never make a perfect plan. Although your plan has been relatively successful so far,

184

Salda has complicated the situation. But the plan could still work. The attack may work out to our benefit if the Salda and the Valda armies destroy each other. In fact, there could be an added benefit. Salda has ex-Talons with them, under a Raptor Clan fatwa for the past ten years."

"So, what do we do next?" I asked. I had heard of the fatwa against the Salda Talons while at the Aerie, a teaching example of what happens to Talons who disobey the Clan.

"I thought you would tell us," Jiang said with a small smile. "The council approved your plan. It needs modification. Who better to amend it than the person who developed it?"

I wondered if Jiang was having fun at my expense. At least, I hoped he was. Worse than that, he could expect me to come up with the next action.

I stalled. "I need more information."

"Very good, Sister. That is the correct response. No one could make a good decision without knowing what hi'Radulf will do and how Salda's army will react. We'll make a better decision with more information. The next few days should be critical."

"Aisha, you were right," Tafadzwa said. He bowed his head to me in respect, locked eyes with me for a long time, then continued. "We did draw out half of the castles' force and my warriors destroyed them. They then sent word to hi'Radulf, who we could have ambushed on the road to Dassel. You planned well. You couldn't have predicted that the Salda would attack Dassel."

"We must now adapt," Anton said as Tafadzwa stared at me with a smile frozen to his face.

"For now, we wait," Jiang ruled.

* * * *

Two Talons frequented the city over the next four days, reporting back to Rhiannon's war council at each evening meeting. We heard the reports of the spies as they managed to find warriors to drink and talk with and bring us back current news.

On the first day, Radulf had tried negotiating with the Salda warriors in command of the castle. He claimed he could

185

starve them out. Salda claimed he couldn't, because reinforcements were on the way.

The second day Radulf tried an early morning assault. It was partially successful and the Salda suffered the loss of 35 soldiers. Salda only had 150 warriors remaining after they secured the castle. Our report said Valda's forces lost about seventy warriors in the fighting.

The next day messengers arrived with the news that the reinforcements from Salda had been ambushed by the Jaddahan, and had turned back. Our spies from the city didn't report more fighting until the following day when Valda again assaulted the castle. Again, both sides suffered heavy losses. I knew that the ex-Talons probably accounted for the heavier than normal losses by Valda.

The next day was quiet, and our spies brought us news of only minor skirmishes.

"Would this be a good time for us to enter the game?" I asked that night after we listened to the reports.

"Why?" Tafadzwa asked.

I felt strange the way he looked at me at times, especially when he thought I wasn't aware he was looking. He seemed to be everywhere I was. He was good looking and intelligent. *He must already know the answer to that.* I gave him a puzzled smile. Maybe he just wanted to talk, and I didn't mind. In fact, I enjoyed his company.

"If we let the Valdans gain the castle with hundreds of warriors, we will never get them out. If we wait until their attack is about to succeed, the number of Valdans and Saldans will be significantly reduced. We could destroy the Valdans, because they will be distracted with their attack, and the Salda will be left with only a small force to defend the castle."

"Warrior Aisha is right." Tafadzwa grinned, a sparkle in his eyes. "If we time it right we might even gain access to the castle at the same time. At worst, the Salda will still control it, but their numbers will be insufficient for a defense." I felt myself color at Tafadzwa's remark. "Warrior Aisha." Warrior had a special meaning to the Jaddah.

"I agree," Jiang said. "Fir'Warrior Tafadzwa, it is time to call in all your warriors. We will move closer to Dassel, tonight."

* * * *

At dawn, we waited for word from Dassel. Jiang had sent in twenty Talons and another twenty Granyans to ensure the city gates remained open when our army advanced.

"Master Jiang," the Talon scout reported, "the attack has started, and the fighting is heavy. It appears hi'Radulf has thrown his entire army against the castle gate. I doubt the Saldans can hold out for more than a couple of hours."

"Fir'Warrior, we move now. We go straight for the castle and hit the Valdans from behind. If they have breached the gate, we follow them in."

We moved towards the city walls, 500 strong. Beautiful from outside the gate, red brick walls towered close to twenty paces high with turrets every thirty paces. The river, splashing in white water as it moved fast over the rocky bed, gave more protection along one side. As we got closer, we saw the gates open and the bodies of the four guards the Talons had killed. I wondered if the city guard had been called to help attack the castle.

As we entered the gate and flowed into the city, the residents scattered. Doors and shutters slammed shut. It was so quiet I could hear the battle cries a good three hundred paces from the fighting.

When we emerged from the inter city into the open area in front of the castle, the battle was at its height, the gate hanging open where a ram had bashed it in. I hung back with Leszek and some fifty warriors, guarding Rhiannon and the war council.

As the Jaddahan warriors stormed the walls, they overwhelmed the Valdan army which was caught between two enemies and out-numbered. The Salda couldn't take advantage of our attack as the main gate had already been breached. In an hour, both armies had been defeated.

"Fir'Warrior, we have secured the castle." The warrior messenger panted from having dashed to find us. "Many are dead or scattered, but we have about 75 captives who

187

surrendered. However, there are some ten Eagles held up in one of the buildings. They are asking for Master Jiang."

"I guess we should see what they want."

"I could order my warriors to attack them. If there are only ten, it should not take long," Tafadzwa replied.

"No, fir'Warrior Tafadzwa. If they are fortified, the toll on your warriors would be higher than they are worth. Let us hear what they have to say. This is a Talon issue. They are under a Talon fatwa."

The castle was not so much beautiful as it was massive and built to be defended. The whole structure including the walls was a circle. The outer walls were fifteen paces high with no turrets but a continuous parapet with crenellations every few paces. A second inter wall was built on higher ground and rose another twenty-five paces and had turrets spaced around it. And rising thirty paces was a rounded keep complete with parapet and crenelles. Inside, the Eagles controlled the top floor.

We passed through corridors and stairways crowded with Jaddahan warriors. I didn't think a mouse could get out of the castle, much less a man.

One of Tafadzwa's sec'Warriors strode up as we entered the audience chamber. He bowed and reported, "Fir'Warrior, we haven't found hi'Radulf and my tri'Warriors report all buildings have been searched. We are examining the dead, but it is unlikely he attacked the walls."

"Keep searching. This is his home. He may have a secret room somewhere." Tafadzwa shrugged in Rhiannon's direction.

"He must die, my brother," Rhiannon said quietly to Tafadzwa.

"Yes, my sister, and he will. You have my word."

We continued walking until we reached the stairway to the rooms the Eagles controlled.

"I'm Jiang Talon. What do you want?"

"I'm Algis Eagle. We Eagles demand a fair fight with you Talons, one on one. We know that we will die, but we demand to die fighting. You swore a fatwa against us. So, enforce it, Jiang Talon." The voice shouted down from above.

"No, you do not deserve the honor of a duel," Jiang said.

"We have fourteen of the women nobles and their daughters up here. We will kill them all. Since we deserve no honor, we have no reason to be honorable," the voice said.

"Wait," Tafadzwa shouted. "Master Jiang, if you will not, the Jaddah will. This will taint my rule if I allow it."

"Your warriors are excellent knife fighters, but will not match well against a Talon trained fighter."

Jiang looked to Anton and Bakaar. They nodded. "We agree, Algis."

"The rules are thus, Jiang. One Eagle will enter the ring with one Talon. The winner may stay in the ring for the next fighter or leave to let another fight the next match. We will fight until all the Talons or all of the Eagles are dead. The youngest girl plus one other will be released as each Eagle enters the ring. Agreed?"

"Agreed. Two knives, no throwing."

"Agreed."

"Give me a few minutes to gather my Talons, Algis."

"You have ten minutes before the first dies."

"Fir'Warrior Tafadzwa, have your men take word to all the Talons they can locate. I need them with me."

We waited, not speaking. Within the ten minutes, Anton and several more Talons joined us. Warriors straggled in to watch as news of the challenge spread. At last, Jiang shouted up to begin.

A middle aged man with the smooth measured stride of a fighter came down first. Tall with long arms and legs, he dressed much like a Talon in black shirt and pants, but with two embroidered eagles on the sleeves. He held a small girl about eight, whom he released when Bakaar entered the ring with him.

I didn't know what to do. War Sigils blazed. If I used my Negation Sigil who would benefit? I decided I should do nothing for now.

"I am to remind you that there are no rules. However, if anyone interferes, our agreement is void and the remaining women will be killed." The man paused. "Master Bakaar, I remember you from the Aerie. You were pretty good."

"I don't remember you, so you couldn't have been that good," Bakaar said as she stared into the man's eyes. The Eagle

189

began weaving an intricate pattern with both knives which Bakaar evaded. First blood went to the Eagle when he slashed Bakaar's arm. Then she moved so fast I couldn't follow it. The Eagle stumbled and fell. Bakaar left the ring where the healer checked the cut on her arm.

"It is deep but not life-threatening," the healer said to Jiang.

"I'm all right," Bakaar replied.

"Rest for a moment, another will fight next."

Another Eagle came down the steps with another girl around ten. He released her and stepped in the ring. The fight was quick with the Talon scoring a slash across the Eagle's chest but had his throat cut in return. The Eagle chose to fight again and Bakaar decided it would be a fair fight as they were both wounded. Her bleeding had stopped. Bakaar won but received two more cuts that weakened her to the point she stumbled as she left the ring. Jiang declared it would be too dangerous for her to fight again.

So the dueling went for the next hour. Four Talons died and six more Eagles. Anton had a deep slash across his chest being tended. I thought the Eagles had lost their edge, but they were Talon trained and dangerous. And they seemed to be better each time. When the ninth Eagle came down the stairs, he had a young woman about twenty-two or three whose dress was ripped and had a dark bruise on one cheek. To my surprise, Master Jiang stepped into the ring.

"Master Jiang, I am disappointed. Aren't you a bit too old for fighting?" The Eagle sneered.

"I should have thrown you out the first year or killed you before your fifth Ordeal, Petras. I knew you would disgrace the Clan," Jiang said in a cool voice.

"Yes, you should have killed me, because today I'm going to kill you." Petras began circling. He moved like a cat. Jiang stood, only moving to keep Petras in sight as he circled. The audience of about two hundred was silent. Petras sprang. Jiang had a knife in his side and a deep slash across his chest. Jiang's knife protruded from Petras' chest up into his heart. Jiang was carried out dripping blood but alive.

"I will take the next Eagle," Anton said. He stepped into the ring in preparation.

"No you won't!" a woman shouted down. "I have five women up here. I want the woman Talon who hasn't fought. Or I will kill them all."

"NO! I forbid it Aisha," Rhiannon shouted, tears forming in her eyes. "I need you."

"I am a Talon like the others, Rhiannon. You can't forbid it. It is my duty. Besides, could you live with five women being killed when I could have saved them?" It sounded harsh, but I was mad. I had seen four of my brothers killed and several seriously hurt.

"How do you know she won't kill you?" Rhiannon asked

"Because, she is a coward. A coward doesn't have the ability to kill me in a fair fight." She was a coward, as were her friends, but they were Talon trained.

Rhiannon stood and said nothing until a woman screamed and a finger was tossed out, bouncing down the stairs, leaving a trail of blood drops.

"Please live, Aisha. I do need you," Rhiannon said and turned to walk away. I gently stopped her with a hand.

"Hi'Lady Rhiannon, emotions kill. I want you to hold my hate, my anger, and thoughts of revenge. Will you do that for me?"

"Yes, I will hold them in my heart, Aisha."

But as I turned toward the ring, Tafadzwa stopped me with a hand on my shoulder. Our eyes met, but he just nodded, squeezing my shoulder.

"Bring the women down. I will fight you." I emptied myself and prepared.

A tall dark woman in Eagle garb appeared leading five women, one with her hand wrapped. They were quickly taken and led away. The Eagle too had a strong War Sigil. I invoked my sigil as I entered the ring, my world expanding. I heard her taunts but not the words, saw every ripple of her body as she, and I moved with the ease of the wind. No hate, no anger, only the fight. Her knifes weaved in the same pattern as the man who fought Bakaar. I knew the pattern and where it was going. Chest, neck, chest. I took the first cut to my chest and then a deep cut to

191

my arm as I rolled out of the way and came up under her guard, one knife slashing her from just under her chest to her groin the other opening the artery on the inside of her thigh. Before she could respond, I scissored her legs throwing her to fall to the side, and I was on my feet. She was still alive, but she did not attempt to get up. Blood pooled under her.

"You bitch." She muttered her last words.

CHAPTER TWENTY ONE

Dassel: Life can be complicated

I woke to a knock at the door. "Enter," I said, assuming it was the healer, Lesedi, who had insisted I needed rest. The knife cut deep, and I had lost a fair amount of blood. I hated being incapacitated, but even Talons needed rest. Bakaar and Jiang had been seriously injured yesterday and would need several day's rest.

To my surprise, fir', no, hi'Lord Tafadzwa entered. I spent years among men and never felt embarrassed being half dressed or being seen in a nightshirt. Now I did. My cheeks flamed as he approached. I restrained myself from making it worse by grasping at the blanket.

"Good morn, Aisha Talon. You look better today." He stood beside my bed, smiling down at me.

"Good morn, hi'Lord Tafadzwa." *Why do I feel so awkward?* I wondered. *Maybe because he is a very good looking man. Tall, lean and muscular, a strong face...stop it!*

"Are you all right?" He took my hand and sat beside me on the edge of my bed.

No I'm not all right. I'm confused. His hand holding mine made my skin tingle all the way up my arm, and my face felt flushed again. *I must be sick; I'm running a fever.*

"You are very lovely, Aisha. Especially in the morning with the early morning light on your face and the color in your cheeks." Tafadzwa ran his hand across my cheek to brush back my hair.

I couldn't think what to say. My mind focused on his hands and the growing heat in my body. *Where is all my control? Gone!* He cupped his hands around my face and bent over to touch his lips to mine, gently at first, but grew demanding. My head was on fire, the warmth creeping down my body. I put my arms around his neck and returned his kiss, my lips parting under his.

193

"Ouch," Tafadzwa moaned as the knives strapped under my breasts dug into his chest, but he didn't move away. I reach behind me and released the harness without releasing his wonderful, sensuous mouth. I guessed it was too late to cut his beautiful throat. I giggled.

His hand slid down, cupping my breast. I lost myself in wave after wave of heat. I was a woman, I mused, as Tafadzwa's kiss deepened. Until now, I had never really considered myself a woman and the others males. We were just Talons.

I sighed when his kisses stopped. Then his breath tickled my ear.

"Marry me, my sweet warrior. Be hi'Lady of Valda."

"Marry?" I squeaked as I shot upward, pain shooting through my injured arm. "I can't."

"Can't or won't?"

"Can't. I'm Clan, I'm under contract, I'm…." words failed me. *Marry. Hi'Lady.* My head was exploding.

"I think I have loved you from the first time we met, Aisha." Tafadzwa slid his arms around my waist and pulled me against him. It was unfair; I had trouble enough thinking without him cheating by holding me. "Don't Clan members get married?"

"Most don't, but some do. But they must still fulfill contracts for the Clan and can't always take their wives. Besides, I'm under contract to hi'Lady Rhiannon." I began to come back to cold reality.

"Yes, I will have to work on my sister, Rhiannon. I may also have to challenge Master Dragos for your hand. But those are minor problems to overcome."

"Challenging Master Dragos would be a terrible idea." I would normally have laughed at the thought, but Tafadzwa' death wasn't funny. "Don't even think such a thing. It is impossible."

"Difficult maybe, but not impossible--"

A knock at the door jerked us both around to face the door. "Who is it?" I asked while he jumped up.

"Rhiannon."

"One moment please, hi'Lady." Tafadzwa took a deep breath before he opened the door.

194

"Good morn, sister Rhiannon. You look well rested, and you brought food. How thoughtful." Tafadzwa sounded pleased with himself and the world.

"Good morn, brother Tafadzwa. You look to be in particularly good spirits. I think my bodyguard is in need of a chaperone." Rhiannon scrutinized Tafadzwa and then, me. "Will you break fast with us, brother? You look hungry, and Lesedi said Aisha needed food to rebuild her strength."

"Thank you, Rhiannon. But I'm afraid I've given your bodyguard a very bad headache." The servants began laying out the food. "She insists on honoring her contract to you, although I suspect it is as much out of affection as duty. She insists on remaining Clan, again, out of devotion rather than honor. And she refuses to marry me, although she loves me." Tafadzwa explained as if he spoke his thoughts out loud rather than talking to us.

"I didn't say that I love you," I squeaked. "And I am Clan. It has nothing to do with devotion. I remain Clan until the day that I die."

"Marry?" Rhiannon blurted.

Tafadzwa tilted his head and looked at me for a long moment before he answered her. "Yes, I've asked her to be hi'Lady of Valda. She has refused for the reasons I just stated, but that doesn't mean I'm giving up."

"You've turned Tafadzwa down to stay with me?" Rhiannon asked in disbelief.

"No, hi'Lady Rhiannon. I am committed to you and will not abandon you. But I am also Clan. It is who I am. Would you wish the same fate on me as the Eagles?" Reality intruded on the illusion.

"Well, I think I shall go see how Master Jiang is doing and issue my challenge to Master Dragos." Tafadzwa rose to leave, but he looked thoughtful.

"Tafadzwa!" I exclaimed, not sure if he was serious. "Don't! He will kill you."

"Since you asked, I won't challenge him, for now." Tafadzwa strode out of the room, with a smirk on his face.

"Goddess. Knife fighting and war is easier than dealing with a determined man." I buried my head in my hands.

"Let's eat, Aisha. Maybe food will help."

* * * *

Lesedi appeared just after the servants had cleared away the food. Rhiannon and I sipped a frothy fruit drink. "Hi'Lady Rhiannon, I need to check on Aisha Talon," she said. I idly wondered what it would be like to be deferred to like that. *By the goddess, Tafadzwa has me actually thinking about being addressed as hi'Lady.*

"Good, I'm as interested as you since Aisha is my bodyguard. I hope she hasn't been overly active." Rhiannon grinned in my direction.

"Aisha, how are you feeling?" Lesedi asked, examining my arm and then my chest. "You look a little flushed, but your arm and chest seem to be healing well. Your temperature feels normal."

She felt my head before adding, "It will be a week or more until we can remove the stitches. You must keep my poultices on the wounds for the next couple of days."

"How long before she can travel, Healer Lesedi?" Rhiannon asked.

"A couple of days, I should think."

"How are Master Jiang and Bakaar Talon?" I asked. I knew they were far more seriously injured than I was.

"Both will recover from their wounds. However, it will be several days before they can be up and around."

"Hi'Lady, I would like to visit them, if you don't mind." I hoped she wouldn't insist I stay in my room.

"Of course, Aisha. You must be concerned for your brothers. I will join you, in case you need help or a chaperone." Rhiannon blushed at what she let slip, and we both laughed.

* * * *

"Good morn, hi'Lady Rhiannon," Jiang said. "Sister Aisha, you look well. I had an interesting talk with hi'Lord Tafadzwa. I understand you are betrothed to the hi'Lord." His lips twitched into a grin totally out of character.

"No! I hardly even know him! I mean..." I broke off. This love stuff was very confusing. Being a Talon was much easier.

"I don't hear your usual decisive tone, Aisha," Jiang said, and this time he laughed, though it ended in a coughing spasm. "I am confident you will find the right answer in time, Sister Raptor. I know marriage is a difficult subject for Talons. But I trust you to make an honorable decision, one that we can all live with. For now, hi'Lady Rhiannon and you must take the army north to Savona."

"We should wait for you to heal, Master Jiang. I can't advise the army." I fought all the conflicting demands on me and tried to see a clear path in the right direction.

"It will be weeks before I can travel, and, even then, I would slow you down. Hi'Radulf slipped out of Dassel while we fought. Anton thinks he assembled 100 troops and headed to Savona, where he has another 100." Jiang paused. "I sent word to Master Dragos to meet you at Terni. By now, he will have about 90 Talons assembled. Hi'Lord Tafadzwa will keep three hundred warriors here in Dassel, but will send two hundred Jaddahans with hi'Lady Rhiannon, plus the Granyans. With Master Dragos' Talons, and the additional Granyans you will pick up on the way, you will lead an army twice that of sec'Tadzio and hi'Radulf."

"But they have the castle at Savona," Rhiannon said.

"And you have the Talons and the support of your people, hi'Lady Rhiannon. Those are two powerful advantages." Jiang stopped to cough before continuing. "Anton Talon will share command with you Aisha, at hi'Lady Rhiannon's pleasure."

"That is most acceptable, Master Jiang. I will be sorry to lose your council. I look forward to seeing you well at Savona castle in the near future."

"Thank you, hi'Lady Rhiannon. I will attend your coronation."

* * * *

The next day, Anton and I went over our anticipated route, stops, and timing. Anton estimated nine days to Livorno and another five days to Terni and another four to Savona. Then we spent another hour going over our strategies.

When I stepped out the door into the corridor, I found one of Tafadzwa's warriors waiting for me with a carefully bland look on this face. "Aisha Talon, hi'Lord Tafadzwa awaits you in the east garden to join him for the midday meal." I raised an eyebrow but followed him without a word.

He ushered me down the stairs and out a narrow doorway into a well-tended garden, a sparkling fountain centered in the swath of grass amid a few blossoming fruit trees. For the first time since we had joined our forces he was not armed, but wore dark blue trousers and a soft belted shirt. A table was set under one of the flowering trees.

He smiled when he saw me, and I couldn't help but return it. He held out a hand. "I think we should talk, Aisha."

I hesitated before I let him take my hand. He rubbed his fingers back and forth across my palm as he looked down at it. When he finally looked up, he had a slightly abashed look on his face. "I rushed you too much, yesterday. I know I did."

I couldn't help the way my lips twitched into a smile. "A little. I'm not used to a man kissing me or wanting to marry me."

As our eyes met, we both relaxed with nothing to say until he raised my palm to his lips. "I'm sorry. I'm used to getting my way, you know, but that's a habit I'm sure you can cure me of—if you will."

I reached up to brush my lips across his. "Master Jiang said that perhaps there is an honorable solution." Then I forgot what I was going to say as he pulled me against him in a long kiss.

When he released me, he beamed, laughed, and motioned toward the table. "The Healer Lesedi says you must eat to get your strength back."

We left two days later. I was anxious to get on the road, but I hated leaving Tafadzwa. We spent as much time as we could together, and every minute was wonderful. I managed to forget about everything except being with Tafadzwa and learning about him and his country. I could envision myself being his wife but not how we could work such a thing out.

"Remember, my sweet warrior, you are committed to me," Tafadzwa said just before we left.

"I will remember, my love. And you, when those ladies chase you, that my knives are sharp." Actually, I wished him happiness above all else.

"Sister Aisha, it must be hard leaving," Anton commented as we rode side by side next to Rhiannon.

"Are you married, Master Anton?" I had never wondered before.

"No, most Talons take their pleasure where they can find it. Few marry. We tend to move a lot, which makes for poor marriages. Your problem is far more complicated, Sister."

"One problem at a time. Savona first." I forced my attention to the war and pushed away thoughts and feelings I couldn't resolve now, maybe not ever.

"Hi'Lady," I said, "we don't want to delay your return too much. But I suggest you spend some time in each village we pass, talking with the people. It should pay off later, and you may pick up additional volunteers for your army."

"I agree, hi'Lady Rhiannon. Your people will help if you ask." Anton added.

* * * *

For the next eight days, we sweat without relief in the saddle under the hot summer sun, faced uncomfortable nights, ate basic meals, and stopped at every village to talk with the people. True to Anton's word, we added 40 soldiers, more than half with experience. We arrived in Livorno on the afternoon of the ninth day.

Lucjan greeted us. "Greetings, hi'Lady Rhiannon. I am pleased to see you looking well. The rumors are flying everywhere, but everyone seems to agree you won at Dassel." Lucjan served us a very lavish mid-day meal, during which, Rhiannon brought him up to date on the events at Dassel and Radulf's escape.

"We believe he and his army is heading back to Savona," Rhiannon said.

"I doubt hi'Radulf could have taken the castle with only 100 men, at least not without a very long siege. But I'm glad he chose to pass us by. My strength is now up to 80. I've managed to recruit another 55 men, many with experience, while you've been gone. Do you need reinforcements, hi'Lady? I can spare, at least, half of my garrison."

"Aisha, Anton, what do you think?" Rhiannon asked.

I looked to Anton who nodded for me to continue. I wasn't sure if everyone deferred to me because I had somehow become Rhiannon's advisor, because she trusted me, or I was being tested. Maybe all of those reasons.

"Sec'Lord Lucjan, I think you should send a token force, say twenty-five, as your support and commitment to the hi'Lady, so that the people of Livorno can take pride they participated in the overthrow of sec'Tadzio and hi'Radulf." I looked back and forward between Lucjan and Rhiannon. Both nodded.

"I will make sure you have my best twenty-five, my hi'Lady, and with your permission, I will lead them."

We stayed two days, which allowed Rhiannon some rest. She took time and visited the town. I went on alert for trouble but none occurred. The people loved her easy going style and the fact she seemed to care about them.

At night, I lay awake, trying not to think about Tafadzwa. I succeeded in putting him out of my mind when I was awake, but I would wake up knowing I had dreamed about him.

* * * *

We arrived in Terni late in the evening, a day earlier than we had planned. You could feel the rising excitement in the troops as we came closer to Savona. You would have thought the Jaddahans were going to a party, not a battle. As Master Jiang had predicted, Master Dragos and ninety Talons awaited us inside the gate. The castle hummed with activity. "Greeting hi'Lady Rhiannon. I see my sister has managed to keep you alive."

"It's keeping her alive that has been the problem over the past few weeks, Master Dragos." Rhiannon's quip surprised me. "But yes, she and your Talons have kept me safe. I owe you my thanks. I will not forget your help in returning order to my lands."

"We have a mutual interest. If we would have had advance notice that hi'Radulf had escaped the battle at Dassel, he would be dead now. Unfortunately, the Talon patrol that encountered his retreating army was insufficient to stop them. There were only nine in the patrol, a poor excuse, but…. They killed 30 and wounded many others."

"I would like to give everyone the chance to freshen up, and then perhaps you, your council, and my war council could meet to discuss Savona, Master Dragos?" I had to admire my charge. Master Dragos could intimidate almost anyone, yet Rhiannon seemed at ease with him.

* * * *

We met two hours later over an elaborate meal of roasted meats and honey-basted vegetables in a small dining room. The troops ate in the larger reception hall, normally reserved for royalty. The war council included Master Dragos and four Talon Masters, three of which met at Dahab for my review, Master Anton, Rhiannon, Awotwi, Lucjan, Sevin, who is the ranking noble at Terni, and me.

Rhiannon and I spent the first hour detailing what had happened since we left Dahab, except for my growing love affair with Tafadzwa.

"The war has gone well," Dragos said. "Sister Aisha's assumptions and unorthodox strategy has proven effective and even decisive. No one could have anticipated Salda's unexpected attack. The Raptor Clan is pleased with you, Aisha. You have served hi'Lady Rhiannon and your Clan well." Dragos both astonished and embarrassed me, but surprises happened a lot lately, not that it changed anything or made my life any simpler.

"The question is how do you recommend we precede now, Master Dragos?" Rhiannon asked.

"You command an overwhelming force, hi'Lady," Dragos said. "However, sec'Tadzio and hi'Radulf hide behind a massive stone structure, and that equalizes the sides. So far, you have won by outwitting your enemy. I would suggest you continue that strategy."

In the end, it was decided that breaching the city gate would be easy, but taking the castle would not.

CHAPTER TWENTY TWO

Savona: A kingdom liberated

We departed Terni with an additional one hundred Talons, forming an army of approximately 500 Granyans, Jaddahans and Talons. Moving such a large army required twice the time of a smaller force, so it took seven days to reach the outskirts of Savona. Each night we reorganized the units and their leaders, met the commanders, and discussed the strengths and weaknesses of each unit. By the time we reached Savona, we were an army, not a collection of guards. On our arrival we made contact with the five Talon scouts Master Dragos had sent ahead.

"Hi'Lady, Master Dragos," the lead Talon scout reported, "the city is wide open. Sec'Tadzio occupies the castle with 100 remaining fighters. The reaction to the rumors that hi'Lady Rhiannon survived is mixed. Most favor her return. Sec'Tadzio faces trouble maintaining control with so few troops, and he can't depend on the city guard, who favor hi'Lady Rhiannon or just hate sec'Tadzio."

"What happened to hi'Radulf and his forces?" Rhiannon asked the question on everyone's mind. I had hoped we finally had Tadzio and the hi'Lord caged. Master Jiang was right. Plans seldom survived contact with the enemy, under no obligation to cooperate.

"Hi'Radulf arrived here six days ago, stayed four nights, and left with all of the Valdan guards, less than two hundred."

"We didn't pass him on the way here, so he headed east." I thought out loud as panic swiped at me. "He probably kept 200 at the eastern Valdan towns of Borkum and Adorf. Added to the force with him, he has a substantial army and will challenge hi'Tafadzwa, especially since he hasn't had a chance to win the support of the Dassel citizens."

"Yes, a logical conclusion," Dragos said. "He has a three day head start. However, following the East Mystic River is slower by a good twenty-five days. We should be able to make the same trip along the West Mystic River in fourteen days. The roads are better and the distance, shorter to Dassel. We have time to take Savona and arrive at Dassel before him."

Dragos turned to Lucjan and Anton. "Anton, take ten Talons and make sure that the gates stay open when we advance on the city. I'll give you two hours to get into position. The Talons and the Granyan guards will move in two hours. Fir'Warrior Awotwi, you will follow in four hours. By then the city will be secured. We don't want to alarm the city with Jaddahans, especially since sec'Tadzio accused the Jaddah raiders of killing hi'Varius."

"What about me?" Rhiannon asked.

"I would like you to ride in with the Talons and the Granyans. We need to parade you through the streets to make sure the citizens of Savona know the rumors of your death are false. They must see you, and that you have returned to claim your rightful place as hi'Lady."

I felt a little let down with Master Dragos directing everything, yet relieved. My duty was simple, protect Rhiannon. There shouldn't be any problem in Savona but one never knew. It would take just one young mixed-up noble who thinks he knows what is right to cause a disaster.

Two hours later, Dragos signaled for the Talons and Granyans to mount up. Minutes later, we moved toward the city walls, which could stop an army larger than ours. But Lord Tadzio didn't have enough troops to man them, so the Talons would easily hold the gate open. Dragos let the Granyans lead the march, Rhiannon, safely towards the back with Talons surrounding her. I approved.

We reached the gate in fifteen minutes with no sign of fighting at the gate. Entering the city at a leisurely pace, the people expecting us crowded the sides of the street, although they were neither hostile nor exuberant as we walked our horses through the town's main streets. Rhiannon waved as we proceeded towards the castle. As she was recognized, the people began chanting her name.

"It's the hi'Lord Varius's daughter. She's alive. The goddess bless you hi'Lady Rhiannon. Long live hi'Lady Rhiannon...." I continuously scanned the crowds but saw no hostile moves. They seemed surprised and pleased that Rhiannon had survived. I doubted that Tadzio would feel the same.

When we arrived at the castle wall, the gates were closed, probably had been closed all along. We kept Rhiannon well back out of archer range but in plain sight as I rode forward.

"Guards of Granya, I am Aisha, pri'Rhiannon's chaperone who accompanied her and her father, hi'Lord Varius, on the trip to Valda with the expectation of forming an alliance with hi'Lord Radulf." I paused and took a sip of water. "As you know by now, hi'Radulf with sec'Tadzio attacked and killed hi'Varius, his guards, the cooks and servants, and the Talons. His daughter, now hi'Lady Rhiannon, survived. She has returned to claim her throne with the support of the Granyans, Jaddahans, and Talons. You have twelve hours to decide who you will support. Hi'Lady Rhiannon has two hundred Talons, in addition to hundreds of Granyan and Jaddah warriors supporting her claim. You will not survive one day. Twelve hours, no more." I turned and rode back to Rhiannon.

"Do you think that will help, Aisha?" Rhiannon asked.

"Yes, those guards are mostly commoners who have nothing to gain by fighting. And they will lose their lives if we storm the castle. The nobles have land and property to lose but not the common soldier. Besides, I doubt sec'Tadzio solicits the same loyalty as you or your late father. If only ten or twenty defect, it will be chaos." As I said this, I realized it was true. The common guards were not Talons who cherished duty above all else.

We turned back from the castle into the city to an elegant inn where the Talons had secured the entire upper floor, so the hi'Lady and her war council could rest and eat in safety. One of the largest rooms had been cleared of the bed and set with a table so we could eat in comfort. Plush padded carpets decorated the floor and elegant silk curtains offset the whitewashed walls. I felt uneasy when Rhiannon frequented the window and pulled the curtains back to look out. I knew an archer wasn't likely, but I was nervous and worried.

Rhiannon watched as sunset stained the western sky. "Aisha, Talons are leaving towards the castle."

"They have been slowly filtering into the city and around the castle for hours, hi'Rhiannon."

"But Master Dragos.... You gave them twelve hours to decide." Rhiannon frowned.

"Hi' Lady, as your advisor I tell you there are no rules in war. The object is to win. The winners are the ones who survive. Sec'Tadzio tried to poison you, and hi'Radulf attacked you without warning or provocation." I paused until she nodded. "If there are men in the castle who would act for any reason, loyalty or to save their own lives, they will act under cover of night. We must have people in place to support them. Our best chance to slip into the palace is while they believe they have twelve hours to plan."

"I need you, Aisha Talon. I'm not ready to rule a castle, much less a kingdom. I need someone who will tell me the truth even when I don't want to hear it. Someone who will tell me when I'm wrong." Rhiannon kissed me on the cheek. "I know I'm asking a lot."

"You have come a long way in a short time, hi'Rhiannon. You don't have to take anyone's advice now that you are hi'Lady, but don't ever forget to listen and you will be a good ruler." I wondered when I had become so wise.

"Leszek, get everyone up and ready." I felt something would happen soon, and I wanted to be prepared.

"We're ready, Sister Aisha," Leszek said. We went downstairs. Rhiannon's guards surrounded us so we could proceed to the castle. Fighting broke out around the gate within half an hour. I knew that grappling hooks hit the walls. One Talon would scale the rope while two stood below with bows notched and ready to fire if anyone appeared above. Normally the tactic would be suicide, but the distraction at the gate and the few guards in the castle made it work. Several would reach the parapets. When that happened, it was all over. In the meantime the Granyans moved to just out of bowshot to go through the gate as soon as it was opened from inside.

In the night, a quarter moon lighting the sky, we stood in the dark well out of bow range of the walls but within sight of the huge gates. I couldn't see the Talons climbing, but knew they must be doing as planned from the lack of shouts or fighting.

The attack came from behind us. In the moonlight, I saw a party of nobles running straight at us.

Leszek moved to the opposite side of Rhiannon so that we sheltered her between us. I drew my sword and held a knife in my off-hand as he did the same. Between the attackers and us, the eight Talon guards silently cut them down. Everyone was on foot, which had allowed the attackers to close in without being seen. The Talons charged into the guards. Several of them lay on the ground, but eventually one would get through.

A young noble jumped over the body of one of his fallen guards, his five men following behind. "Kill the girl!" He charged straight for her. I was about to throw my knife at him when the Sergeant, running beside him, spun around to slice through the noble's neck. The Sergeant stopped along with the four others beside him and dropped to his knees. Two others dropped their weapons. "Hi'Lady Rhiannon, we served this worthless traitor because we thought you were dead. We pledge our lives to you." The Sergeant bowed his head.

When I looked around, a second noble was lying dead, his arm severed at the elbow and only a couple of other attackers injured. They hadn't fought very hard, in fact, held back.

"Your name, Sergeant?" Rhiannon asked to my amazement.

"Sergeant Indar, hi'Lady."

"Well, Sergeant, will you join the fight to free the castle?"

"Yes, hi'Lady Rhiannon." He rose and waved to his men to follow him towards the castle.

"Now I've seen it all, Sister Aisha," Leszek said as he shook his head. "This is the strangest fight I've ever participated in. Nobody is going to believe me when I tell them."

"Well hi'Rhiannon, it is obvious that the people support your claim. I'll bet most of the guards in the castle surrender." Leszek was right. It was a strange night.

The castle was secured within just minutes after a group of 20 guards opened the gates and they dropped their weapons immediately. Another forty surrendered within minutes and the remaining 40 were dispatched within an hour. Tadzio was captured alive by two Talons, who disarmed him with ease.

Surrounded by her Talon guard, for the first time in months, Rhiannon entered her home. Walking through the corridors usually so full of bustling functionaries and nobles seemed strange. I told Rhiannon to wait while we sent guards ahead to be sure that no supporters of sec'Tadzio lurked anywhere inside.

Rhiannon stood quietly talking to Awotwi as we waited for a report that the castle was clear when a captain rushed in. "Hi'Lady, we found a young woman in one of the upper dungeons. She claims to be Master Healer Luminita, and she has a small boy with her. She's asking to see you."

Rhiannon jumped up and laughed. "Captain, escort the lady and her child here, and find Leszek Talon. Tell him I want to see him."

Five minutes later Leszek arrived. "You wanted to see me, hi'Lady?" he asked. Confusion painted his face. Rhiannon merely raised her hand and indicated he should wait. Five minutes later the Captain arrived with Master Healer Luminita and her son.

Leszek froze as his son darted to him, grabbing him around the leg. "Daddy, Daddy," the adorable dark-eyed boy cried. Leszek grabbed Luminita's shoulders, looking her up and down. She was thin, her healer robes, rumpled and dirty. Luminita reached up to cup his face and said nothing for a few minutes, but kissed him soundly on the lips.

"Pardon me, hi'Lady Rhiannon." Luminita released Leszek from her embrace. "I had to convince myself he was alive and well. When they said the caravan had been attacked and you were killed, I knew my Talon husband would have died to protect you." Her eyes welled, but a smile brightened her face.

Leszek picked his son up, running a hand over the boy's back, and then he put his arm around Luminita's shoulder, leaning his cheek against her head.

"I am glad to see my healer is safe and back where she belongs," Rhiannon said, "with me. Leszek, perhaps my Master Healer should examine you to make sure you are fit to accompany us to Dassel. You are free until we leave."

Leszek had said nothing and remained speechless as Luminita led him and their son, clinging to his father's neck, out the door.

Rhiannon and I exchanged a look as they left, her eyes sparkling with joy.

* * * *

The next morning Rhiannon sat on the throne that had been her father's. Talons lined both sides of the room, swords and knives drawn. Awotwi stood to her left and me, on her right. I surveyed the audience. The room was crowded. The Granyan guards had admitted 100 merchants and business owners, from a tax list found in Minister Lucas' office, and the first 50 commoners waiting at the castle gate.

Granyan guards ringed the walls. Ex-lord Tadzio stood in shackles at the bottom of the platform. His face was pinched, his clothes, wrinkled, soiled, and torn in a few places. He had spent the night in the dungeon, guarded by Talons. Master Dragos wasn't sure whether a Granyan would try to save him or kill him, so he set Talons to guard him. Two other nobles had survived the fighting along with Minister Lucas, who was determined to have supported ex-Lord Tadzio's attempt to seize the throne.

Rhiannon stood. The noise in the room died.

"Citizens of Granya, sec'Tadzio, in consort with other nobles, plotted the overthrow of my father, hi'Lord Varius. They began with the assassination of my mother, hi'Lady Varius, my older sister, and my younger brother. They subsequently tried to poison me. And in desperation, they formed an alliance with hi'Radulf, who crossed into Granya with five hundred troops and murdered hi'Varius and over a hundred guards and civilians. I escaped. I have formed an alliance with Jaddah and together we have freed Savona, Terni, and Livorno. We have taken the city of Dassel. Know that the Jaddah are not only our allies but also our friends. Fir'Warrior Awotwi, son of hi'Baqir, stands at my left hand in witness and as my betrothed. Without his help and his father's, Granya would be in the hands of killers who would hand Granya over to the Valdans. And, if it were not for the Talons, I would be dead."

She paused to let all of that sink in, looking into the faces one by one around her before she continued. "Tomorrow at dawn, sec'Tadzio will be hanged in the public square for his crimes against Granya."

* * * *

The war council convened around the dinner table after the servants had cleared away the dishes.

"Hi'Radulf must be pursued immediately," I said. "If we don't, he will be free to build an army and will challenge either Granya or Valda again."

"Do you have a special interest in protecting Valda?" Lucjan, who led the Granyans against the castle, asked. "I hear that you and hi'Lord Tafadzwa are betrothed."

"The rumor is true but meaningless. Everyone here has a reason to pursue hi'Radulf. The Granyans, because he killed the hi'Rhiannon's father. The Jaddahans, because the hi'Baqir's son is now hi'Lord. The Raptor Clan, because he broke his contract with us and killed Talons. If that were not enough, the Jaddahans were the first to provide armed support to free Granya and hi'Rhiannon is betrothed to the son of hi'Baqir. The longer we wait, the more costly the bill." I looked around the room daring anyone to dispute my reasoning.

"Aisha," Master Dragos said, "I leave you and Master Anton in charge of pursuing and killing hi'Lord Radulf. The older masters and I are returning to the Aerie. War is for the young. We would slow you down. Besides, you have done well without us."

"I want Aisha Talon to stay with me," Rhiannon said, frowning with determination.

"She is under contract to you, so it is your decision." Dragos looked at me. I said nothing, although I felt a knot in my stomach.

"Master Dragos, I would like to negotiate a contract with you," Rhiannon said, "today."

"For Aisha? You already have a contract for her. Do you want to lengthen it?"

"I want to negotiate Talons for Granya, Valda, and Jaddah." Rhiannon cracked a slight smile as her eyes twinkled. "And include Aisha."

Everyone took the hint and departed except for Master Dragos, Anton, two other masters, Rhiannon and me. I started to

209

leave, but Rhiannon held up her hand to stop me. "Master Dragos, I would like Aisha, my advisor, to stay. I understand she can't negotiate with you or advise me on negotiating with you, but she can help me determine my needs."

"That is acceptable, hi'Lady," Dragos replied as a small laugh emerged. "Master Jiang and hi'Blessed Tasilaba were right about you, hi'Blessed Aisha. You were the right choice."

"Hi'Blessed Aisha? But she has no sigil tattoos." Rhiannon's eyes grew wide as she shook her head before my face.

"I know, but hi'Blessed Tasilaba called her hi'Blessed. Neither would explain. Another mystery about our sister, Aisha."

"She obviously isn't going to explain it to either of us. Never mind. I want sixty Talons and Aisha Talon." No one in the room, including me, could believe the number.

Eventually Master Dragos asked, "For how long, hi'Lady?"

"A hundred years." The room went silent as the Talon masters looked at each other in disbelief. "And I want the number of women Talons increased."

"And who is going to pay for this?" one of the masters asked.

"The contract will be with me. I believe the hi'Lords of Jaddah and Valda will share the cost, but I will be responsible for payment even if they don't. You may rotate Talons at your discretion, except for Aisha."

"That would not be fair to Aisha. Rotations are to give the Talons time to rest and recuperate," Dragos replied.

"Aisha is my bodyguard, advisor, and…sister. I will take care of her needs… and my future brother." Rhiannon bit her lip as she tried to hide a grin.

"How are we to ensure that we can provide you with "more" women Talons. Few women apply and fewer survive the Ordeals?" Master Dragos asked. Rhiannon looked to me. I sat there in silence for what seemed hours, in reality, minutes, with everyone staring at me.

"Well, hi'Blessed Aisha?" Rhiannon asked.

"I think few apply because they know they aren't wanted and aren't expected to survive. I know because I have heard the stories about how Bakaar struggled to be accepted. I would have never applied if I hadn't been desperate. If you try to recruit more women and accept them once they are recruited, more will apply and that will mean that more will survive the Ordeals."

The negotiations went on for five hours. Rhiannon had drinks served but would not stop until the contract was completed.

"You are a hard bargainer, hi'Lady. Did you learn from your father?"

"No, from my advisor. She usually proposes first death as a negotiating position. I thought I'd try first exhaustion."

"It worked," said Dragos.

After everyone had left, Rhiannon looked at me long and hard. "You need to make arrangements for us to leave tomorrow. We are going to Dassel."

"Why?" I was so confused.

"You were a terrible chaperone. You refused me the respect I thought I deserved, but you protected me with your life. You are a terrible advisor, telling me the truth and forcing me to make difficult decisions. And you are a terrible tutor, teaching me duty." Rhiannon paused to smile. "I owe hi'Lord Baqir and his sons my kingdom. How can I sit in this warm, comfortable, castle in luxury when my brother is in need? I can't fight, but I can show my support by being there. And I can take my army to support him."

CHAPTER TWENTY THREE

Race to Dassel: Usurper killed, peace restored

"I wish I were going with you, hi'Lady," Lucjan said as, we prepared to leave the castle. The army was mounted and ready to move as soon as Rhiannon gave the signal.

"I need someone I trust to remain and rule the city, let the citizens feel things are back to normal, get things running again. The people need to know that they are safe, sec'Lucjan. Hopefully, we won't be too long finding and destroying hi'Radulf and his army." Rhiannon looked to me, her signal to leave. I raised my hand to Anton who ordered the army forward.

Anton and I had advised Rhiannon to keep a large contingent of Granyan guards and to recruit more. The war reduced the army to less than a quarter. Although Granya now had allies, soon to be family, on all her borders. At full strength the army's presence would preclude nobles who would challenge Rhiannon's reign. Her recent contract with the Raptor Clan should discourage adversaries.

Rhiannon led a procession of 200 Granyan soldiers and 100 Talons through the city. Crowds lined the winding streets, cheered and waved at hi'Lady Rhiannon as she passed. Tadzio still hung from the gallows in the town square, as did three other nobles and Minster Lucas. They would remain for a time, a sobering reminder of the potential consequences for those who would rise up against the hi'Lord or hi'Lady.

Soon we passed the city walls and joined Awotwi and his Jaddahan army. Awotwi rode beside Rhiannon as the Jaddahans took the lead on the road to Terni. I was glad to see them talking as they rode, smiling at each other, happy in each other's company.

We traveled from sunrise to sunset and reached Terni late on the second night. We lodged two nights, so the horses could rest. Another two days' travel, we reached Livorno, and stayed two nights. At each city Rhiannon walked through the town in the daytime and talked with the citizens. Everyone seemed genuinely pleased with the new hi'Lady.

The ride to Dassel strained men and horses. After five days of hard riding, Rhiannon was exhausted, but she didn't complain. She spent each evening talking with the warriors of Granyan, Jaddahan, and Talons. I had no doubt that by the time we reached Dassel, she would lead an army who would die for her. Even the emotionless Talons were in love with her. I know I was.

"Welcome, Rhiannon, my sister. It is always a pleasure to see you." Tafadzwa greeted hi'Rhiannon as we rode into the castle courtyard.

"I suspect you are happy to see me," Rhiannon quipped with a sly smile, "because my advisor is along, my future brother. But never mind, it is nice to be among family. I hope in the future we will be frequent visitors, just for the joy of being with family and among friends."

"Yes, I too look forward to that day. Is that not right, Awotwi, my warrior brother?"

"Yes, Tafadzwa. I am a lucky warrior." He looked at Rhiannon and seemed genuinely happy.

"My betrothed, it has been a long time." Tafadzwa smiled and took my hand.

"It has only been a few weeks," I said. Actually, it seemed like we only left yesterday.

"But it has seemed like years." Tafadzwa helped me down from my horse. I felt foolish, a Talon being helped off a horse, yet giddy, held in his strong arms. He took my hand as he turned towards the commanders. "You all look tired. I have had your rooms prepared for you. We can talk after you have refreshed yourselves."

"I must go with hi'Lady Rhiannon." Tafadzwa didn't release my hand.

"Your room is mine. She does not need you to help her freshen up. My mother and sister will look after her. Father has sent another hundred troops to me along with my mother and two sisters. Mother is looking forward to being formally introduced to you since we are now betrothed." Tafadzwa grinned and I blushed. I had to stop blushing, it wasn't becoming for a Talon.

* * * *

The dinner was typical fare for Jaddah, many small bowls, each with a different dish. I couldn't have named half the food. I remembered his mother from our earlier meeting with Baqir and his family. But this time I wasn't Rhiannon's bodyguard. I was the center of her attention. After all, I would be her son's wife, the mother of her grandchildren.

"You are Talon and trained at the Talon fortress, Aisha?" hi'Lady Sauda asked.

"Yes, Lady. I spent ten years there."

"You had no trouble there among all those men?"

"No, hi'Lady, no trouble." I paused, then added, "No lovers." I knew that was what she wanted to hear. She smiled and nodded in what I saw was approval on her face.

"You are a strong woman and warrior," Sauda said. I thought it was a statement of fact until I realized the hidden question. *What kind of a wife will you make?*

"Yes, I am a warrior, as is Tafadzwa. And I'm a woman. Someday I would like children of my own. You see, I love Tafadzwa as he loves me." The discussion, while somewhat uncomfortable, helped me come to terms with the situation. I didn't know how this was going to work, but I wanted to try. The questions went on for some time, with everyone paying more attention to us than the food.

"Enough, Mother," Tafadzwa said. "You will scare my beloved warrior away with all your questions."

"I doubt that my son. She is not the type to be scared by me...or by you. I like her." Sauda rose to leave. "May Tiamat bless you, Aisha."

Now only the war council remained. "So, now that we have eaten and my mother satisfied her curiosity, what brings you here with such urgency? Savona has been liberated, yes?" Tafadzwa settled back against his cushions.

"Hi'Radulf eluded us in Savona," Anton said, "with 100 troops. He deserted Savona several days before we arrived. Aisha and I believe he is headed for Borkum and Adorf, two

Valdan towns on the East Mystic River, to raise an army. With those garrisons, his new army could number 400 warriors."

"The question, then, is whether he will be content to stay in the east, go back into Granya or attack Dassel." Tafadzwa wrinkled his forehead in thought. "If I were him, I would attack Dassel. He has partial support of the citizens."

"Yes, Anton and I believe that is likely, hi'Lord Tafadzwa," I said. It sounded funny to call him by his title.

"And what do you suggest we do, hi'Lady Aisha?" Tafadzwa mocked me with a new title, mischief in his eyes, and made me blush again. *Damn the man.*

"I say we kill hi'Radulf. That should resolve the situation and give you time to unite the kingdoms under your rule." *He was far too handsome.*

"That would be convenient." Rhiannon blurted. "I mean, he is not alone or seen in public."

"No, but he will have to travel from Borkum or Adorf to Dassel. That will mean they would camp in the Ebowood forest and travel the roads," I said. "His soldiers defend castles and fight with swords. The Jaddah and the Talons are superior with bows and knives."

"So, we assassinate him in his camp or ambush him on the road, employ attacks designed to kill him rather than to destroy his army?" Tafadzwa stroked his jaw in thought.

"Armies tend to be quick to disengage when their leaders are killed," Anton said and laughed. "I will send out scouts tomorrow. The army will move the next day. I will leave 200 with Awotwi and take four hundred. With the Talons and Granyan troops, that will give us over six hundred warriors. just in case the Valdans don't have sense enough to disperse after we kill hi'Radulf."

* * * *

I felt guilty not guarding Rhiannon or at least sleeping in the next room, even though Leszek had Talon guards in the hallway and at the door to her room. We were in the next hallway. I had little time to feel guilty since Tafadzwa kept me wrapped in his arms. Mostly, I was lost in a magical paradise where no evil men lurked and only good, exciting things were allowed to happen. Dawn broke the spell.

215

"Good morn, my love," Tafadzwa whispered in my ear. I must have dozed off because I jerked awake not sure where I was for a moment. Fortunately, my knives lay scattered around the room or Taz wouldn't be laughing.

"Morn, my love," I answered as I relaxed back into his arms.

"Waking you is an exciting way to start the day." He lay back and laughed. I hit him.

* * * *

The rest of the day we prepared the army to leave. Tafadzwa spent it with the Jaddahans. Anton worked with the Talons and formed teams for assassination in the forest. Rhiannon and I spent it arguing about her role and mine.

"If you're going, I'm going." Rhiannon pressed her lips together in determination.

"What purpose would that serve, hi'Lady?" I searched for reason.

"To keep you out of trouble!" She defied reason. "Besides, hi'Radulf killed my father. I want to be there when he dies."

In the end, we both won. Rhiannon was going along and Tafadzwa insisted we stay in his party so I would be close to him. Ironically, my first concern would have to be Rhiannon. With me, Leszek, who had a perpetual smile on his face, and his eight Talons, she would have plenty of protection.

* * * *

We left the next day. Our scouts reported no sign of the Valdan army. We stopped 25 leagues from Dassel and set up our ambush. The roads from Borkum and Adorf merged five leagues down the road. Tafadzwa divided his army, 100 soldiers on the north side of the road, 100 stationed on the south side, and 200 located a league closer to Dassel, in case Radulf's army broke through toward Dassel. Tafadzwa established a command post with the Granyans, which provided a mobile force, if necessary. Anton led the Talons to find Radulf's camp for the attempt at an assassination; the Talons had a blood debt to settle.

Rhiannon and I camped with Tafadzwa's force a half league off the main road. Five days later the scouts rode into camp, jumped off their horses, bowing to hi'Lord Tafadzwa, and reported that Radulf had been sighted on the road from Adorf. His army numbered 400, seen by the scouts with their scouts out about a league down the road and 100 paces into the forest. They expected Radulf's army would make camp tonight about ten leagues short of the merge.

The Talons returned, believing Radulf would make camp tomorrow night, well short of Dassel, to rest his troops. They planned their attack just before dawn. Whether they killed Radulf or not, they would retreat toward Dassel, where they would ambush any pursuers. Anticipating that the hi'Lord would remain at the rear of his army, Tafadzwa split off two hundred troops; he would let the Valdan army pass and close in behind them.

The next night I paced with frustration. My brother Talons prepared to engage our sworn enemies, and I sat in safety, babysitting. That wasn't fair. Rhiannon wasn't a baby, but protecting her was important for Granya, and my duty. And I was close to Taz. But I missed the excitement of the action.

Just as the gray light of dawn approached, we started receiving reports. Anton appeared out of the woods. "Aisha, our brothers hit hi'Radulf's camp an hour ago. We killed about a quarter of his force and retreated. It was a hard retreat, Sister. We lost seven and another ten were wounded. We could have killed more as we retreated but that would have stopped their following us." Dirt-smeared and dripping sweat, Anton wound a cloth around a cut on his arm as he spoke. "Within the next ten minutes, those chasing us should hit the ambush."

"Do you know if you killed hi'Radulf?" I asked. This was Talon business and Tafadzwa stayed out of it. That was good. I loved him, but if we married, I would have Talon business to take care of. He had to understand that.

"He may have been wounded, but he was moving, the last time I saw him. I believe he knows it's a trap and will retreat east to Adorf."

"Good!" Tafadzwa said. "My warriors will cut him off."

An agonizing hour later, a Jaddahan warrior rode in on a lathered horse with news. "Hi'Lord Tafadzwa, we have crushed the Valdan army that chased the Talons. Maybe 200. We killed

150, captured 30, and the rest escaped into the woods. Fir'Warrior Fassi ordered us not to pursue."

"Excellent. Tell fir'Warrior Fassi to hold his position for now," Tafadzwa said. He smiled at Rhiannon. "It is just about over, my future sister."

Three hours later, a large force of Valdan soldiers charged out of the forest from the south, screaming war cries. Radulf rode his big warhorse in the lead and a standard bearer galloped at his side. A second group burst through from northeast. Leszek and I moved in closer to Rhiannon as her guard encircled her. I lost track of "Taz" as I focused on the fighting, watching for anyone breaking through our guards. Radulf had us out-numbered and in the kind of fighting, that gave them an advantage.

We had to hold until we got reinforcements. The guards surrounding us backed their horses closer as Radulf pulled his rearing steed up and motioned his warriors toward us. With Radulf in the lead, a line of them charged. The Talons broke into two lines, four behind. Four dropped from their horses, swords drawn. With no lances or shields, the Talons were out-matched. Leszek and I drew and pulled our bows taking aim at a leading charger. One went down to our arrows then another. The charge hit, and the kneeling Talons rolled under the horses, slashing their bellies and legs.

Horses went down with screams. I couldn't get a shot at Radulf with Talons in the way. I dropped my bow and let my throwing daggers fly. Two daggers flew through the air. Leszek and I picked the same soldier. I nudged my horse ahead of Rhiannon. Radulf rode over one of the Talons, hooves slashing. He ignored me, striking my horse in the neck instead. As my horse went down, I leapt, catching his arm and yanking him off his horse. We both landed on the ground unhurt. He rolled to the side, jumping to his feet almost as fast as I did. We stood facing each other, but then I heard the thunder of horses behind me. Backing up a step, I glanced around. We were surrounded by Jaddah warriors, drawing their bows. I waved them off.

Sword in hand, Radulf smiled. I met his eyes calmly. The time had come for him to pay for the Talons he had killed. I dropped my sword and drew my knives. This was going to be up

218

close and personal. He charged, his sword coming down to split my head in two. I twisted, the sword whistling by my face as I stepped close inside his guard. With a swipe, I cut his throat with my right dagger and stabbed his belly with my left. He fell and cheers rang around us.

Several warriors jumped off their horses, picking up the dead hi'Lord and tying him face down to a horse. "Taz" had ridden up next to Rhiannon while I was fighting Radulf and sat staring at me and shaking his head.

"Hi'Lord Tafadzwa," a warrior said, beside the dead body. "May I present to you your predecessor, ex-hi'Lord Radulf. I'm afraid he can't accept your generous terms of surrender. He's dead." He smiled broadly.

"He antagonized my future wife. I'll have to remember not to," Tafadzwa said. The steely tension faded from his face. Turning to Rhiannon, he said, "Your father's murder is avenged, my sister."

Rhiannon blinked back tears, but managed a shaky smile through them. "The war is over. We have work to do. Rebuilding."

"Celebration first. Then we will think about work."

The ride back to Dassel was glorious. For the first time in months, I felt no strain of miscalculating and losing everything. I had much to look forward to. I was bodyguard and advisor and friend to hi'Lady Rhiannon. I was betrothed to hi'Lord Tafadzwa and in love. Almost drunk with exhilaration, I joined up with Tafadzwa and Rhiannon and we entered the city.

That night Tafadzwa held a feast inside the castle for the senior members of the combined forces and invited influential local merchants and business owners. Rhiannon's Talons stood guard everywhere. I felt out of place sitting with Tafadzwa and Rhiannon. I felt like I should be standing behind her.

"Sister Rhiannon, I can't believe you have contracted twenty Talons for me. I am forever in your debt." Tafadzwa kissed her on both cheeks. "For how long is the contract?"

"100 years," Rhiannon lowered her head shyly with an impish smile.

"What! I sit between two beautiful and dangerous women." He laughed, then rose and the room quieted.

219

"Citizens of Valda, welcome. Today you see me as a conqueror in your lands. I hope that tomorrow you will see me as a just ruler. I am a plain desert man, not interested in the luxuries and excesses of your previous ruler. In addition, trade between Valda, Jaddah, and Granya will be easier, because we are family. My father, as you know, is hi'Lord Baqir and my future sister is hi'Lady Rhiannon." Tafadzwa helped Rhiannon to stand. He then turned to me, and helped me to my shaky feet. "I would like you to meet my future wife, and new hi'Lady, Aisha Talon. The wedding will take place in three days."

I sat in numb silence as hi'Lady Sauda came over and sat next to me.

"We have a lot to do in three days, my daughter Aisha. Fortunately, you have me and my daughter, and Rhiannon to help." I think I nodded affirmatively. *But when I find Taz alone, we will have a long discussion about making decisions and announcing them without talking to me first!* I felt dizzy with shock.

The next fifteen minutes were a blur as people trooped by to congratulate the hi'Lord and me. Someone had arranged entertainment, an illusionist with a powerful Illusion Sigil, who created a beautiful array of flying birds and other creatures. Several dancing girls moved so sleekly, they seemed not to have any bones.

When the illusionist finished, a juggler entered the center of the U-shaped table arrangement. I sensed the presence of a strong War Sigil, which seemed strange for a juggler. Almost automatically, I activated my sigil nullifying his. He was excellent, beginning with plates, then balls, then knives from the table. He had eight in the air when suddenly he caught one drawing his arm back for a throw.

I screamed, "Leszek!" I dived across the table and hit both Taz and Rhiannon in the chest and knocked them backward. When I looked up, the juggler stood with two daggers in his neck and four in his chest. He collapsed as I watched.

I sat up and blinked at the knife in my leg, blood dripping. The pain began to reach me through the shock.

Everyone crouched down, some under the table, others in the process of going after the juggler. The Talons had swords and daggers drawn and scanned the room. Taz picked me up in his arms and turned towards his guests.

"Obviously, our juggler was not as good as he thought. Please stay and finish your dinner. My betrothed needs my attention." He turned to his mother. "We need our healer in my room."

"Is she all right, Tafadzwa?" Rhiannon asked, wide-eyed with fear.

"I'm fine, hi'Lady, or will be, once the healer gets this thing out of me." I gritted my teeth.

"I hope you're not trying to get out of our wedding." Tafadzwa scowled, but I saw the twinkle in his eyes. "Because it won't work."

* * * *

For the next three days I felt like royalty. I almost lived at the seamstress, my long hair trimmed, my body massaged until it glowed, and my skin smooth as ripe fruit. But I wasn't allowed to see Taz. Rhiannon informed me, laughing hysterically, that she was my chaperone for the next three days.

The day of the wedding they bathed me in some sweet smelling bath oils, fitted me into a simple but glorious dress, and fixed my hair, as I giggled through the entire morning. The wedding, the feast, and the night were everything any woman could ask for.

I'm now hi'Lady, hi'Blessed, and Aisha Talon Tafadzwa. Only the goddess knows what lay ahead.

partnership with an alien. She successfully qualifies and wins one of the coveted ten positions. Of course everything comes with a price—the alien is a parasite that inhabits the body and mind, and is there for life. Is it a dream or nightmare come true—or maybe both?

The Riss Proposal
Book II in the Riss Series
Science Fiction/Fantasy

Nadya, hosting an intelligent parasite, is now an experienced naval officer with two battles against the Raider's cruiser packs. But she continues to be seen as an alien, generating disgust, fear, raw hate, and attempts on her life.

To add to her problems, the Raiders have identified her as contributing directly to their bad luck and have designated her a dybbuk—demon—and have set a price on her dead or alive.

With the Raiders a continuing threat to the SAS, life has become a little too interesting.

The Riss Survival
Book III in the Riss Series
Science Fiction/Fantasy

The Raider clans have been defeated and their planet under the supervision of the Riss, with Captain Reese the station commander. But while Reese sees the Raider clans as on probation, many in the SAS task force she commands, perceive them as prisoners and hope to break the Treaty and get revenge.

As Nadya attempts to maintain the fragile peace, the three empires are being invaded. They know the invading force is far more technology advanced than the SAS. But who are they, where did they come from, and what do they want?

One thing appears certain. The SAS cannot defeat the aliens alone. But can they overcome their prejudices against the Riss, hatred of the clans, and long years of distrust of the other empires, to combine forces and technology to meet the challenge. The fate of the three empires, Riss, and the Raider clans may depend on it.

Kazak Guardians: Lynn's Rules
Book I of the Kazak Series
Urban Fantasy/Adventure/Romance

If the Kazak Guardians had a recruiting poster, it would have read: WANTED: A select few insane men to fight professional Assassins with super-human abilities. Good medical plan provided.

Because surviving the training program to graduation was dangerous, even the first challenge to gain entrance could get you killed. But training was the easy part. Staying alive afterward was the hard part. Kazaks guarded individuals whose lives were deemed critical to the security of the United States. These individuals attracted fanatics and the best professional assassins money could buy—Liars who could tell lies you believed, Ghosts who could become nearly invisible, and Illusionists who could appear to be anyone, among others.

But Lynn wanted no other life--the Kazak Guardians gave her life purpose. She had grown up in the foster care system, neglected and abused, at the mercy of people who didn't care. Even when she finally ran away, her freedom wasn't the renewal she had hoped. So when a friend told her about a unique organization that trained individuals to protect VIPs, she knew it was the life for her.

She survives years of training and five deadly challenges to become a Kazak Guardian, and entered a world of extremists and assassins, where each assignment became a deadly contest between Kazak and assassin, with the prize the life of the VIP.

Kazak Guardians: The Unthinkable
Book II of the Kazak Series
Urban Fantasy/Adventure/Romance

Lynn the Fox has been a Kazak for several years and thought she had seen it all; after all, she's a Master Kazak having killed more than five Assassins—professional killers with wizard-like talents. But life is unpredictable

There is a new kind of Assassin—a Mind Bender—who has caused two Kazaks kill their clients.

The unthinkable happens—and a client turns on her.

An unknown member of the secret and powerful Committee who funds and directs the Kazaks is a traitor.

And what should have been a simple misunderstanding at a State Department security checkpoint results in a life and death encounter with a SWAT team.

But there are fun moments, if you don't mind people trying to kill you and your client. Lynn gets to play the part of Afghan Warlord's daughter, a college student, and a homeless woman—an eagle covered with dove's feathers.

Talon of the Unnamed Goddess
Fantasy/Adventure

Alisha is the newest Talon of the Raptor Clan, mercenaries prized by rulers, nobles, and the wealthy as elite bodyguards. Like all Talons, she survived the five Ordeals and ten years of grueling training.

Alisha is not the strongest mercenary in the Raptor Clan, but she is the craftiest. Only tricking her opponents into underestimating her got her through the long years of clan training. Those years honed her weapon skills, but not as much as her sharp wits. Even the ability she gets from the rune she was given by the Unknown Goddess depends on her guile.

Her first assignment for the clan, to guard a young princess, requires all Alisha's skill, wit, and her newly acquired rune to keep the young heir to the kingdom alive.

Women of Power
Fantasy/Adventure

Nisha has trained all her life to develop Qi--her internal energy--exceeding the raw power of any Qi'advisor in several generations. But before she is ready to take her place, the unthinkable happens. Rhybac's king is dead; the kingdom is in chaos. War breaks out and their enemies out of the Sands are circling for the kill. She chooses to become a Qi'advisor, although still untried.

As Qi'advisor to a duke, she must risk her life to negotiate with the greed, the treachery one of the dukes, and the desperation that fuels the war in order to reveal what others cannot or refuse to see. The fate of Rhybac, its people, and even its enemies are in her young hands.

Blood Duty
Fantasy/Epic

Ixich, huge demons summoned through a savage blood ritual, lead an army through a mountain pass, slaughtering all who would stand in their way. Tamra, Captain of the Guard of Wayfare Keep, and an allied army from the city of Madrian mount a desperate defense against the onrushing enemy. When their army is defeated and her lover is lost in the battle, Tamra is devastated but must somehow struggle on.

Even worse lies ahead as the secrets of her past come to light and her loyalty is tested. Yet, she must protect all those who trust her against the ixich horde. In her darkest hour, haunted by loss and with defeat imminent, can Tamra fulfill that trust and do her blood duty?

Scales of Justice
Fantasy/Epic

A hundred years ago, a treaty jointed the seven provinces under a king and created a system of equal justice for nobles and commoners. The Sisters of Astraea were proclaimed the judicators of the land because they had gold vipers that could tell truth from lie. A gift bestowed on each judicator by the god Naga.

Now many nobles want to go back to being above the law. Duke Chaney is using this discontent to raise an army against the king and the judicators. Jola, a newly promoted judicator starts out with her mentor, Tenzen, to investigate the growing unrest. They encounter revenge, greed, and the desire for power, and become targets of the growing hostility as they attempt to discover who is behind the rebellion.

Laughing Hounds
Urban Fantasy/Horror

After what were thought to be dogs kill her mother and attack her, Annette discovers she has become the last female descendant of a line of women who, for over a century, fought and died fighting Countess Lenuta, her sons, and their packs of Werehyenas. Annette learns she has inherited her ancestors unique ability to make Tone-wood sing—the only weapon that can kill the Werehyenas. As such, she represents the last threat to their existence.

With only Annette remaining, Countess Lenuta and her sons see an opportunity to kill the last of their century-old adversaries. Their first attempt fails, and Annette must choose to hide for the rest of her life or accept the legacy of her ancestors to stop the Werehyenas. She chooses to fight.

With the help of ex-Green Berets her father hires to protect her, the battle soon escalates into a series of attacks and counter attacks that become fiercer as the tactics of each side evolve. The winner will be the last one standing.

Freedom's Sword
Scottish Historical Fiction
A Prequel to the Black Douglas Trilogy

Before William Wallace ... before Robert the Bruce ... there was another Scottish hero ...

In 1296, newly knighted by the King of the Scots, Andrew de Moray fights to defend his country against the forces of the ruthless invader, King Edward Longshanks of England. After a bloody defeat in battle, he is dragged in chains to an English dungeon.

Soon the young knight escapes. He returns to find Scotland under the heel of a conqueror and his betrothed sheltering in the hills of the Black Isle. Seizing his own castle, he raises the banner of Scottish freedom. Now he must lead the north of Scotland to rebellion in hope of defeating the English army sent to crush them.

A Kingdom's Cost
Book I of the Black Douglas Trilogy
Scottish Historical Fiction

Eighteen-year-old James Douglas can only watch, helpless, as the Scottish freedom fighter, William Wallace, is hanged, drawn, and quartered. Even under the heel of a brutal English conqueror, James's blood-drenched homeland may still have one hope for freedom, the rightful king of the Scots, Robert the Bruce. James swears fealty to the man he believes can lead the fight against English tyranny.

The Bruce is soon a fugitive, king in name and nothing more. Scotland is occupied, the Scottish resistance crushed. The woman James loves is captured and imprisoned. Yet James believes their cause is not lost. With driving determination, he blazes a path in blood and violence, in cunning and ruthlessness as he wages a guerrilla war to restore Scotland's freedom. James knows he risks sharing Wallace's fate, but what he truly fears is that he has become as merciless as the conqueror he fights.

Countenance of War
Book II of The Black Douglas Trilogy
Scottish Historical Fiction

Fourteen-century Scotland is a conquered nation, at the mercy of England's brutal King Edward. James Douglas continues his guerilla war to reclaim his stolen birthright and drive out the English tyrant. But as Edward's attentions turn again to subduing the rebellious Scots, James must deal with the tortuous, conflicting demands of duty and love.

The clash of two nations and the destiny of a man coming of age in a violent time springs to life in this novel of passion, loyalty, cunning and ruthlessness.

Fourteenth-century Scotland suffers under the heel of England's King Edward, but James Douglas refuses to submit to the conqueror. Above all else, James fears that his life and his own dream—of a free Scotland—might be lost to Edward's lust for conquest. As James wages a guerilla war to drive out the invader and reclaim his birthright, Edward brings a vast army to crush the Scottish resistance. In the midst of the brutal war, even the woman James loves is threatened by his implacable duty.

In a conflict poised to reach its bloody finale, the Scots and English cross swords in a reckoning that will determine Scotland's survival.

Not for Glory
Book III of The Black Douglas Trilogy
Scottish Historical Fiction

All over Scotland, crops are burning and people have fled. The English army led by King Edward has invaded, and the Scots meet them in an epic battle at the waters of the Bannockburn. When the battle is over James, Lord of Douglas, emerges a hero and has his orders from his liege lord, Robert the Bruce, King of the Scots. In order to force the English to the peace table, James sweeps through the north of England like a storm, burning and wreaking devastation. But the English king instead brings another army north to try to conquer Scotland. With the city of Berwick under siege and Scotland yet again facing conquest, James takes a desperate risk. He leads his army south to York in an attempt to capture the English queen. When the outnumbered Scots seem to be trapped, James and his men, his enemies, and the fate of Scotland meet at a apex of violence and heroism.

23991005R00128

Made in the USA
Lexington, KY
01 July 2013